A LYNX IN TI

Shifting Desires 1

Marla Monroe

MENAGE EVERLASTING

Siren Publishing, Inc.
www.SirenPublishing.com

A LYNX IN THEIR DEN

Shifting Desires 1

MARLA MONROE
Copyright © 2014

Chapter One

What on earth is that god-awful noise?

Serenity Jones squinted at the time on her computer monitor and sighed. It was nearly eleven p.m. She'd been working on the last part of the program for nearly four hours straight. No wonder her back hurt. But what was making that terrible racket at this time of night?

She shuffled down the hall to the living room and pushed the curtain aside to look outside. At first nothing really jumped out as unusual to her. She lived in a cul-de-sac at the end of a long road outside of the small community of Talmadge, Montana. There was only one other house in the cul-de-sac, and it was empty right now. She liked it that way.

"What the…" Unfortunately, it looked like someone was moving in.

Serenity groaned. Until now, her nearest neighbor had been nearly half a mile down the road. Now she had someone living directly across from her. She could only pray they would be quieter once they got moved in. And why were they moving in the middle of the night, anyway? Usually you moved *out* in the middle of the night, not in.

She turned on her porch light and unlocked her door to step outside. The night air had turned much cooler since the sun had gone down some six or seven hours ago. Summer in the mountains was much different than it had been in the south growing up. Where the sun sank all the way to the ground down there, up where she lived now, the mountains tended to hide it much sooner.

A large moving van had backed up to the garage, and the horrible noise she'd heard earlier had probably been them opening the back or pulling out the ramp from the bottom of the truck. Now she could see several very large men milling around in the light coming from the garage. She wasn't able to scent if they were human or shifter with the wind blowing the wrong direction, but at least it wouldn't be blowing her scent in theirs if they were shifters. Why hadn't anyone told her someone had bought the house across from her? Serenity had hoped it would remain empty for a little while longer. Maybe she should have bought it when she had the chance.

Then the house would have slowly deteriorated, bringing unwanted attention to her. If she'd kept it up despite no one living in it, the costs would have been more than she was willing to part with as big as the place was. It didn't matter now. The place wasn't on the market any longer, and now she had new neighbors to worry about.

Sound carried in the cooler night air in the mountains, but the men gathered at the edge of the garage spoke softly enough that she wasn't able to make out their words, just that they were talking. She tried to count how many there were but only managed six before they started moving around so that she couldn't tell if she'd already counted them or not.

After another five minutes of discussions, the men finally started unloading the van. As they walked back and forth between the van and the garage, it became obvious that they were shifters with enormous strength and agility. They easily moved the furniture without the normal grunts and curses humans made when they moved. Serenity could appreciate the fact that they were trying to remain quiet despite the initial cacophony of screeching metal when they'd first arrived.

She sat and watched them for about thirty minutes before deciding she really needed to get in bed. The program she was working on was due to her client by Monday morning. It was now nearly twelve thirty Saturday morning. If she stayed up much later, she wouldn't be able to get out of bed at a decent hour to get back to work on it.

Serenity prided herself on always delivering her completed, flawless products on time. Her reputation as a programmer earned her more work than she could handle at a price that kept her more than comfortable. When she stood up from the chair to head back inside, her back reminded her that she'd neglected to move around enough and would be stiff and sore the next day because of it.

Or I can take a nice hot shower and sleep in my lynx form tonight. I'll be right as rain in the morning.

She smiled to herself and walked back inside, making sure to turn all three deadbolts before she padded back down the hall to her bedroom and en suite bathroom. In less than a minute, she had her clothes off and the water going in the shower. As it warmed up, Serenity thought about the big shifters across the road. What flavor of shifter would they be? They all looked much too large to be wolf, which was the most common of the shifter groups. Still, there were some large wolves out there. She'd seen them.

Once the water reached her favorite heat level, barely below scorching, she stepped in and sighed at the invigorating sting of the shower against her sensitive skin. After washing off, she turned and let the pulsing showerhead do its thing to her back and shoulders. She swore that next spring she was going to have her bathroom completely redone into one of the luxury spas she'd coveted on HGTV. She had enough money to redo her entire house now if she wanted to, but that would mean allowing strangers into her sanctuary. So far, she'd talked herself out of a new bathroom two years in a row. Would she make it three?

When the hot water began to cool to warm, Serenity growled and turned it off before stepping out of the shower. She quickly toweled off and brushed her teeth then, after turning off the light, walked back into her bedroom. Already her back felt better, but sleeping in her lynx form would have her loose and relaxed when she woke up the next morning. With that thought, she picked up the large pet bed that was shaped like a cave of sorts and positioned it on the bed so that she could see both the window to her right and her bedroom door through the narrow opening. Then Serenity let out a breath and relaxed into the magic that brought the change.

She hardly ever felt it anymore unless she hurried it. The breaking and tearing and splitting that went on during the shift no longer affected her as it had when she'd first started learning to control the change. As a kit, babies followed their mother's change, flowing into and out of their lynx without thought or pain. It wasn't until they grew old enough that they had to control it that the pain came. While they learned to master their shift, the interruption of the flow caused pain. Once they could control without thinking about each part of it, the pain went away except in times of stress or when trying to hurry the shift along.

In less than half a minute, a golden lynx shook out its fur and stretched on the floor before walking around the room to check that everything was in its place. Once assured that everything was as it should be, the lynx hopped up on the bed and nosed the added sanctuary until she was happy. She slipped inside, turned around a few times, then lay down and covered her nose with her tail to sleep.

The lynx had wanted to go check out the intruders across the road, but Serenity refused. The lynx didn't understand why the human side of her wasn't much more upset over their territory being invaded. The human side couldn't make the lynx understand that, for humans, there were boundaries that had to be observed called property lines. They weren't on hers, so she couldn't do anything about it.

They lynx didn't care about property lines or boundaries. She'd marked her territory, and the others were in her area. She slept, but she was never unaware of everything around her. If they tried to breech her den, she'd know.

* * * *

Creed North stretched after unloading the last box from the moving van. His brother Shayne set the one he had carried off next to it. They exchanged looks and nodded in agreement. Unpacking could wait until they woke up later. It had been a long day of driving, and everyone was ready to crash.

While they'd been unloading, two of the others had been putting together beds complete with sheets and pillows. With the ten of them, the work had gone fast. It was only a little after three, so they could easily get a good five hours of sleep before needing to get up and start unpacking.

"Is the fridge cool enough we can unload the coolers?" Shayne asked one of the others as they walked inside the house.

Eason, a hybrid black bear and grizzly mix, opened the fridge door and checked. "Feels cool to me. I think we can do that."

Shayne and Zeth, a black bear and the youngest of the group, carried the first of the coolers over and set it down in front of the huge industrial-size refrigerator and started unloading it. Creed and Warren pulled the other one over and opened the lid. Warren was a grizzly bear who seemed to have a special connection with Eason, who most thought was unstable because of his bear mix. Together, they were a team who could deal with most anything that came up, and Creed trusted them.

As soon as his brother and Zeth had finished the first cooler, Creed carried the empty one out on the carport and left it on its side to drain overnight.

"As soon as you finish that one, call it a night, and let's all get some sleep," Creed told them. Turning to his brother, he nodded. "Let's check the area before settling in to grab some shuteye."

Without needing to be told, Shayne shifted to his bear form. Creed followed as soon as Shayne had finished. Zeth let them out the back door, and they immediately began combing the area surrounding them for any hint of a threat. Both he and his brother were Kodiac bears with Creed being the Ursus of his sleuth and Shayne his Zashchita, or second. Normally he would have had his Ruka, Locke, a grizzly bear, with them, but it had been a long hard day for all of them, especially Locke.

As Ursus, Creed was the leader, or alpha, of the group, which with bear shifters was called a sleuth. He saw to it that they were all cared for and followed shifter rules. His brother was his second-in-charge, known as the Zashchita of a sleuth. He helped Creed maintain order and helped run the sleuth's main businesses and handle minor problems among the sleuth.

His Ruka, Locke, was the enforcer of the sleuth. He saw to their safety and was a personal bodyguard for Creed, though he rarely needed one. Locke took care of anything major among the sleuth and any threats from outside as well.

As they circled their new den, a scent crossed his nose, setting his bear on edge. It took all of his control to rein in brother bear. He wanted to go after the scent. Female—mate. She belonged to them.

Shayne suddenly reared up on his hind legs and growled, turning toward Creed. Aw, hell. Shayne's bear had also caught her scent. With both bears reacting, Creed had no doubt they'd locked onto their mate's scent. If Shayne was having nearly the amount of trouble that he was keeping the big Kodiak from giving chase, his brother seemed to be winning.

Creed shuffled over to his brother and butted his head at the other bear's side to get him to stand down. He knew there was no way their bears would allow them to return to the den without locating the origin of the scent first. He led the way with his brother following close behind. Despite their size and weighing close to two thousand pounds, they were relatively quiet walking through the trees and brush as he tracked the origin of the sweet smelling scent of their mate.

It led them in a roundabout way to the only other occupied house on their street. She literally lived right under their noses. The sweet scent translated to a mixture of honey and cinnamon on his tongue. The next thing that hit him was that she was feline. He wasn't sure what type of cat, but she was definitely of the feline side of the shifter world.

Shayne chuffed at him, obviously wanting a closer look. With the house appearing dark and the late hour, he decided it wouldn't hurt to get a bit closer. They couldn't hide the fact that they'd been this close anyway, they might as well go for broke and trespass onto her personal territory as well. He nodded, and his brother eagerly shuffled ahead.

Creed watched Shayne move in closer to the house but remain clear of the more open area surrounding the structure. With her blinds drawn, they wouldn't have been able to peek anyway. At this point, a bear with the scent of his mate would stoop to just about anything to get a glimpse of her. Still, he was pleased that they wouldn't be crossing that bridge of depravity.

He turned toward the other side of the house and explored in that direction, knowing his brother was under control. When their mate woke later in the morning and ventured outside, she'd know immediately that they'd been there and what they were. Hopefully it would prepare her to accept them as mates. Had she been a sow instead of some type of cat, he wouldn't have worried about her acceptance of them, but he knew next to nothing about felines and their breeding habits. With there being so few bear shifters, interbreeding was fairly normal among his clans, but usually the opposite mates tended to be wolves or even African wild dogs. Hell, their aunt Sonya had been a panda shifter. Rarely had there been a feline mating that he could recall.

Creed stopped in front of her house and chuffed for his brother. Shayne hurried around to meet him. Together they rubbed against the trees near the front door then raked their claws down the bark to mark it. Any other males would recognize that they'd laid claim to the female inside, and she would know of their intentions when she saw it. How she took it, though, would be the big question.

He and Shayne walked back to their property, and after making one more round, walked into the garage and shifted. One of the others, probably Seth, had left jeans for them. He was the mother of the group, though he'd probably beat anyone's ass who said as much to his face. The Kodiak bear stood over 6'4" and weighed over two sixty, so it was hard to associate him as motherly until you watched him constantly making sure everyone was well and had what they needed. None in the group ever made the mistake of pointing this out to him, though.

They quickly pulled on their jeans, and while Shayne closed the garage door, Creed walked into the mud room to wait for him.

"What are we going to do about her?" Shayne asked, his eyes flashing with the after effects of sensing their mate nearby.

"First we'll introduce ourselves," he said. "Then we claim her."

"She's feline. I've never been around a female feline before. Their males normally keep them sequestered when we've met with them for some reason. What if she refuses us?" he asked.

Creed cocked his head. "We convince her. Felines are very sexual. That is one thing I do know. If need be, we will seduce her. She is our Ursa, our queen, and will be the mother to our cubs. Fate decreed it. She'll adjust with time. It's our job to make her happy and keep her that way. She's the life blood of our sleuth and will draw other mates out for the den."

"I hope you're right, Creed. This move was hard on everyone. None of us wanted to leave," Shayne reminded him.

"I know, but the clans have become too inbred. It has lowered the number of cubs born to us. The elders are right that once a clan becomes too large it tends to breed from within, and the sleuths become weak blooded so that fewer cubs are born. There was need for new blood, and moving was the only way to accomplish that. Our bears will locate mates no matter where they go. By moving far enough away, we ensure that they are from different sleuths and clans." Creed knew Shayne already understood it, but it was obvious they all needed reminding while they were unsettled.

"Looks like ours is going to be from a different species all together. At least she isn't a bunny rabbit or squirrel," Shayne joked.

"I don't believe there are any non-carnivore shifters. Omnivores, of course, but herbivores? I truly doubt it. We require way too much protein to power the shift to get our energy from anything except meat." Creed smiled. "I'm looking forward to having a little pussy for a snack. What about you, little brother?"

Shayne chuckled quietly. "I can't believe you made a joke. You never joke. Of course, if our future mate hears how you talk about her…" he began.

Creed growled in warning. "Don't make me hurt you, Shayne."

Shayne grinned but ducked his head. "You know I'm not going to do anything that will hurt our future with her. Wait until we tell the others. They will be jealous but pleased since it means theirs are not far behind."

"Enough screwing around. We need to get some rest. There is much to do tomorrow, and the truck has to go to the nearest turn-in station by noon," Creed reminded his second.

"I've already made sure that Eason knows to take it in tomorrow. He and Zeth looked up the location on their cell phone earlier." Shayne yawned and stretched. "Okay. I'm heading to bed. Wake me if you get up before me in the morning."

Creed smiled. "Don't worry. No one is sleeping one second longer than I do tomorrow."

He watched his brother head to the stairs. The main reason they had settled on this house was due to the huge basement that would work well for the sleuth's den. They were going to enlarge it to make up most of the back part of the property over time, but for now, it would easily hold all of them and their mates once they were all found. Until then, they all slept above ground. There were five bedrooms. The master was downstairs on the other side of the living area. The other four bedrooms were upstairs.

He took the master, but once they had their mate between them, his brother would join him there. The others were sharing rooms for now with Otto sleeping in the living area until they got the main suite downstairs completed where he, Shayne, and their new mate would take up residence. Then his Ruka would take the master on the first floor so he would be close at hand to defend the den.

As he removed his jeans in the bedroom and stepped into the master bath, he wondered how things would work in their den when it came to his bears finding their mates. Would they all end up with a mate a piece, or would they pair up as the older, original sleuths did? His father felt that with him and Shayne pairing up in a bond as they had to break off from the clan, it was highly possible that they would settle into the earlier culture of sharing mates. It had been how sleuths worked many years ago when there was much more danger from hunters and other shifters.

Before The Awakening, when full humans knew nothing of the shifters and shifters fought each other, it was safer for the males to share a female to help keep her safe. While one hunted, the other guarded. If their sleuth returned to the old ways, it might cause some problems initially between the bonded pairs. He hoped not, but all the men who'd chosen to go with him and Shayne were strong, dominant males. Sharing when it wasn't something they'd grown up with might prove to be much harder for them.

Then technology got too sensitive and it wasn't possible to hide their existence any longer, especially when it came to forensics. With the encroaching populations spreading into more and more of the wild areas previously untouched, it was only a matter of time before someone witnessed something they shouldn't have. And that's what happened.

One day a family went out hiking in Yellowstone National Park and strayed off the beaten path to see a wolf cub change into his human form and dress right in front of them. He'd been upwind of them and hadn't known they were there until it was too late. At only thirteen, he'd run home, afraid that he would be killed for allowing them to see him. He'd ended up very lucky in that they had been so shocked, they hadn't remembered to take any pictures.

It had served as a wakeup call to the elders of each group, and the decision was made to reveal themselves to the humans so they could control the fallout as best as possible.

With the knowledge that it could all go bad, they chose someone who was already a much-loved popular figure among the humans. Andrew Fisher, a popular music star known for his friendliness and straight living, held a press conference surrounded by other shifters from all walks of life and The Awakening occurred. Humans became aware of things they'd only dreamed and fantasized about in books, movies, and TV.

At first they'd embraced the knowledge, comfortable with them walking the streets and living in their neighborhoods, but soon secular groups began to form protesting the shifter's rights, saying they weren't human, so they shouldn't be treated that way.

Like humans, shifters sometimes had deviants among them who broke the laws of all shifters as well as human laws. Once one of them was determined to have killed someone, humans began questioning every death that occurred, trying to turn all of them into shifter kills. And so the Rogue Hunters were born to police the shifters and bring down those who broke the law.

Unfortunately the hunters didn't much care what a shifter was allegedly guilty of. It was all the same to them. When it came to taking them in, if they resisted or protested that they were innocent, likely as not they ended up shot under the pretense of being a dangerous animal who just needed to be put down.

Lucky for them, they had quite a few shifters in key official offices, both nationally and throughout many of the states. Most humans were fine with shifters and being around them, but like anything or anyone who was different, they developed a following of haters who made it their mission in life to destroy them any way they could.

He quickly showered off. Once he was dry, Creed climbed into the big bed, wishing his mate was already there with him. While he and Shayne would share her, there would be times they each spent time alone with her to keep their bonds tight. He would love to curl up around her right now and have her rest her head on his arm or shoulder. His bear rumbled in agreement.

The comforting scent of cinnamon-spiced honey lingered in his nose as he considered how to approach her. He wished he'd had more interaction with felines before they'd moved. It had never occurred to him that his future mate might not be bear or wolf. They had moved directly into the middle of bear and wolf country when they'd chosen the Talmadge Community at the edge of Glacier National Park. It had seemed to be the most similar to where they'd moved from out of Alaska. Finding a feline up here wasn't unusual, but he'd have thought most felines would stay a little farther south. Maybe she was a snow leopard, he thought to himself. That would make sense.

Visions of a pretty snow leopard leaping from rock to ground and across snowbanks made him smile. Worries over the future with him now, the Ursus of a sleuth shoved the lighthearted thoughts down. He had set up Talmadge Sleuth with the hope that they would grow to be their own clan one day. When it had all been theory, plans, and dreams between Shayne and the others, the pressures hadn't seemed unbearable. Now, in the early morning hours of his first day in their new den, Creed fully appreciated the difficulty and stress his Ursus had been under in their old home.

With change came challenges, and with success came sorrow. It was one of the many things his great grandfather Papa Bear had taught him many years before he'd gone to the Father five years ago. His kind lived long lives, but as Papa Bear had said to him just before his death, great age and great wisdom might join hands for most. Few are allowed the privilege of sharing it with their mate, and it made for a sorrowful time. Papa Bear's mate had died nearly fifteen years before, leaving his great grandfather alone and lonely.

He and his brothers had all taken turns staying with him when they were growing up. It had kept the older bear busy and helped him live through the long days. More than that, it had helped them to learn things they might not have had they not spent the time with him. He and Shayne had spent a lot more time with their Papa than their three other brothers. He prayed they'd used that time wisely to learn what they would need to know to nurture and protect their new sleuth.

I promise that I will make you proud, Papa Bear. Thank you for sharing your wisdom and time with Shayne and me.

Creed pushed the button on his cell phone to check the time and winced. He needed to be asleep already. With one last thought of his yet-to-be-claimed mate, he let sleep claim him.

Chapter Two

Serenity's feline half woke seconds before her human half did. The lynx sniffed the air and relaxed before yawning and opening her eyes. Once her human side stirred, joining in the start of a new day, the feline crept out of the mini-den and jumped off the bed before stretching. Seconds later, the lynx retreated, and Serenity's human side stood to her full height of five feet, four inches.

As she moved around the room, pulling on clothes and pulling her hair back into a ponytail, all of the stiffness from the night before was gone, as she'd known it would be. Sometimes being a shifter proved to have some advantages after all. Then the memory of new neighbors of the shifting kind crashed her good mood.

"Damn and double damn!" She stomped into the kitchen to pick out her coffee, thankful she'd managed the nearly seven hours of sleep she'd gotten after drifting off sometime around one thirty that morning.

Serenity settled on a fairly strong morning brew since she had a feeling the day was going to be challenging with her deadline as well as new neighbors. All she could hope for at this point was that they would want to keep to themselves and leave her alone.

Just give me until Monday to finish this project without interruptions, and I'll play nice when they come visiting. I promise.

Right. She wasn't living out on her own, a female shifter without a mate, for no reason. Serenity's name didn't reflect her nature, or even her personality, by a long shot. Her mom had been dreaming or wishing when she'd named her youngest kit Serenity. Chaos would have been a much better label for her. As in, anytime she was around, chaos ensued.

She sighed and waited for the Keurig machine to do its magic before continuing on to figure something out for breakfast. By the sound of her belly, it had been longer than eight hours since her last meal. When she was in the middle or on deadline with a project, eating only occurred when she could no longer think over the noise of her protesting belly. Until then she ignored the sounds.

"Looks like eggs and toast and—eggs. Time for a supply run." Had it been that long since she'd been to town?

Normally Serenity only went to town once every two weeks, but knowing that she was going to submerge herself in the computer program until it was finished, she could have sworn she'd stocked up on everything to last her three weeks. Since the project was due on Monday, according to her deadline program that counted down the days for her, it had already been three weeks, and she was out of food.

The scrambled eggs, toast, and jelly settled her hunger pains for the time being, so she took her coffee and her preprinted grocery list outside to make notes on what she needed to order and pick up in town. The instant she unlocked and opened her front door, the scents attacked.

"What the…" Serenity took a step back then forced herself to walk out onto the front porch.

Leaving the grocery lists and coffee cup on the table by her favorite chair, she walked down the steps to stand a few feet away from the trees on either side of her sidewalk. Here she had no trouble determining what brand of shifter had moved in next door. Nor did she need to talk with them to find out what the relationship between their homes might be. They'd introduced themselves and staked their intent for all the world to see in her front yard. At least every shifter who might pass through would know their business once inhaling and viewing her trees.

Her new neighbors were bear shifters, and they were claiming her as their mate—their mate, as in two of them. She could smell two distinct scents and could tell the differences in the claw patterns they'd left behind on her trees. Why were there two of them, and were they planning on fighting over her? Hell no. She wouldn't have either of them, so there was no reason for them to fight over her. End of story.

She turned her back to the mess, and after grabbing her coffee and the food list, walked back through the house to the back porch and settled out there to commune as best she could. Though there were no claw marks marring her trees back there, their scents were still potent and irritating to her feline constitution.

"Even my lynx knows it will never work." At least that was what she hoped since the feline had been so quiet since picking up the bears' scents.

By the time she'd finished her coffee, Serenity had a makeshift list of her needs for the next two weeks and was chomping at the bit to head to town. That in itself should have warned her that she was freaking out. Serenity never eagerly went anywhere other than for a run around her territory. She hated going to town and dealing with pesky humans who were either scared to death of her or too curious for their own good. Somehow going to town edged out staying in close proximity to the bears as the lesser of two evils. This was proving to not be the easy clean up day she'd envisioned for finishing the program.

Serenity set some program tests into play to work while she was gone then set up a new program that would keep track of things she monitored in various forums around the Internet. If anything was posted that included certain target words or phrases, it would mark the location and time so that she could review them when she got back.

With the majority of the world now active with technology, threats of all types emerged for not only humans, but shifters as well. She kept up with as much of it as possible and sent out reports to those who might be interested to follow up on or not. She maintained her anonymity through careful re-mailers, switch stations, and recycled temporary e-mail addresses. It wouldn't do for her cover to get blown. She'd be either an enemy or a major resource to be owned, controlled, or eliminated. Serenity's goal was to be none of the above. She belonged to no one, and no one told her what to do.

With everything set into motion to keep her programs going while she was gone, she grabbed her bag and, after checking to be sure there was no one around the carport, raced out the back door to her SUV. She felt a little foolish acting like a teenager sneaking out of the house under her parents' noses, when she'd never done so as a teen in the first place.

The drive into town took over thirty minutes with so many people on the road out to enjoy a pretty Saturday. Everyone knew how soon winter would be slipping in to force hibernation for those without alternate transportation.

Hibernation? Where did that word come from? I don't use words like hibernate.

She suppressed a growl over the unintended reference to bears. She hadn't even had a confrontation with them yet, and already her subconscious was focusing on them.

At the local department store where one could find anything from grapes to pipe cement, Serenity parked and mentally prepared herself to deal with the humans and any other shifters that might be out shopping. With her unusual eye color of pale light green and the otherworldly aura that gave humans goose bumps or had their hair rising all over their body, she had no illusions that she could shop undetected. While there were some lucky humans who were *other* unaware, or as some shifters called them, danger dumb, the majority of the human population sensed something when around them.

Since their secrets had been revealed out of resentment by someone in the armed forces seventy years earlier, the whole world knew of their existence now. When anyone felt that odd feeling around someone, they automatically assumed they were shifters. In fact, the military had known about them for nearly one hundred years when science had begun to progress faster than the shifters realized the dangers of their blood and tissues being tested. Once it was discovered, the shifters worked a compromise with various governments to keep their secret safe.

As long as they didn't go on killing sprees and promised to supply a percentage of their men to serve as soldiers in special units, the government would keep their secret and allow the public to continue living in the dark but side by side with them. Then someone got their feelings hurt, citing preferential treatment without knowing the entire situation, and their days of anonymity were over.

Using her list that had been tailor created for that store, Serenity started on the opposite end of the food side of the building and worked her way up and down aisles containing things she needed with a single-minded determination to get through the ordeal without arousing interest or losing her temper.

Her plan failed halfway through the school and office supply department.

"There she is. Told you she was still around." The soft whiney voice of a male human reached her ears from somewhere ahead of her.

"What does she need that much printer paper for? Do they use it for toilet tissue? Hell, even the store brand is softer than that," another male voice said.

"Who knows what they do. She's kind of pretty for an animal. I'd do her in a minute," the first guy said.

A snorting chuckle pinpointed their location for her as across the main aisle, looking in the sporting goods. Typical for a pair of non-sequiturs like them, she thought with a shake of her head.

"Yeah, a minute is all it would take for you, Jim."

"Shut the fuck up, Mike. They got keen hearing. You want her to hear us?"

She had to bite her tongue not to laugh at that. They were almost shouting, she could hear them so well. Didn't matter. They'd never have the balls to put anything they might think up into play. They weren't the ones she had to worry about. It was the ones like the lone male standing near the back of the store on the same aisle watching her. He hadn't said anything, and she didn't watch him back. She'd picked up on his heartbeat and the scent of his arousal just after she'd honed in on the two idiots talking trash. That man she needed to be wary of and stay out of his way.

Even though she kept his scent and features in the back of her mind, she really didn't think he'd try anything. His type were capable of it and had the balls to follow through, but normally they were only interested in running scenarios in their heads for the brief adrenaline high they got in psyching themselves up for something dangerous and challenging. It was a lot like having an erotic daydream about your favorite movie star or sports player.

She nearly chuckled out loud at the thought of some stranger having erotic thoughts about chasing her down, chaining her up, and raping her before killing her so he could mount her head as a trophy when she changed to her lynx. In lynx form, all tests came back to be normal for the animal they changed form to. No one would know he'd murdered a shifter—except another shifter who would be able to scent one of their kind.

Once in the grocery area, she relaxed some. There would be fewer men in this section intent on *stalking* her through the store. They'd be much too obvious among the fruit and vegetables. Now all she had to contend with were the nosey women and occasional child still young enough they paid attention to their inborn instincts that warned them of possible danger.

"Hi. How are you doing? We met a few weeks ago when my car wouldn't start. Remember?" A tiny older woman with graying hair had stopped her cart near hers next to the bread.

"Oh, um. Yes. I remember. Did you get new battery cables?" she asked, remembering that the woman's cables had been old and rotted with exposed wires.

"Yes, I did. Thank you so much for helping me that day. I was scared standing alone like that. Normally several of us come to the store together, but last week Jane and Clara were ill, so I came and did all our shopping. I just don't know what I would have done if you hadn't stopped to help me," she said. Doris. That was her name.

"I'm glad everything worked out for you. Do you have your emergency number with you in case something happens?" she asked.

"Yes. We all have two numbers we can call if we need help. I wanted to introduce you to my friends. They're right over there by the peanut butter." Doris pointed at two women who looked a little older than her reading labels off of jars.

"Oh, I..." She found herself pulled along by the old woman's strong grip.

Unwilling to harm the woman by jerking away, Serenity allowed herself to be dragged toward the two women in a heated discussion over the merits of one brand over another.

"Girls, girls. Look who I ran into. It's Serenity. She's the woman who helped me when my car wouldn't start," Doris presented her like a prize-winning show cat, complete with arm flourish.

"Hello," she managed to get out before the other two women descended on her, hugging her and squeezing her cheeks. She wasn't able to stop the soft growl that erupted from her chest.

To her surprise, the women burst into laughter but stepped back, giving her some room.

"I told you not to crowd her. Shifters don't like to be cornered. You're lucky she recognizes us as helpless and not a danger to her. She could have attacked us all." Doris didn't seem the least worried about that possibility though since the other woman patted Serenity on the arm.

"We're sorry," the shorter of the two women said in a cracked voice.

"We're just so excited to actually talk to an honest to God shape-shifter that we forgot Doris's warnings," the other woman said with a broad smile.

"Shh. Keep it down," Doris admonished them again.

"I'm sorry I growled, but like Doris said, we don't like to be touched by non, um, family or cornered by anyone." She pasted on her brightest smile to soften her earlier threatening growl.

"That's okay. You can't help it. You're so pretty!" the taller one whispered loudly.

"Um, thanks. It was great to meet you, but I've got to be going." She kept the already faltering smile plastered on her face and started easing her cart away from the three women.

"Wait," Doris said with a panicked expression on her face. "I was hoping to see you so I could tell you that there's a new group in the area who are anti-shifter. They are circulating pamphlets and recruiting people into their hate group. You need to be very careful, honey. Here."

Serenity took the folded up papers the older woman shoved in her hand but didn't look at them. The woman obviously thought it safer to hand them to her on the sly, though she failed miserably at being stealthy. Serenity could appreciate the woman's courage. No doubt she would enjoy thinking about her contribution by informing a shifter of the new threat when she sat on her rocking chair later.

"Thank you." She didn't get a chance to say anything more since Doris hurried her cackling group of chicks farther along the aisle.

Shaking her head, Serenity stuffed the folded papers into her back pocket and continued filling her cart with the items on her list. As she neared the check out stations, a scent teased at her nose. At first she couldn't place it or why her cat woke up to take notice. Then the finicky feline purred and urged her to drop everything and locate the source of the mouthwatering aroma.

Fuck! They're here. Or at least one of them is.

Her mates were somewhere in the building, and her cat was on the job, interested in pursuing them. What had changed since this morning when she'd first discovered their scents and visual intentions?

Mates. Mine.

"Yeah, well, not right now," she muttered under her breath.

Need.

"Rein it in, girl. You don't need anything or anyone. Remember?"

Serenity rushed through checking out, throwing things on the belt, just barely saving the eggs from being broken and the fruit from becoming bruised. The clerk had eyed her warily as if she would jump over the counter and pounce on her. Maybe the poor girl wasn't entirely wrong about that. If she hadn't been very efficient in checking her out, Serenity might have done just that.

Why now? I've just gotten to the point that I don't look over my shoulder and can afford anything I need.

It had been nearly eleven years since she'd escaped the den's confines and rules. The first two of those years, Serenity had kept on the run, moving from one big city to the next to hide her scent beneath the choking fumes of humanity where her kind couldn't track her among the stench found in the more industrial areas. She'd suffered the misery of foul air, reconditioned water, and processed food in order to remain free of the den's influence and directives.

Then, once she'd felt that they would no longer be looking for her, Serenity had settled across the country in a small community where there was a college she could attend. It took her five years of working and going to school, but at the age of twenty-five, Serenity held a dual degree in computer programming and microelectronics. From there she worked her way up two different companies until she had enough money to branch out on her own using her ideas to fulfill her goals.

Total independence from all forms of power over me and a feeling of worth outside that of my uterus.

She had a thriving business and enough money to do pretty much anything she wanted. Her needs were simple and her wants few. She loved to read and loved listening to music. Her frequent runs around her property in her lynx form kept her other side happy. She didn't need or want a mate, and certainly not two of them.

After settling the last bag in the cart so that she could still steer and see over the stack of bags, Serenity pushed through the automatic doors and rolled toward her SUV parked about eight cars down the aisle from the store. The SUV beeped when she pushed the button on the key fob in her hand, and the back hatch opened automatically for her.

The thin trickle of unease down her spine had her glancing around as she loaded her groceries into the back of her vehicle. Nothing stood out as unusual. There were no groups of men hanging around or even one or two who looked suspicious. The sky's pale blue hue stretched from one mountain range to the next, uninterrupted by clouds or birds. And that was what had her cat pacing beneath her skin.

Serenity didn't see or hear a single bird in the area when, normally, they were fighting for prime space on the cart returns and empty baskets to get first dibs on abandoned food wrappers that littered the ground.

Danger!

"No shit, Sherlock," she ground out between clinched teeth. "Be of some real help and tell me which direction to watch."

No such luck. All she could do was finish piling the bags into the back then haul ass home where she would be on her own territory and able to defend herself against an attack.

An impending attack.

Because she knew it was coming. The knowledge that something was coming churned in her gut like a good Evinrude motor through a crystal clear lake. The interesting thing about what was to come was that her cat knew it as true danger, whereas the mate claiming bears hadn't been seen in that light. Well as far as Serenity was concerned, they both equaled threat to her way of life. She would avoid them both if at all possible. If not? Well then. The fight was on.

"Told you there were shifters 'round these parts," a young, barely teenage male voice all but shouted.

"Shut up," a second, much more controlled voice answered.

Cold, numbing fear iced her veins as Serenity fought to continue what she was doing without showing that she'd heard them. Had she been human, she wouldn't have. It wasn't that someone knew she was a shifter, and it wasn't that she was afraid of those two per se. It was the sound of the man's voice that had her fear factor climbing to the top. Quiet calm had filled those two words that would have barely reached the stupid kid's ears. Only those experienced in hunting shifters for the enjoyment of killing something as lethal as their animal side but with the intelligence of the human side could manage that amount of calm confidence free of fear.

Fuck!

Hunt!

"No," she mumbled more to herself than to the lynx pacing and snarling inside of her.

She needed more information. Knowledge was power, but first she needed to make sure they didn't follow her home so that they knew the location of her den.

Protect the den—always.

It was her last stand of defense should all else fail. No, what she needed to do was lose them, regroup, and find out who was in town and why. The crumpled papers in her back pocket suddenly didn't seem like such a joke any longer. She'd grown lax in watching for signs of hunters when none had ever shown up in her little garden patch of the world before. Now she was behind instead of ahead of the game.

Even though hunters technically didn't exist in the new order of the world, they had never really gone away. They'd simply moved underground to pursue their prey. Instead of hunting only when they had a sanctioned kill order from a government judicial agency, they hunted off the radar and hid their kills, often disguising them as random violence among shifters that did occur on occasion.

Serenity reined in her speeding heart and forced her breathing to remain normal as she pushed the button on the hatch for it to automatically close while she rolled the cart over to the return rack as if there wasn't a hunter somewhere nearby. He wasn't east of her or she'd smell him, and he wasn't north since that was open without anyone standing around. Her enemy would either be to the south or west. She could glance around behind her sunglasses as she opened the door and climbed up into her SUV.

Almost. She almost made it to the driver's door before her earlier threat trumped her escape plan.

Chapter Three

The instant Creed closed his hand over the sexy feline's upper arm, he knew he'd screwed up. She turned so fast he nearly missed the fist plowing right for his throat. Thankfully, he could move just as fast and stepped back, throwing her momentum off as he pulled her around with him. Shayne caught her curled up hand in his before she ended up smashing it through the side window of her vehicle.

"Let go of me," she hissed out just like the cat she was.

"I'm sorry. I shouldn't have grabbed you like that, but I wanted to talk to you and didn't think," he admitted as he cautiously let her arm go.

"That's what's wrong with males. They don't think before they speak or act." She turned to walk around him as if she planned to leave after all of that.

"Whoa. Don't just walk off," he said, his voice grumbly to his own ears. "We need to talk."

"Not in the middle of a parking lot, we don't. There's a hunter watching us, and I'd like to give him as little of me as possible to sharpen his scope skills with." Again, she turned away from him and managed to get her door open before he twisted and grabbed the frame to keep her from closing it.

"Move over. I'll drive, and my brother will bring our jeep to be sure we aren't followed." He attempted to scoot her over but she didn't budge.

In fact, she buckled her seatbelt and started the engine, glaring at him with enough anger he would have sworn he saw flames in her eyes if she hadn't had shades on.

"Don't go straight home. Drive around and let us throw him off your trail," he finally said in a half snarl.

"I've been taking care of myself without a male to hinder my efforts for years now. I think I can lose a hunter without your help. Move!" she demanded, grabbing the door in an effort to close it.

Creed stepped back as she slammed the door closed and nearly ran over his toes as she backed out of the slot and drove off. He and Shayne hurried back to where they'd left the Jeep when they'd scented their mate nearby. Thank goodness no one had stolen the damn thing while they'd been following their noses and their dicks.

He had the Jeep in gear before Shayne even had his door closed. His brother cursed but didn't growl at him. They had to keep up with their mate and keep her safe. That was all that was important now.

"It looks like we have a fight on our hands," Shayne said with one hand clutching the *oh shit* bar and the other bracing on the dashboard.

He didn't bother answering that redundant statement. He was too busy trying to catch up with the sassy feline. Hell, his jeans chafed at his aching dick.

"Maybe she's upset about the trees. She could be funny about her yard like Aunt Stacey." Shayne's annoying tendency to go off on tangents when they were knee-deep in crap gave him the urge to reach out and touch his brother with a fist.

"Watch for tails, and shut the hell up, Shayne," he finally said.

"So far nothing. I'm watching. Maybe that was just to throw us off so she could get away."

"Brother Bear didn't think so. She tasted of fear, raw fear. The scent was so thick up close to her that it coated my tongue with it. There was someone there all right. Hunter? I don't know—yet," Creed bit out.

"Besides," his brother said staring over his shoulder. "She knows who we are and that we already know where she lives. No point in trying to get rid of us when we'll just show up on her doorstep, clawing up her trees again."

"She doesn't care about the fucking trees, Shayne. She doesn't want bears as mates. We'll seduce her and prove to her that we can more than take care of her and our cubs. Then she'll settle down," he said, his voice deepening to a growl as a fresh surge of heat traveled from his balls to his shaft at the mere mention of sex.

"Still nothing following us. I don't think they even attempted to follow us, Creed."

He had been feeling the same way when no glimpse of them showed up in the rearview mirror. Now all he had to do was follow their mate as she led them on twisting turns that, had he not had a GPS system for back up, Creed might have been a bit worried. Brother bear would have found the way home, but it would have entailed leaving the Jeep and the few perishables they'd picked up and traipsing cross country since bears saw no reason to follow roads that didn't make sense. Why go around a stream when you can go right through it and maybe catch a tasty snack on the way.

"What's the plan once we catch up to her?" Shayne the pain asked with a smirk.

"We talk to her. Explain that we understand she's not keen on having bears as mates, but we'll take things slow so she can get to know us," he said. "I'm sure she'll be reasonable and react logically. Finding our mates is instinctual and crucial for males just like it's critical for a female to have a male to keep her safe. Without her mate, the female is always in danger and isn't equipped to adequately protect herself. Females have that innate need to breed and create life. Just being around us should kick in the need, and she'll probably all but attack us once that happens." He stopped talking when he heard what sounded suspiciously like a snore.

Tearing his eyes off the road for a second, Creed growled loud and thickly at his brother who had crossed his arms over his chest and proceeded to pretend to be asleep, making loud obnoxious snoring sounds in the process. He threw a punch at his sibling's stomach, enjoying the *whoosh* sound and grunt when his fist made contact with the man's abdomen with a loud *thump*.

"Really, Creed. Are you that out of touch with the real world? I know we grew up spending time with Papa Bear, but some of his teachings had to be taken with a grain of salt and some tasty honey to go down. Women aren't needy like that out here," Shayne said, frowning.

"Women? I'm talking about our mate, a female. Women are human. Their logic and thought processes don't make sense to human men, much less shifter males. You can't compare our little kitten to a human woman, Shayne." Creed wanted to spit in disgust. Just thinking about that left a bad taste in his mouth.

"I'm telling you that *our* little feline isn't operating under normal shifter logic. She's living out here alone, outside of a den, and without other relatives around her. That tells me right there that she's independent and won't appreciate your backwoods view of how she should act and react to finding her mates. Let's not even add to this issue the fact that there are two of us, not just one." Shayne glared right back at him, finally giving in to rub circles around the spot he'd hit.

"Regardless of why she's where she is now, it's going to change in the near future. She's ours and we protect what's ours." Creed focused on the road ahead of him, trying not to let his brother's ideas lead to doubts.

Damn him!

Why was their little kitten living alone outside of even a human town? There hadn't been a male or even another female scent anywhere around her home when they'd checked it out the night before. Sure, there had been a few faint human scents near the front of the house, but not strong enough for them to have lived there or even be a frequent visitor. It made him wonder what she was hiding from. It was the only plausible explanation in his mind.

Finally, they turned onto a road he recognized by scent and sight as one that would take them around the back way to their little cul-de-sac. He relaxed his hands on the wheel, wincing at the sight of pale knuckles turning pink once more. Between her stubbornness and his brother's suppositions of their chances with her, Creed teetered on having a meltdown.

I don't have meltdowns. I'm the Ursus. My control has always been faultless among all our bears. Nothing riles me, and I've never lost my cool under any circumstances. It must be the need to mate and have her safe in our den.

As he pulled into the drive behind the feline's car, Creed drew in a deep breath and slowly released it, willing his unease to leave with it. Shayne looked over at him with one arched brow and a barely hidden smile.

"Are we going to get out and help her with her groceries, or what?"

"You're going to take ours over to the house and put them up. Come back when you're through, and you can help," Creed said with a snort.

He heard his brother's soft curse as he opened his door. Creed opened his and managed not to jerk when his brother's door slammed. No reason to call him on it. Instead he focused his attention on his mate as it should be and had to swallow hard to keep from growling at the sight of shapely legs exposed a little too far from under sinfully short shorts. Her ass was heart shaped with large, soft looking globes he couldn't wait to squeeze.

Fuck! He was actually salivating at the thought of what she had hidden under the short shorts. Soon. Right now, he needed to focus on winning his way into her good graces so he and Shayne could claim her and get her settled in their den where she belonged. He wanted nothing more than to spend his days making her happy and his nights making her scream in pleasure.

When he walked up behind her, she stiffened noticeably before turning around to stare up at him. Bright green eyes like new pine growth flashed daggers at him even before he spoke. He realized that his brother might have been on to something, which was a real bitch. He didn't like to have to admit anything to the younger bear.

"Hi. Why don't you unlock the door, and we'll bring in your groceries," he said with a broad smile.

She looked as if she were going to say no with a lot of emphasis on the *hell* part in front of it, but then she seemed to change her mind. She nodded once, tersely, before turning on her heel and all but stomping to the back door. If the sight of her ass swaying hadn't distracted him, Creed would have had a load of groceries in his arms and been behind her before she'd managed to get the door open, but he couldn't tear his eyes away from her delicious ass until she'd disappeared inside the house.

"Aw, hell."

Creed picked up as many sacks as he could handle and strode up to the door, pausing for a second to inhale the scents from his mate's home before stepping inside. Nope. No one else shared the space with her, and there were only very light scents of one human female.

"Put them on the table, and I'll sort them out while you bring in the rest." The female was smart and planned to use them to unload her car then probably planned to kick them out once it was done.

He carefully settled the various bags on the table then turned and walked back out the door to meet his brother with a load of bags in his hands heading in. Shayne winked at him just before they passed each other. He groaned inwardly, wanting to call his brother back and demand he behave himself. Instead he rushed to the car and grabbed a couple of bags to run back to the door where he stopped short of walking inside. The sight before him had his cock growing even harder if that were possible.

His brother had set down the bags he'd been carrying and was standing next to the table starring at their mate as well. She was bent over the pull out drawer of the fridge that housed the freezer section, rearranging food in order to squeeze a few more things in. Her ass up in the air, swaying with her every move, was like a red flag to a bull to him and Shayne. A thin edge of lacy red panty made an appearance every time she moved something in the drawer. His incisors had lengthened and were poking his lips. His earlier fight to rein in control seemed to have been for nothing. Creed was on the edge and knew it.

Their bears were clawing at their thin control to claim their mate. There she stood, already in position for a good fucking. Brother bear couldn't understand why Creed wasn't already over there ripping her clothes out of the way. He was scared to even guess at how his brother was fairing in the fight with his bear half.

The sound of a low throaty growl startled him enough to snap out of the frozen trance he'd been in to stare at his brother with worry. If Shayne lost control and changed there in her kitchen, she'd never trust that they were strong enough to protect her when they couldn't control their other selves in her house. The growl came again, and Creed realized with horror that it was coming from him, not Shayne.

* * * *

Serenity straightened up at the sound of a low growl coming from behind her. Turning around, her eyes widened at both of the bears from the parking lot earlier standing in her kitchen. She was almost afraid to move for fear of setting them off. She didn't know which one of them had growled, but both of them were displaying their elongated teeth and panting through their mouths. She knew what she'd find if she looked down their amazing bodies without dipping her eyes.

They were turned on, and with the mating heat riding them, they were having a devil of a time controlling themselves. If she hadn't been their focus, it would have been funny as hell to see two huge males reduced to slobbering dogs—uh, bears.

The taller of the two males stood nearly six and a half feet tall with a broad chest challenging the T-shirt he had stretched across it. His equally wide shoulders accented how, once you got past his amazing chest, it tapered down to a narrow waist. She'd already noticed his ass. She loved a man with a squeezable butt. It would have been a shame for someone that looked as ripped as he did to be stuck with a flat ass.

The coffer of goodness didn't stop there. The big bear had beautiful dark brown hair that was rich in color and thick from the looks of it. It appeared shaggy but not long enough to pull back. He kept a close cut beard sculpted to his face that complimented his sharp features, almost softening them, but not quite. But it was his warm brown eyes the color of mocha that captured her attention in the end. Even now as they flashed from that warm brown to dark gold, they compelled her to stare in to them, holding hers until the movement of the other bear, his brother from their similar scents, jarred her attention to him.

This one stood two or three inches shorter than his sibling but was just as muscular and sculpted. His coloring was lighter all over than the other male with brown hair a shade lighter and long enough to pull back in a ponytail at the nape of his neck. She could almost say the color was a chestnut color. Then there were his eyes. Like the other male, his eyes were amazing in their lighter color that almost didn't seem real. When his flashed with his bear, the gold was much lighter.

His step closer to her was what had grabbed her attention from his brother. Yet he stopped when she stared at him, not moving another inch, as if just having her gaze on him now settled his bear enough that the male was able to regain control. She studied him while she waited to see if they would regain control for good or not. This bear was clean shaven and had slightly softer features without the harder planes of his brother.

That they were both dominant males was clear, but from the flare of power coming off of them, Serenity began to wonder if they weren't high in their sleuth. She'd never met bears in person before but had been told all about them. They were just as fierce as the cats and wolves but were usually more laid back in their family hierarchy and intersleuth relationships. There wasn't a lot of infighting amongst them unless it was over a female. Bears tended to be born into their positions with similar males just moving on to find another sleuth rather than fighting to usurp the other.

But when it came to their cubs, mates, or a potential mate, bears were ruthless in their protection. Though males were referred to as boars and females as sows, most bears didn't appreciate outsiders referring to them that way. They might refer to each other in those terms, but an outsider only opened themselves up to attack over the slight.

So now, as she waited for them to calm down, Serenity reviewed everything she knew about the shifters. Where her lynx had started to react to the bears now that they were both right in front of her, she was desperately trying to convince her to ignore them. Why couldn't she refuse to mate with them since they weren't lynxes, and what ever happened to one mate per cat anyway? There were two of them, and from what she could tell, they expected her to take them both on.

Hell, no!

What was wrong with bears that there were two of them? It shouldn't require two males to mate with one female. She hadn't heard that about bear shifters. They sure didn't do that in the wild.

The larger bear seemed to pull it together first and slowly walked over to where the other one still stood with his mouth slightly open, his breathing coming in light pants. The big male laid his hand over the other one's shoulder, and instantly the room lost the feel of an impending disaster about to break free. Serenity realized it was easier to breathe and hadn't realized it had been all that hard before.

"We need to talk as soon as you have the remainder of your supplies stored away," the apparent leader of the two said in an unnaturally deep and raspy voice.

"About what?" she asked, despite it being obvious.

"Who was after you, and why?" he asked, surprising her with the question.

"I don't know for sure. There are hunters in the area. A new group of shifter haters, intent on destroying us all." She figured talking about their mutual enemy was a much safer topic than their elephant of a problem hovering in the room.

"I didn't see them, but I felt danger when I approached you. Do you know what they look like—their scent?" he asked.

"No. I didn't see them, but I did hear them. They were probably west of me based on the wind's direction. One was a kid in his early twenties. The other sounded like an older man in his thirties maybe."

"It's not safe for you to remain alone in this house," the big bear said.

"I can take care of myself," she huffed out, thrusting her chin up and her hands on her hips.

"Told you," the younger and slightly shorter male said, softly.

His sibling growled a warning at him, making Serenity smile. Maybe they would argue, and she could just slip out and go for a run. They'd never be able to catch up with her in her lynx form. The cat purred at the thought of a run.

But the big male ignored the other one and stared intently at her. "My name is Creed North, and this is my brother Shayne."

Serenity hesitated. Finally she sighed and realized that withholding her name was nothing but childish. They could find out easily enough considering that they lived just across the way from her.

"Serenity Jones. You're bear shifters."

Creed nodded with a hint of a smile on his face. "And you're a feline shifter, but we don't know what flavor."

"Flavor?" Somehow that didn't sound all that friendly to her.

The shorter male stepped forward, a much more obvious grin in his expression. Despite his large frame, the bear moved smoothly without any sign of clumsiness. She knew it was a shifter trait, but seeing it with these two massive mountain sized males really drove it home.

"Type, Serenity. We're just wondering what type cat you turn into when you're furry."

"Lynx."

She lifted her chin once more and waited for the raised eyebrows and snorts of laughter since she wasn't sleek and thin like other female lynxes. No, instead of a normal lynx female, Serenity turned into a slightly plumper version of the lean felines that were known for their stealthy ability to slink around like the fox.

The snorts and laughter didn't come. Neither did she see either male lift a brow or look her over in disbelief. They just stared at her with interested smiles. Maybe they hadn't really thought about what a lynx actually looked like and compared that image to her yet. The mating heat was obviously working on them with how deep and growly Creed's voice was and how Shayne kept testing the air by breathing it in through his slightly open mouth.

"I can't wait to see you change, sweetness. I bet you're a beauty," Shayne crooned.

Confusion ate at Serenity as she slowly started to put her groceries away once more. They had her mind perplexed, muddled to the point she couldn't string two thoughts together. She hated it. This wasn't her. Serenity was always calm and had a clear picture of where she was going and what she was going to do when she arrived.

The entire time she put her kitchen back to rights, Serenity could feel their presence in the room with her despite the distance they kept by remaining by the kitchen table. Neither of them took a seat, just stood there waiting for her to finish. It was interesting how they were able to remain so still when beneath their skin lay fur, and beneath that lay a living, breathing animal supposedly absorbed with the mating frenzy that shifters fell victim to at times.

Serenity had seen the wildness that her kind exhibited when a true mate was encountered and their animals demanded to seal their mates to them. A male would always feel threatened that another male would take his intended from him until he had marked her as his. The female, more often than not, didn't fight once she'd assured herself the male was worthy of her acquiescence. Some tried to run from the one nature had picked for them, and it always ended up with the male subduing the female to mark her. She'd refused to allow that to happen to her, so she'd left.

Now, years later and thousands of miles across the nation, Serenity was faced with the very thing she'd run from with added irritants to the issue. They weren't lynxes, or even felines, but bears, and there were two of them, not one.

She finished folding the last of the bags and, after stashing them in the pantry, turned to face the two barely contained bear statues taking up space in her kitchen eating area.

"I don't need a mate, let alone two. I don't want mates. Nothing personal, but I don't plan to be part of a den or a sleuth. I'm sorry that you are going through this, but it can't be helped. Once your bears realize I'm not changing my mind, they'll settle down." She didn't smile, not wanting to seem unkind or vindictive. She really did feel for them, but she refused to get caught up in the entire thing.

Her lynx growled, clawing at her from the inside. Serenity winced as she tried to get out to see her potential mates. What had happened to her animal's strong agreement not to have anything to do with the opposite sex of any species? If the feline didn't settle down, there'd be trouble for sure.

Neither of the two big males moved from their spot next to the table. Instead, power radiated off of them, filling the room until it was nearly suffocating. She began to wonder if they would lose control with her rejection and attack her. She'd never heard of that happening before, but then she'd never known of a mate to refuse the mating before.

The lynx fought her for control, not understanding Serenity's choice one bit. She'd agreed with her when they'd been back in her home den where the males had little to offer her. Now, it seemed that the finicky feline had changed her mind. With her lynx battling her from within and the two massive bears pouring out their power on the outside, Serenity felt as if she were about to implode from all the power directed at her. Real fear began to seep into her bloodstream and drift from her pores.

She saw the instant the bears became aware of it. Their nostrils flared as their lips drew back to expose their sharpened teeth while they breathed in her fear. Something changed in their eyes. She'd pushed them too far. They were going to tear her apart for denying them as her mates. She hadn't outrun her fate after all. She'd just changed the location of her demise.

"Ours," Creed growled.

"Safe," Shayne added in a slightly less harsh voice.

"Mate," Creed said. "Our mate."

Serenity didn't dare say anything to set them off again. She'd let them settle down then talk with them under calmer circumstances. This was not a good time.

The doorbell rang, startling her so that she jumped with a slight shriek. The two males lifted their noses and frowned.

"Wild dog, female," Creed said. "Do you know her?"

Serenity had to make herself think. Her heart raced to the point of pain. What was going on? She'd rarely had any visitors at her house in the years she'd lived there, and now she had not only two huge male bears in her kitchen but an unknown female wild dog at her front door. Had the cosmos hiccupped or something?

She shook her head but turned and walked into the living area to answer the door. The female at the door knocked again before she got there. Whatever was going on it seemed to be urgent. She unlocked the multiple deadbolts and swung the door open wide, aware that she had two overly cautious bears at her back.

Before she managed to ask the female standing there with wild multi-shaded hair what she needed, the wild dog rushed inside and slammed the door behind her.

"They've figured out who you are. You've got to get out of here. They're coming for you."

Chapter Four

Shayne stepped up in front of his brother. "Who's coming for her? Why?"

"How do you know me? I've never met you before," Serenity said, taking a step back. Large, warm hands settled lightly on her shoulders.

"I'm Wren Angles. I live in town with my pack. We've been staying off the radar ever since we noticed that over the last few months strangers have been moving in and staying but not putting down permanent roots. Some are renting cheap hotel rooms by the week. They all meet up in a roundabout way at Phill's bar every Friday night." Wren's words tumbled out of her so fast it was difficult to follow her.

"Slow down," Creed said in a much more controlled voice. "Tell us who they are."

"Rouge Hunters. They're not the ones the government sanctions to hunt down shifters who've murdered humans. These are shifter haters. They believe that all shifters should either be killed or locked up. They've figured out that Serenity is a shifter and plan to come get her." Wren looked back and forth between them all. "You've got to hide her before it's too late."

"Nothing will happen to her. She is ours. We'll protect her with our lives," Shayne assured the little female. Wren stood an inch shorter than their mate, but seemed just as fierce as Serenity appeared to be.

"How do you know they are aware of Serenity being a shifter?" Creed asked.

"I'm really good at hiding my shifter abilities, so I've been spying on them. I'm a bartender there on Friday nights when they meet. Since I'm a shifter, I can pretty much hear everything they say," she told them.

"Why didn't you tell Serenity about this before now? It's Sunday already," Shayne asked.

The female all but stomped her foot at them. "Look. You're wasting time drilling me when you should be getting her to safety. We can discuss the particulars later."

"Talk," Creed growled.

The little wild dog growled right back at Creed, clearly unimpressed by his attempt at menacing her. Instead, she bared her teeth and looked to Serenity.

"Look. I know you don't know me, but I'm telling you the truth. Your life is in danger. I was working last night when they all showed up and sat at the back of the room. They normally didn't meet on Saturday nights. I was delivering a round of drinks when I overheard them verify that you were a shifter based on something someone saw you do. I don't know what it was or when it was, but they've outed you. You need to hide while we all figure out how to get them to leave the area."

"How do you know me and where to find me?" Serenity asked. Shayne began to feel the prickles of unease as they stood there talking.

"I saw you for the first time in the grocery store today. That older woman you were talking to said your name when she introduced you to her friends. From the description I overheard on Saturday night, I knew you were the one. I tried to follow you to your car but saw two of them watching you several rows over. Then those two showed up, and the men disappeared. I followed you but had a difficult time carrying my clothes and running at the same time. I just managed to get dressed and locate your car again, so I knew I had the right house. Now. Are you going to believe me and hide, or wait around and let them catch up with you?" Wren stuck her hands on her hips and glared at them.

Shayne felt that glare all the way to his toes. She was deadly serious. The dangerous feeling grew stronger.

"Creed," he began.

"Yeah. We need to go." Creed nodded his head toward the kitchen. "While Creed grabs your perishables, you need to pack a bag for a few days until we can figure out what to do, Serenity."

"I'm not leaving my home. I have a job to do. I can't just walk away like that," she said.

Shayne hesitated for a second, but then turned and left them to handle his mate while he gathered anything that might not make it for a week. He could hear their voices in a low murmur but resisted the temptation to listen in. He needed to stay focused on his job for the moment. He could find out what was going on later.

As soon as he'd repacked her dated food in their Jeep, Shayne hurried back to the front of the house to find it empty. Following his nose, he located Creed in what must have been her office, dismantling some computer equipment.

"Need some help?" he asked.

"Yeah. Grab those and take them out to the Jeep. I'll bring this when I finish getting it unhooked. Serenity and Wren are in her bedroom packing. At least I hope that's where they are right now."

"I'll check on them when I get back from carrying this out," he said, hoisting the equipment and carrying it back out to their vehicle.

Stepping into his mate's bedroom was a step into heaven. Her scent permeated everything in the room, right down to the paint on the walls and the finish on the wood floors. He wanted to roll around on her bed to cover himself in her scent, but refrained, reminding himself that he could do that with the real thing soon enough. They would soon have her in their den.

"Do you have anything ready that I can go ahead and carry out?" he asked from the doorway.

Serenity turned toward him, and for an instant, he saw fear in her eyes before she covered it up with an irritated scowl.

"That suitcase is ready. I'm almost finished with the rest," she said.

Shayne could see Wren in the bathroom filling a case of sorts with all the things women used in the bathroom. The case wasn't as large as a suitcase but did look large compared to the small shaving kit he carried when they traveled. Shaking his head at the secrets of being a woman, he carried the heavy, packed suitcase out of the bedroom toward the kitchen and the back door. He met Creed returning from the Jeep.

"Did you get everything she needed out of the office?" he asked.

Creed frowned. "Almost. One more trip, and I'll have it. What about her things from the bedroom?"

"There's two more that I'm aware of. One is a smaller version of the one she is packing now. The little wild dog is packing it out of the bathroom." Shayne grinned at the exasperated expression his brother exhibited at the mention of the wild dog. Someone had rubbed him the wrong way.

"I'll go hurry them along," Creed said with a soft growl in his words.

Shayne just nodded and continued to the Jeep. Somehow he didn't think anyone could hurry their mate if she didn't want to be hurried. He couldn't stop the grin from spreading across his face. They were going to have a fight on their hands with her, and life would never be dull as long as she was in their den. He meant to make sure she remained in their den as long as there was breath in his body.

Just as he walked back into the kitchen, he heard the argument in full swing growing closer by the second. He remained where he stood in the middle of the kitchen and waited. Wren entered the room first with an amused expression on her face with Serenity in a not very serene mood right behind her.

"I'm not going home with you. You can't make me. That's kidnapping. I plan to go to either Flat Head or Echo Lake. I can rent a place there until this blows over. They'll get tired of looking for an easy target and move on eventually. Then I can come back home." She glared at Creed as he walked through the door carrying a suitcase in one hand and the odd-looking round case that had come from the bathroom in the other.

Shayne walked around the two females and took the cases from his brother so he had his hands free. He knew his brother. The poor male was not far from picking up their mate and throwing her over his shoulder. He wanted to be sure he was out of screaming distance when that happened. A female's enraged screams tended to be shrill on a shifter's hearing. He didn't envy his brother's position one bit in that moment. No doubt his ears would be ringing for hours afterward.

Just as he closed the jeep's back end after shoving the cases inside, the hair on the back of his neck lifted. They were already here. As normally as possible, Shayne walked through the small walkway and back inside the house. Without waiting to see what was going on, he growled to get their attention. Everyone's head snapped toward his warning of danger.

"They're already here. I can sense them outside. We need to go, and we can't go home until we're sure they aren't following us or watching the area."

"Fuck." Creed stared at the two women. "Don't struggle, or we'll all end up dead."

"Struggle?" they both asked in unison with a question clear in their eyes.

He grabbed the female wild dog just as Creed picked up Serenity, throwing their mate over his back. Shayne followed suit and led the way outside through the walkway to the Jeep. To his surprise, neither female made a noise in protest. In fact, the wild dog female remained completely still and limp as he raced around the front of the vehicle and opened the back door, shoving her inside before slamming the door and climbing in the front passenger side. His door closed at the same time that Creed's did. When he turned around, it was to see both females hunched down in the back.

Nothing happened as his brother started the engine and backed them out of the garage. It wasn't until they drove down the drive and reached the street that anything out of the ordinary happened. As they raced down the road, a Humvee turned down the road heading in their direction.

"Stay down," he called back to them. "They're coming up the street now. Maybe they don't realize you're with us."

Shayne didn't turn to make sure they followed his directions so as not to tip off anyone in the approaching Humvee that there might be someone in their back seat. He saw Creed's eyes check the rearview mirror though. He seemed satisfied, so Shayne trusted that they were behaving.

As they passed the other vehicle, the tinted windows kept them from seeing inside even with their enhanced eyesight. He felt sure by how the tires appeared that there were more than three or four men inside.

"They stopped at the bottom of her driveway," Creed told them. "Don't get up yet. They can still see us. It looks like they are blocking the drive to keep you from trying to escape if you decide to make a run for it."

"That wouldn't have slowed me down. I'd have gone through the yard," Serenity huffed out with a slight growl to her voice.

Shayne couldn't stop a snort at that. "More than likely they would have caught you unawares and captured you. There were probably more than five men in that thing. They'd have surrounded the house and caught you no matter which door or window you went out."

"Idiot. I wouldn't have gone out the normal way. I've been living there for several years and had escape plans in place. I have an underground tunnel that leads to the garage, and one that leads deeper into the woods. I'm not stupid or helpless," she hissed from the back floorboard.

Shayne winced, looking over at his brother. The other bear didn't look very pleased either. They were digging their graves with their mate. She was on the defensive already. With the present turn of events, they were only reinforcing her belief that they thought her incapable of protecting herself. Of course, Creed, the big oaf, pretty much believed that from what he'd said earlier that day. How were they ever going to win her acceptance in the middle of something like this? Their bears would never allow her out of their sights now and would be overbearing bastards before it was over with to keep her safe. Her safety was all they would live for right now, no matter what it took to ensure it. He sighed and resumed watching for a tail.

* * * *

What was going on? She'd lived by herself for years in that house and had never given away anything about her nature when she was in public. Now she had crazies after her and two mates that turned into bears all in the space of twenty-four hours. How had that happened?

Shayne started talking to someone about what was going on. Evidently he'd called someone because he wouldn't rehash everything to Creed when the other bear had been right there with them. Who was he talking to? What did he expect them to do with all the information he was giving the other party?

She looked over to where the wild dog female crouched next to her wearing a scowl of her own. She obviously hadn't expected to get caught up in the mess when she'd raced to warn her about the Rogue Hunters. Wren was pretty with her odd-colored hair and pert nose that turned up slightly at the end. Her hazel eyes seemed to swirl with color when she was mad as they were doing now, and her variegated brown and gold hair hung forward over her shoulders like a thick curtain.

"So the first time you'd ever seen me was at the grocery today?" Serenity asked.

"Yeah. I've lived here all my life and only met a few other shifters out this way. The area is too remote and gets so cold in the winter that few shifters are comfortable this far north," she said.

"Shifters have become soft and too dependent on technology and the comforts they have since The Awakening," Creed snarled from the front seat.

"You sound like my da," Wren mumbled.

Serenity heard Shayne's snort from the front seat. "I kind of agree with him. My den back home had gotten to the point that they spent so much time with humans that they were adopting a lot of their nasty habits."

"Is that why you left—moved here?" Shayne asked.

She started to ignore him, but figured now was a good time to make sure they understood her stance on mating while they were stuck up front and she had Wren back there with her. The sudden tightening of her skin as her lynx made her displeasure known reminded her that she couldn't protect herself from her cat.

"No. I left because I refused to mate with any of the males in my den, and the Rufus, the alpha leader of our chain, had decided that he would choose for me. I refused to accept his choice as well and left." It had been much more than that, but she wasn't about to tell them the entire sordid story. She didn't know any of them well enough to bare her soul to them.

"He would have forced you to accept a male you didn't want?" Creed's voice still had that growly quality to it while his brother's had calmed somewhat.

"Yes. It wasn't uncommon for him to choose mates in our den. I hated that and had already decided that once I was old enough to support myself, I was going to leave. He started harping at my parents to push me to select a mate. He liked the females to all be mated by the time they were eighteen. My parents refused to force me to choose so young. He let it go for a few years, but as soon as I turned eighteen, he insisted I choose my mate and get on with the business of producing more cubs. I'm not a baby factory." It had infuriated Serenity to be told it was what she was born to do, care for her mate and have his cubs.

"Why don't you want cubs, Serenity?" Wren asked.

"It's not that I don't want them. It's that I want to make that decision for myself and not be forced to have them to strengthen the den and improve my mate's standing to the Rufus. A lot of the females in my den were abused by their mates because they didn't stay pregnant and give them lots of sons. No male will ever lift a hand to me. I'll scratch his eyes out if he tries," she said with a hiss.

"Your Rufus wasn't a good leader. Females are to be cherished, never abused," Creed said in that growly voice of his. Serenity was beginning to wonder if that wasn't his normal sound.

"Yeah, well tell that to the Rufus. I left. I hated leaving my parents and brothers, but I knew I would end up dead if I had stayed. The first cat to touch me like that would have known just how well my brothers taught me to fight. They would have tried to declaw me, and I would have fought them over it."

"Declaw you? Are you serious?" Shayne sounded appalled.

"Yes. They will declaw a feline they feel is dangerous if they feel like that feline is still needed in the den. As a female, I was considered a breeder, so my life would be spared but I would be made helpless so that I had to depend on my mate to keep me and our cubs safe. I'd rather die," she spat out.

"I can't imagine anyone being that cruel," Wren said, shaking her head. "Is a chain what you call your den? We just use den to describe ours."

"Yeah, as a group we are considered a chain and we live in our dens."

"You can get off the floorboard now. I'm sure it's not very comfortable," Creed said.

Serenity sat up and stretched before settling back on the seat and fastening her safety belt. Looking around, she recognized that they were close to Echo Lake already. They were going to take her there after all. She relaxed.

"Do you mind if I call my brother and let him know where I am?" Wren asked. "He'll get worried if I don't show up at home soon."

"Go ahead. If you need me to talk to him, I'll assure him that we will keep you safe," Creed said.

"It's good." Wren pulled her cell out of her back pocket and pressed a button, holding it to her ear. "Hey. I'm fine. Remember that conversation I overheard at the bar Saturday night? Yeah. I found the shifter they were talking about and warned her. That's where I am right now. I just wanted to let you know I'm safe."

Serenity could tell from Wren's expression that her brother was fussing at her. All males were alike, thinking females had no abilities outside of cooking, cleaning, and spitting out young for them to brag on.

"I'll call you once I know where we're going to stop. Yeah, we're on the road right now. We're not alone. Her mates are with us."

Serenity started to dispute that, but the look on the wild dog's face had her relenting and letting that pass for now. It was obvious she was trying to keep her brother from going off the deep end.

"They're bears, so I think we are pretty safe, Roco. They're probably six and a half feet each and huge. Um, yeah. I said mates. She has two. I don't know. It's none of my business. Look. I'll call you later. Just tell everyone I'm fine." She pressed the end button and sighed, sticking her phone back in her pocket.

"Everything okay?" she asked the female.

"Yeah. He's my oldest brother and tends to baby me. It's good." The wild dog settled back in the seat and looked out the window.

"When we get to where we're going," Creed began, "you can let your brother know, and he can come pick you up. We won't be going back right away."

Serenity's eyes shot to where his watched her from the rearview mirror. What did he mean they weren't going back right away? She chided herself over jumping to conclusions. They needed to talk, and obviously they couldn't with Wren there. She slowed her breathing and jerked her eyes away from Creeds to stare out the side window, much like Wren was doing.

After what felt like forever, they finally pulled into the little community outside of Echo Lake. She wondered what Creed planned to do until he pulled up outside a mom-and-pop motel. It looked pretty run down, but beggars couldn't be choosy. She could sleep in her lynx form if the place was terrible, but she hated the idea of setting up her computer equipment in a nasty place.

"Stay here. I'll be back in a minute," Creed said.

Shayne didn't budge, so she wondered why he'd bothered to say anything. With his brother watching over them, they weren't likely to attempt to run off. Besides, they *did* need to talk. The sooner they got that over with, the sooner they could all go on with their lives. Well, once she got the damn Rogue Hunters off of her tail.

Creed returned much sooner than she would have believed, making her wonder if they were full or just not open any longer. Once he had climbed back behind the wheel, he turned to look over the seat at them.

"They don't really rent rooms out much anymore. They just keep them up for when family is in town. They aren't expecting any until next month, so they said we could camp out for a few days."

"That's fine. It will give me time to decide where to go from here," she said with a defiant look at Creed then Shayne.

Neither male said anything, but a nerve ticked at the corner of Creed's mouth. For some reason, Serenity had the urge to lick it until it relaxed. She shook all over like a wet dog then cast a quick glance in Wren's direction. She hadn't meant that as an insult. Thank God the other shifter couldn't read her mind.

Creed drove the Jeep around to the back of the building and parked in front of a faded orange door with the number fourteen on it in just as faded black numbers. Creed shook his head to stop them all from getting out except Shayne, who took the key from his brother and eased out of the vehicle. It was obvious that he was going to check the room to be sure it was secure. What were they expecting, that the hunters had already set up shop there waiting for them? They had no idea where they might have headed.

Shayne returned after propping the door open with a chair. He walked over to the driver's side, and Creed rolled down the window.

"It's not bad at all, just musty. If we leave the door open for thirty minutes or so, it should be okay. We can unpack everything, and by the time we have her computer set up, it should be fresh enough to close it again."

"Fridge?" Creed asked.

"Yeah. Apartment size, not dorm size, so it's got a little room."

"Unload the perishables and food. Wait on the computer and clothes just yet," Creed told him. Then he turned to look back at them. "We might not stay here. We'll unload the computer a little later if we decide to stay."

Serenity wasn't going to argue with him at this point. She respected the need to be careful, and if he wasn't satisfied with where they were, she would trust him and his instincts on this—for now.

I might as well face it. I want to trust them with more than my safety. Refusing their mate claim isn't as easy as I thought it would be.

Ours, her lynx whined. *Safe. Strong.*

She and Wren stepped down from the Jeep and followed Shayne inside as he carried several bags of food. She took them from him when he stopped next to the refrigerator and put away the milk, eggs, cheese, and meat she'd bought. At least they hadn't brought any of the frozen things with them. She watched Wren set the bags of nonperishable items on the little table that was probably intended as a dining table. When she looked around, she noticed that there wasn't a desk anywhere around that she could use for her computer anyway. There was no way her computer would fit on the table. Besides, the piece of furniture wasn't strong enough to hold it up anyway.

"There's no desk." She stated the obvious, pissed at how aware of the two bears her body was.

"Don't worry," Creed said with a feral appearing smile. "We're not staying here too long."

"Then where are we going, and why did we even bother stopping here?" she demanded.

"We're taking you home, to our den, where you belong."

Chapter Five

"If you were going to take her to your place, why did you bother driving all the way out here and get a room?" Wren asked when all Serenity could do was open and close her mouth.

"We live next door to her, so taking her right next door with them so close wouldn't have helped us at the time. Now we are safe and can make plans to go back," Creed said.

"We have den brothers back home who can help," Shayne explained.

"What can they do?" Serenity asked, finally able to speak again.

"For one thing, they can watch to see what the hunters do and find out if they are following us," he said.

"Is that who you were talking to earlier?" she asked.

"Yeah. They were already wondering why Shayne and I hadn't shown back up with cream for the coffee," he said with a rueful smile.

She frowned. "Who takes cream in their coffee?" Was there a female bear over there? And why did that possibility make her angry?

Not her. Her cat.

Bitch!

The lynx was jealous and had no reason to be when they weren't keeping the damn bears in the first place. She wanted to swat at the feline, but she knew it was impossible. She'd only have to endure the vindictive feline's tricks if she tried something.

Shayne chuckled. "That would be Otto. He's from Russia and a little, um, different."

She frowned. "Why do you have a bear from Russia as part of your den? Is he related to you somehow?" she asked.

Creed had stepped away when Shayne had first spoken up. She could hear him talking low to someone over the phone. She ignored him and concentrated on what Shayne was saying instead.

"Sit down, and I'll tell you about the others." Shayne indicated the small living area where there was a love seat and two chairs, one on either side of the loveseat. She chose a chair while Shayne sat on the side of the loveseat closest to her.

When she looked around for Wren, it was to find that the other shifter had disappeared. Before she began to worry, she noticed that the bathroom door was closed where it hadn't been a few seconds ago. More than likely she'd gone in there to give them all some privacy, or for her own privacy while she called her brother again.

"Serenity?" Shayne's voice snagged her attention once again.

"Sorry. You were telling me about why you had a Russian shifter in your den," she prompted.

He smiled, a slow grin that told her he had a very mischievous streak and was probably thinking naughty thoughts.

Don't go there, Serenity. You've got enough going on without steering your mind in that direction.

She forced herself to concentrate on what he was saying and not what his expression made her think of instead. He was telling her about finding the house and knowing that was where they were supposed to be because it was perfect for them.

"Why?" she asked, even though she already knew what he would say. It had a nearly finished full basement, which was something her cat and the bears would both appreciate.

"One reason was because it had plenty of bedrooms for us if we shared," he said winking at her. "The main reason was because of the huge basement. We like to den underground as much as possible."

"Yeah, so do we," she said before she could stop herself. She frowned.

To his credit, Shayne didn't push her to reveal more, choosing to let it go and continue with his explanations.

"There are ten of us in our sleuth. We've chosen to call it the Talmadge Sleuth and are claiming the area as our territory. Creed is our Ursus, our leader much like your Rufus, though yours in particular is a worthless asshole. I'm the Zashchita, Creed's second," Shayne explained to her.

"You and Creed are the leaders of your sleuth?" Panic clawed at her throat, threatening to choke her on the realization that they could very easily force her into a mating with them. She didn't want that—to be forced. She wanted to choose her own mate when she got ready to.

Not only that, but they would never allow her to do anything on her own. She'd be surrounded by guards all the time and rarely allowed out of their eyesight. It would kill her, suffocate her to be forced to live that way. No. She had to get away from them. Her sanity, maybe even her very life, could depend on it. The one thing she knew beyond all doubt was that confining her would drive her insane.

"...introduce you to all of them when we get there," Shayne was saying.

She nodded absently, her mind in turmoil over finding out that her predetermined mates were not just bears, but the leaders of their sleuth. The odds were unimaginable, yet there she sat with one of them right next to her and the other one merely across the room. No wonder her cat hadn't put up much of a fuss. They made her feel safe, and she was starstruck. Female cats looking for a mate never settled. They would search for years until one that instilled a sense of safety and the knowledge that their genes were superior to others could be found. Cats tended to be slightly snobbish when it came to continuing their bloodlines where wolves could care less about bloodlines as long as the potential mate was strong and able to protect them and their pups.

Serenity looked back toward the bathroom. She didn't know what wild dogs did or thought when it came to mates. She'd never been around one before. The only thing she knew about them was that they could be crazy when riled and were fierce in a fight. They were about the only shifter group that would willingly attack and fight a hyena or jackal clan. Now *they* were crazy.

"Serenity? Are you okay?" Shayne's voice slipped into her thoughts, confusing her for a moment until she realized he'd spoken out loud and hadn't spoken to her in her head like it had sounded.

"Yes. Sorry. I started thinking about something and stopped listening." She smiled to soften the insult of not paying attention to him.

"Yeah, well, ancestry and such is really boring. Suffice it to say that because our home sleuth's bloodline was beginning to weaken from all of the inbreeding, it was time for some of us to break off and form our own. Two of our brothers went toward the New England states around Maine. Personally, I'm thankful we chose here. It's similar to home, while still offering a little nicer weather more often than home." He grinned and touched her cheek before she realized what he was going to do.

The calluses of his fingers and the pads of his hands rubbed not uncomfortably against the softer skin of her cheek, stimulating a need she'd never felt before. Serenity wanted to roll against his body, cover him in her scent while taking on some of his at the same time. Her lynx stirred at the sudden change in her body temperature, sniffing to determine what had aroused her in more ways than one.

"More importantly, though, it's where we found you, our mate. Nothing is better than finally locating our other half and becoming whole. Until that happens, we're incomplete and restless. Our mates still that wanderlust in our soul and keep the wilder side that is always just beneath the surface a little calmer. You give us control that we don't normally have," he said.

She scoffed at that, breaking the spell he'd somehow weaved around her with his touch. She'd felt warm and safe for a minute with his hand gently caressing her face. All of that flew away like a butterfly on the wind in the face of that one word, control.

"Obviously it only works on one mate, not two. Creed is anything but in control as far as I can see. He's growling at me anytime he talks to me," she nearly snarled.

Shayne burst out laughing. It pissed her off that he'd laugh at her. She started to get up and stomp to the bathroom and ask Wren if she could come in, but Creed walked over, shoving his phone into the case attached to his belt.

"What's so funny?" he asked.

Shayne had gotten up when Serenity had. Now he blocked the path to the outside door while his brother stood in the way of getting to the bathroom without brushing past him. She wanted to yowl in frustration.

"She thinks you're out of control because you keep growling at her when you talk," Shane explained between chuckles.

Creed frowned deeper and spoke to Shayne without removing his gaze from her. "What have you been talking about that my being out of control would even come up?"

"He was telling me about why you were in Montana and picked the house next to mine. Then he said some crap about how important it was for bears to find their mates. They help settle you down some, help you control the bear." She smirked at him, daring him to try and tell her it was true.

His mouth slowly widened into a smile, one that reached all the way to his eyes, turning them into warm chocolate brownie orbs that twinkled. They actually twinkled with laughter. It captured her in his spell so completely that she didn't hear the bathroom door open, nor did she notice the female wild dog walk up behind Creed.

"Shayne's right. Mates are like a mild dose of a tranquilizer. They calm the raging beast that lurks in all of us. Of course not even a mate can calm one that senses danger to their other half. They'll fight to the death to keep their mate and young safe," Wren said matter-of-factly then plopped down on the love seat and propped her bare feet on the coffee table.

And they were big feet, not so much wide as long. Serenity stared at them trying to figure out why she was angry. Then when it hit her, she glared at the other female.

"You're not in this conversation. I've never heard of mates calming each other before. I'd think someone might have mentioned that to me if it were true." She scowled at all three of them before brushing past Creed to stomp toward the bathroom.

No one tried to stop her, which was fine with her. She needed to think and that wasn't going to happen around them. How had she managed to end up stuck in a hotel room with two bears and a wild dog anyway?

I made the mistake of thinking I could outrun fate. I guess this is payback.

It wasn't like the two bears weren't good-looking men. Hell, they were hot! Just being near them kept her breasts tingling and her clit throbbing for relief. Still, it was the principal of the matter. She hadn't wanted to be forced into a mating. This—this pull she felt was just another type of force. There was no way they loved her after only one day. Hell, she wasn't sure she even liked them, much less loved them. Okay, maybe that wasn't quite true. She did sort of like Shayne. He had a sense of humor and wasn't nearly as overbearing as Creed seemed to be.

But mate both of them? I might as well throw away my career and everything I've worked for if I give in to them.

Did she have a choice? She had run away from her old den, and could have run away from Creed and Shayne as well if it weren't for one small issue. The mating heat. It had them from what she'd noticed so far. Their scent was slightly different than it had been in her front yard from the night before. Had it only been that morning she'd become aware of them for the first time? If she left now, they could and very probably would go insane hunting her down. They would be dangerous bears to anyone they thought might be in their way.

More to the point, though, was the fact that she had started feeling it now, too. It wasn't the lust that plagued her anytime she caught sight of their purely masculine bodies or inhaled even a hint of their scent. With her, it concentrated around the cat's need to reproduce— to fuck. Felines were cursed with a raging libido when they went into heat, and hers was just about to hit at the worst possible time.

Normally it wouldn't phase her, making her belly hurt some and her breasts tender all over, but without a male lynx or other feline around, she handled it just fine. Add to that the fact that she rarely went into heat, maybe twice a year instead of once every three months like most of the females in her den, and she knew she wasn't prepared for what it was already throwing at her. If she'd had any doubt that the two bears in the other room were her mates before, there was no doubt anymore. Any other shifter outside of a feline or her mates wouldn't have triggered her heat so soon since her last one had only been about two months back. The building discomfort in her pelvis along with a slowly growing need to be fucked assured her that her fate had already been sealed without her agreement.

"Serenity?" A sudden pounding on the bathroom door shocked her out of the miserable stupor she'd settled into. "What's wrong? Open the door."

Creed's voice elicited shivers along her spine with how deep and growly it had grown. She was sure his bear was reacting to her discomfort. Even though they hadn't shared the mating bond, any shifter could sense when another one was in distress if they were close enough or if they were family or an alpha from short distances.

"I'm fine," she lied then covered the lie with the truth so he'd believe her. "I'm upset, okay? I've got Rogue Hunters after me, and I need a minute to regroup. Leave me alone, Creed."

"You don't have to be afraid, kitten. Shayne and I will never let anything happen to you."

She wanted to scream at him but drew in a deep breath to calm her lynx before she said something she would regret. They were just as much a victim as she was in this. They had no more control over nature's method of making them comply to her will than she did. They just didn't bother fighting it or see it as a problem. They were males. They already had their freedom.

"I know, Creed. I know. Just let me be for now." She swallowed once more and gritted her teeth. "Please."

A complete second passed before his soft *okay* reached her ears, and his scent faded as he walked away. The strangled sound of that one word ate at her guilty conscious. As much as Serenity had always wanted to have choices, she'd never been one to willfully hurt another before. It didn't sit well in her soul now. What was she going to do?

* * * *

Creed walked away from the bathroom door with a sick feeling in his gut that their mate really didn't want anything to do with them. Reluctance born of fear of the unknown or the need to impress on them her importance by making them work for her affections he could have handled—had expected to handle. But this seemed much more serious in his eyes. Serenity didn't act like any mate he'd ever been around or heard about in the past.

"What is it?" Shayne asked quietly when Creed walked over to the window to carefully peer outside through the slit in the drapes he'd created.

"Nothing. She's anxious about the hunters and is getting control of her emotions. She doesn't seem to be one who wants anyone to know when she's upset." He continued to watch for any sign that they had been discovered. It was still too soon for his bears to arrive.

"You could have fooled me," Shayne said with a snort. "She didn't seem to have any trouble earlier telling us how she felt."

Creed pinned his brother with a heavy gaze before returning to stare out the window. Evidently Shayne got the message loud and clear because he stomped over to the little table and rummaged around in the bags as if hungry. Creed knew better. He was attempting to rein in his own emotions over their mate's obvious rejection. His bear paced and growled as if he thought Creed should be bursting down the bathroom door and forcing her to accept them.

Maybe in the woods a flesh and blood bear could get away with something like that, but not when his mate was also part human.

Hell, my human side almost understands how she feels. It might have been harder for me to accept her as my mate if I hadn't been attracted to her from the beginning. If she's not attracted to us as males...

Well, that thought didn't sit well at all. The idea of trying to control brother bear if their mate refused them and didn't change her mind scared him. Not only would he lose control over his den mates, but the pain of her loss might be enough to turn him feral. God help them all if he lost control.

Glancing over to where Shayne stood with his back to him as he ate something he'd found in the bags, Creed realized it would be doubly bad for everyone, shifters and humans. Brother bear seemed to catch on to his human half's unease and began to whine to get out. If Creed wouldn't do something, brother bear would.

Not yet, brother. Give me time.

"You don't have a clue, do you," Wren said from her position on the loveseat.

Creed looked over at the tiny wild dog female. "What do you mean?"

"Males are so arrogant. They think that just because they want someone that they should want them back."

"She does want us. I have smelled her interest. I don't understand why she fights it," he said shaking his head.

"With males, the attraction is all they need to start with. Over time, they form the deeper emotional connection that a female needs right from the beginning. Physical attraction for sex is just scratching an itch. You can handle not really liking or caring about someone if the sex is good, but when a long-term relationship like a mating is on the table, females don't want to end up stuck with someone they don't even like talking to, much less want to be around for the rest of their lives," Wren told him.

"Our bears wouldn't have chosen someone we wouldn't be compatible with long term, Wren. This is a true mating. Nature made the choice for us. This has nothing to do with shifters who choose their mates instead of allowing their other half to lead them to the right one for them."

She huffed out an irritated breath that sounded much more like her wild dog than her human side. "That's all hype. There's no truth to those old stories. What was the first thing you noticed about her? That is what drew you to her."

Creed smiled and shook his head. "I'd never set eyes on her when brother bear announced her to me."

Wren frowned, her eyebrows drawing together almost comically. "Then how did you know she was the one?"

"We've just moved in across from Serenity last night, and once we'd unloaded the moving van, Shayne and I went to check the area before we settled down for the night. Before we'd gone far from the house, her scent awakened my bear from a deep slumber. He had no doubt she was our mate." Creed folded his arms across his chest and watched the little shifter.

Her brows remained drawn as she seemed to think his words over very carefully. He didn't smell distress in the air surrounding her. Instead, he smelled something surprisingly close to relief wafting from her skin. Why would she be relieved that she had no say in a mating? Unless she thought that there was no chance she'd ever find her mate and could hide behind wanting to wait for her true mate. Her brother was going to kill him, Creed thought with a grunt.

Before either of them could say more, the bathroom door creaked open. He watched as Serenity stepped out and walked directly to the fridge. She opened the door and peered inside for a second, then closed it and ran her hands through her hair.

"I'm going to walk around to the vending machine I saw next to the office. I need something cold with caffeine in it." She walked toward the outside door, but both Shayne and Creed reached it before she could.

"That's not a good idea. We're trying to keep our presence here quiet, Serenity," Creed told her.

Her expression changed from one of confidence and determination to one of near desperation. His bear roared inside of him, nearly making it all the way out of his throat. Their mate shouldn't look this way. They had to fix this.

Shayne stepped in. No doubt his bear had demanded the same thing. "I'll get you whatever you want to drink. Just tell me what you like. I probably should get something for all of us since we have plenty of food but not much else."

Creed nearly held his breathe. Unease flowed down his spine like a rushing stream after a spring shower. If she insisted, he'd let her go but follow to be sure she remained safe. It went against his instincts to let her go alone.

"Okay. I want Diet Coke. I need a Diet Coke," she said.

Creed relaxed enough that he didn't feel as if his skin was going to crack open under the strain. "I don't remember seeing any in your fridge, and there weren't any in the groceries you bought."

She hissed at him, her eyes flashing brightly. "I try not to drink them often. They tend to make me hyper."

"Um, maybe I should grab some milk instead," Shayne said with a worried look toward Creed.

This time she didn't just hiss but growl, but it was directed at his brother this time. She stalked closer to him with near rage in her eyes.

Creed quickly wrapped his arms lightly but securely around her, pinning her arms to her sides where deadly claws flexed and extended at her side. He was sure his eyes were huge considering his brothers were as he stared at her hands.

"You can partially shift," Shayne said in amazement.

"Of courssse I can." Her hissing words let Creed know she was still angry, and evidently her mouth had shifted some as well. More than likely she was talking around an impressive set of fangs.

"I've never known a female who could before," Creed said. "Do all of your female lynxes partial shift?"

She grew still in his arms, her heavy breathing slowing even as her razor sharp claws slowly receded. Once she seemed to have calmed down some, he let her go and moved slowly around her so that he could watch her expressions.

"I guess I haven't thought about it before. Our queen could, but I don't remember seeing anyone else now that you mention it. Of course, there hadn't been many times a female had needed to before I left." She looked from Shayne back to him and cocked her head much like a cat. "So sows don't partial shift in your sleuth?"

"No. I've never heard of a female anywhere who could. Unlike your den, we've had our share of reasons a female could have used such a talent, so I'm sure if they could have, they'd have done it." Creed looked over at his brother and nodded.

Shayne slowly backed toward the door to leave. Just as he turned the knob, Serenity spoke up.

"Better get you a pot or two of honey while you're at it, bear boy."

Shayne burst out laughing and quickly left, closing the door with a soft click before their mate recovered from shock that he was laughing.

"Sweet Serenity. That was no insult to us. We do love honey, and I can promise you that once we get between your tasty thighs we will lick our fill of yours. Did you think Shayne was trying to insult you when he suggested milk instead of soda?" Creed asked, watching her flexing hands warily for any sign of change.

"Wasn't he? I don't like people being condescending around me, Creed. I'm not some simpering female who needs a big strong male to keep me safe or make me happy."

Creed nodded solemnly. "We don't need a female incapable of taking care of herself. Our mate would have to be strong and self-sufficient in order to handle the stress and strain of setting up a new sleuth. Just because we want to protect you and see to your every need doesn't mean we don't think you are capable. It just means we care."

"How could you possibly care about me or trust me with your new sleuth when you know nothing about me?" she asked with a deep tired sigh.

"That's what we want to do, Serenity. We want to get to know you, and that takes spending time together, but you won't even give us a chance. How do you know you don't want to be our mate if you don't give us a chance?" Sadness laced his words. He hadn't meant to do or say anything that might sound like he was laying guilt at her feet to force her to give them a chance, but he was tired. It had been a long, long day after an equally long night.

She lifted her eyes to meet his. Something flitted across them that he didn't catch. He had to strain to hear her words then replay them slowly through his disbelieving mind.

"Okay. I'll try."

Chapter Six

Shayne felt the difference in the air as soon as he walked back into the room. Something had happened while he'd been gone. He'd tread on eggshells until he knew what had happened and what it meant. If his brother had managed to calm their feisty mate down some, Shayne didn't want to undo whatever he'd accomplished.

"Here you go, Serenity," he said, handing her an ice cold can of Diet Coke. "I'll put the rest in the fridge."

Wren walked over while he unloaded the bags he'd brought in. "Did you happen to get anything besides Diet Coke?"

He grinned. "I have Dr. Pepper, Ginger Ale, and"—he whispered the next word softly—"chocolate milk."

Wren burst out laughing before covering her mouth and looking over her shoulder at where Serenity sat on the loveseat next to Creed watching the only channel the older model TV picked up. At least it wasn't one of the old fat tube TVs. Serenity looked up and shot Shayne a very unladylike gesture but didn't say anything.

Shayne relaxed a little more and watched as the female wild dog reached in the fridge and pulled out a can of Ginger Ale. He thought that was funny since the only reason he'd gotten it was because he knew Eason and Warren were the two from their den that would be there soon. Eason loved the stuff. As a hybrid bear holding both grizzly and black bear in him, his control was not as perfect as it should be. Living with two different bears sharing his body left him always on edge with a tight grip to remain in control. It was one of the reasons he'd wanted to come with Shayne and his brother. Warren was going, and for some reason, the crazy grizzly helped Eason remain in control.

It had caused a stir in their old sleuth. Their father hadn't wanted to risk him out in the world and away from familiar, home territory for his bears, but Creed had stepped up and assured their father that they could handle Eason and his bears. Shayne was sure that Eason would do everything in his power to not cause trouble for his new Ursus after Creed had gone to bat for him like that.

He wondered what Eason would say when he found out that a spirited wild dog had appropriated one of his sodas. It would be interesting. He liked to see the dual bear male get pissy now and again. He spent so much time trying to remain in control that Shayne felt he needed to lose it now and again so it didn't stay bottled up inside. If he didn't let off steam occasionally, he was in much greater danger of going off the deep end as far as Shayne was concerned.

"Glad I picked something you liked," was all he said, though.

"I don't drink soda as a rule, but I like Ginger Ale," she said with a shrug. "It's better than drinking water out of the tap."

Shayne couldn't fault her there. He had no desire to taste what the water was like in the place. He didn't like drinking anything but fresh spring water, preferably right from the source.

"Hand me a Dr. Pepper," Creed said from the loveseat.

He grabbed one and one of the individual chocolate milks and walked over to where his mate and brother sat. Creed snagged the Dr. Pepper from his outstretched hand as he took a seat on one of the chairs. Serenity had her head leaning back with her eyes closed. She looked so vulnerable there like that. It wasn't until she opened her eyes that you saw the strength shining through. It would be easy to underestimate her. He wouldn't make that mistake. She deserved to be herself. It sounded like in her old den they had wanted her to conform to their idea of what a mate should be. He could see how that would have chafed at her. She isn't a conformist, he thought with a small smile.

"Is the Diet Coke good?" he asked when she'd taken a sip again.

"Mmm. Good." She didn't open her eyes again.

"Eason and Warren should be here soon," his brother said.

"Did they ask many questions?" Shayne asked. He and his brother hadn't talked much alone, so he didn't know the entire plan.

"Not after I told them our mate was involved. They just asked what they could do after that."

Shayne smiled. He just bet they did. The fact that he and his brother had found their mate already bode well for them. Once the alphas mated, the others would soon find theirs. It had something to do with cementing the den as a unit. Until the alphas found their mate, the others knew it was rare for another bear in the den to locate their mate. He was sure they were already anticipating theirs. They wouldn't question anything the Ursus said or asked where the safety of his mate was at stake. Keeping her safe trumped everything except the safety of their own mates and cubs.

"Wren, have you called your brother to come get you?" Creed asked.

"Yeah, but he won't be here for at least another hour. He was working on a bike and had to have it finished today." The wild dog cocked her head oddly. "Someone's here, though."

Shayne was out of the chair about the same time she announced they had company. He'd heard the crunch of gravel on concrete about the same time she had. The little shifter had good ears. Few shifters could beat his senses. Even Creed didn't have the hearing he did. Of course, his brother's sense of smell and eyesight couldn't be topped.

Looking out the window behind the edge of the curtain, he saw Eason's big four-wheel drive pull around from the front of the hotel. It eased down the lot before parking two doors down and cutting the engine.

"It's them. They should be knocking in a minute," he told the others.

As he watched the two bears climb out of the truck, Creed stood up from the couch and stretched. His brother's power flared slightly around him. It took him by surprise. Turning around, he noticed that his bear had moved closer to the surface, filling Creed's eyes with a honey-gold glow.

"Creed?"

"Brother Bear doesn't like another male being around our mate while the bond isn't secure." Creed shrugged.

"Crap," Shayne said. "We don't need this right now, Creed."

"Tell me your bear isn't putting up a fuss at the thought of those two coming in right now," Creed snapped.

Shayne relaxed and thought about it. He could feel the unease in the pit of his stomach, but his bear wasn't gnawing at him to get out. Instead, the wily ole beast was watching and waiting.

For what?

Brother will take care of this.

Shayne smiled, looking at his brother. "Seems that my bear is letting you handle this one. He'll take the next one."

He heard a snort and turned to see Serenity stand up with a disgusted look on her face. She obviously wasn't one of the females who enjoyed seeing males fight over her. He frowned. Maybe it wasn't such a good idea for Shayne to let Creed handle this one after all.

* * * *

What was it with males that they had to beat their chests and proclaim their testosterone was thicker than everyone else's? She wasn't meant to fight over. Serenity sighed and walked around Creed and his growly breathing. She didn't need this. It was one of the reasons she didn't think agreeing to their mating was a good reason. Of course her lynx had an entirely different opinion on the matter and didn't mind making it known to her.

"This is ridiculous," she snarled at the two men.

Before either of them knew what she was going to do, Serenity threw open the door to two very startled bears who took a step back when she did. Her eyes were immediately drawn to the odd male with rich brown eyes and the most unusual hair she'd ever seen. Instead of dark brown or deep black strands, this one's hair was multicolored all over. The variegated strands hung just past his shoulders and weren't like anything she'd ever seen before. There was no way this one could ever have been mistaken as anything but *other*, shifter. Humans didn't get hair like that. Not even from a bottle.

The other male with him had the darkest brown hair that couldn't be mistaken for black that she'd ever seen. His eyes had the liquid quality of dark chocolate syrup without a hint of laughter showing. Both of these bears were solemn and controlled as if they'd purposefully locked themselves down. Maybe they had. They were coming to meet their Ursus and Zashchita's mate for the first time and had probably guessed that the mating wouldn't have been completed yet with trouble brewing. She sighed.

"Come in. Don't mind the homicidal bear standing behind me. He isn't going to hurt you because he knows I'll walk if he does." She added that last bit a little louder and firmer for Creed's benefit.

She thought she saw the second bear's lips twitch as he walked into the room, but it could have just been a fluke. As both he and the first bear stepped into the room, closing the door behind them, she walked over to where Wren had retreated near the fridge. The other female looked almost sick. Maybe she didn't like being among so many dominant male shifters either. She sure didn't like it.

When she looked back at where the four bears were still standing by the door, she realized that the two new bears weren't even looking at Creed and Shayne. They were looking at them. A low growl erupted from Wren. She bared her teeth at the four bears across the room. Before Serenity could ask her if she was okay, the female wild dog stalked into the bathroom, slamming the door behind her.

"What's wrong with her?" Shayne asked, the puzzled expression on his face almost comical.

"I don't think she likes being in the middle of a group of dominant males any more than I do. Add to that the fact that Creed is all but beating his chest and all four of you are bears, I don't blame her for putting some space between you," she said with a laugh.

Creed drew himself up to his full height and glared at her. She didn't lower her eyes, despite the danger in defying him. She was a feline and didn't follow directions if it didn't suit her. It didn't suit her right then. Instead, she sauntered up to stand between the two new shifters who looked far from happy to have her there. They both stepped to the side, placing plenty of room between her and them.

"Why don't you introduce me to your den brothers?" she asked, letting her voice go deep and throaty.

"You're playing with fire, Serenity," Shayne said in a hushed voice.

"Serenity?" the variegated-haired bear asked. "Her parents seriously named her Serenity?"

Creed growled much louder than before while she fought not to burst out laughing. She totally agreed. Her mother shouldn't have given her that name. She had never been serene in her life.

When Creed took a step toward the other male, she stepped in front of him. "Stop it, Creed. I'm about as far from a Serenity as you are from Teddy. Now suck it up and tell me what the plan is, or I'm going to leave with Wren and her brother when he gets here."

"No," Creed said in a gravelly voice.

"Then straighten up." She turned to face the other two males who, though their heads were still held high, their eyes had been averted. "I'm Serenity Jones. I'm sure you can tell that I'm a cat shifter. I'm a lynx."

Shayne took up there. "This is Warren and Eason." He pointed to first the one with the amazing multicolored hair then the slightly shorter one with deep shade of brown hair.

She held out her hand. "I'm pleased to meet you."

When neither bear reached to shake her hand, Serenity sighed and glared over her shoulder at Creed. What was she going to do? Serenity had no doubt that she was stuck with the two bears for mates, but nothing said she had to stay with them if she didn't want to. It might hurt and cause a lot of stress for her cat, but if Creed was going to be like this, she would rather live with that misery than to deal with someone like him.

"Creed. Calm down. She isn't looking at Warren or Eason as potential mates. All you're doing is pushing her away with the attitude," Shayne said, gripping his brother's shoulder.

Serenity didn't think there was anything that would calm the big brute down. Her lynx disagreed. She listened to the whispers of the cat in her head and shrugged. It was worth a try. She wanted to go home, and as long as Creed was acting like this, they weren't getting anywhere. She walked slowly toward him, his eyes jerking from the two bears to focus on her. His brown eyes followed her like a tractor beam as she eased closer to him. As soon as she was within touching distance, Creed turned his eyes back to the two bears at the same time he reached out and grabbed Serenity, hauling her next to him in a gentle yet unrelenting grip. There was no getting out of his hands now. Maybe she'd made a mistake.

"Mine," he grumbled in his chest.

"Mine too, Creed. Ours," Shayne said, slipping up next to her so that she was sandwiched between them.

Creed changed the "mine" to "ours" and reiterated it with the two bears once again. They didn't argue, nor did they say anything else. Both of them seemed completely fine with that proclamation. While Serenity wasn't, she let it go. She'd pick her battles, and with there being four huge male bears in the room and her in between, that time was not now.

"What's the plan to get out of here?" she asked.

Creed nodded at the two new arrivals before clasping her hand in his and pulling her toward the loveseat. He sat then pulled her onto his lap as Shayne sat next to him. It was a tight fit.

"We're going to take the truck Eason and Warren drove here in and drive home. When we are close to town, you will stay down until we're safe inside of the garage where no one can see you," Creed told her. His voice slowly reverted back to his normally deep tone as he spoke.

"What about them? How are they going to get back? If they show up at your place in that truck, it might tip the hunters off. They saw you leave in that truck and might put two and two together," she pointed out.

"We're going to park it somewhere for a few days until the coast is clear," Warren said.

She didn't see where they had much choice, but the truck looked expensive. She was worried something would happen to it and it would be her fault, but Serenity didn't have a better idea.

A knock at the door made Serenity jump. She hadn't heard a car pull up or sense anyone near. She'd been so wrapped up in the issue with the hunter and her own problems with being mated to two bears that she'd relaxed her normally astute senses. None of the bears seemed worried, though. She watched as Warren stood from the chair he'd sat in and walked over to the door. While he didn't exactly throw it wide open, he didn't hesitate much once he got there.

Creed's arm wrapped around her waist, securing her to his lap. He didn't feel tense exactly, but she could tell he didn't want her to leave his embrace. They must have sensed whoever it was as another shifter.

Sure enough, a tall, thin, dirty blond shifter walked into the room, his eyes moving from one male to the next before he settled himself with his back to the corner behind the door and crossed his arms.

"Where's my sister?"

"Mojave! I told you they were fine. Don't go insulting them before you get to know them." Wren walked out of the bathroom directly to her brother.

Serenity noted that she carefully avoided looking in their direction, though. What had spooked her when she'd been fearless earlier? The wild dog glared at her brother but didn't let her gaze rest on any of the other males in the room. Instead, when she looked over in their direction, she focused on Serenity.

"They can't just leave an expensive truck out in the open somewhere or it will get stolen. Besides, if they recognize the truck, all they have to do is run a check on the license plate to find out who they are and where they live," Wren pointed out. She still didn't look at any of the bears.

"What other choice do they have?" Serenity asked, already catching on to Wren's thought process. She wanted her brother to offer them a place to hide the truck.

Evidently her brother had figured it out, too, but he didn't like it. He glared at his sister then sighed. "They can park the truck at my garage. There's room."

"Thanks, Mojave," Wren said before nodding at Serenity. "We better go."

"Are you sure? We don't want to cause your pack any trouble. Your sister has already put herself in danger by warning Serenity," Creed said.

"We can handle ourselves. If it wasn't Serenity, it would have been another shifter, maybe Wren. You can follow me," the other shifter said.

"There's enough room in Eason's truck for all of us. Once we drop off mine, we'll all return home in his. We'll duck down once we get close in case someone is watching either house," Creed added.

It didn't take long at all to load everything into the big four-wheel drive. The back had a cover, so all of the groceries would be safe back there. Before she climbed into cab of the truck, she thanked Wren for her help, then watched as the other shifter hurried around the bears standing between the two trucks to get into her brother's truck. Serenity couldn't help but wonder why she'd been so freaked out by Warren and Eason. She'd been fine with Creed and Shayne. They were much scarier than the other two bears. Maybe, like she'd first thought, it had been too many big males in one room.

Creed ushered her out of the room with Shayne following behind her. They all got into the big new truck Warren and Eason had driven in. The other two bears took the black truck. There was plenty of room in the big four-wheel drive so that she didn't feel as if she were squashed between the two big males. Even so, her nerves were already strung tight from being on the Rouge Hunters' radar. That was bad—real bad.

A chill ran down her spine as it finally sank in that she'd been identified by them for extermination. Why? She'd done nothing to bring attention to herself. She kept a low profile and stayed away from humans anyway except when she needed supplies. It didn't make sense.

Shaking her head, Serenity fought hard to find some of the calm that her mom thought she'd gifted her with when she'd named her. It wasn't happening though. Panic amped up her heartbeat, tightening her throat until she started making odd whining sounds. This was not like her. She didn't lose it like this.

"Easy, honey," Creed told her, losing his hold on the steering wheel to take her hand in his.

Shayne squeezed her knee before leaning closer to kiss the outer corner of her eye with the lightest of kisses.

"Shhh. It will be fine, Serenity. We won't let anything happen to you," he said. "It's been a long day. As soon as we get back to the den, we'll settle you down to take a nap."

"I don't understand what's wrong with me. I'm never like this. I don't get shaky or terrified like this," she said.

"You've had too much happen in a short period of time, Serenity. We'd just claimed you to be our mate, then you find out that you have hunters after you as well. That's a lot to deal with in one day. I'm sorry," Creed told her.

She felt his sincerity, and, despite that she didn't want to be anyone's mate right then, she appreciated that he had offered his apologies for adding to the ordeal.

"It's okay. Nature has a way of blindsiding you when she wants to." Serenity blew out a breath. "I just wanted to be allowed to make my own choices."

"No one is forcing you, Serenity," Shayne all but whispered next to her.

"Having a fated mate, or mates in this case, is the same as force. I can't change how my lynx feels or how your bears feel. At least I didn't have to end up with some asshole that would try to keep me under his thumb." She realized she'd accepted her fate and just confessed as much to the two bears on either side of her. To their credit, they didn't give a loud whoop of triumph.

They soon reached the outskirts of the Talmadge community where she bought her supplies and where Wren and Mojave seemed to make their home. She wondered how many wild dogs lived in their pack. Then she wondered if the other woman would mind if she called and talked to her sometime. It had hit her as they had sped away from danger earlier that day that she didn't have any friends to talk to. If she was going to be mated to two bears, she would need a female's prospective at times, and just maybe she could count the other shifter as a friend. Serenity had a feeling that having a friend during her transition from lone lynx to the status of a mated female was going to be a rocky one. Having a wild dog female sympathizer on her side could help keep her out of trouble.

I have a feeling I'm going to need all the help I can get.

Chapter Seven

They drove around the back of a large brick building that had multiple pull-down garage-type doors on it. A high fence enveloped the entire area, but someone opened it as soon as they drove up, closing it behind them. Serenity stilled her nerves that ran up and down the skin of her arms like an army of ants. They weren't her enemies. They were helping them. As a rule, dogs and cats didn't get along, but they were shifters and alliances had been formed in the past for the sake of their existence. She could do this. Wren had gone out of her way to warn her of danger, putting herself in the line of fire in the process.

Wren and her brother pulled off to one side, Mojave waving them inside one of the bays with a long muscled arm out his window. Once they'd parked, the rolling doors slammed down, causing her to jump between the two bears. Immediately Shayne settled a calming hand along her shoulder, rubbing over it and down her arm in a light caress. She couldn't stop her smile of appreciation.

"It's okay. We can trust them. I'm very good at reading people and these African Wild Dogs are good shifters." Shayne smiled back at her.

Before she could reply, both doors of the truck were opened for them to climb out. Well, the bears stepped out while she had to climb out with Shayne's assistance. Looking around, she realized there were five of the wild dogs in the bay including Wren and Mojave. He walked over with his sister on his heels.

"Your truck will be safe here for as long as is necessary. I would like to set aside some time as soon as possible to talk about the situation that has developed here. I understand that you are new to the area and setting up your sleuth with several male members. I think it would be to all of our advantages to work together and develop a relationship to ensure all of our protection. The hunters are not going away," Mojave said.

"You have more information on these hunters?" Creed asked, crossing his arms over his chest.

Serenity couldn't stop herself from poking him in the arm. Hello, talk about closed-off body language. He needed to relax if he wanted cooperation. Creed looked down at her with a puzzled frown. She pulled at the crook of his arm until he uncrossed them. When he did, she smiled and clasped his hand in hers to keep him from doing it again. As a result, Shayne claimed her other hand with a mischievous grin. Creed merely grunted but didn't attempt to pull his hand from hers.

"One of my pack brought information a few minutes ago that one of the old hunting lodges outside of town has been bought by one of the men suspected of being a member of the Rogue Hunters. To add to that, several more people have arrived in town and are actively looking for rental property in the area."

"Does sound like they are setting up shop since they bought something they can use as a headquarters," Creed agreed. "Why are the ones coming in only renting then? You would think they would stick around and set up a home to blend in better."

"I think they are moving them in and out to keep the suspicion off of them. If several new faces move in and act as if they are going to settle down all at one time, it would get our suspicions up for sure. They think we are so much of our animals that we won't notice what it going on," Wren said.

"In the meantime, we need to remove Serenity from their radar," Creed said. "Once we've identified who is behind the hunt for her, we can eliminate the threat."

"Eliminate?" someone said from the back of the bay. "What do you mean by eliminate?"

The newcomer wasn't a wild dog, but close. Serenity wasn't surprised to see a wolf, but she was surprised that he'd shown up out of the blue, without being invited. She shifted her eyes over to where Wren stood by her brother.

Or had he? Mojave didn't appear upset or surprised by his appearance, but Wren looked anything but pleased. She shifted closer to her brother and slightly behind him. It was then that she noticed how Eason and Warren instantly came to attention and all of it on Wren, something to file away for later. Right then, she needed to focus on what this meant.

"Alex," Mojave began. "This is Creed, the Zashchita of the sleuth. They have just moved here…"

"And already their mate has come to the attention of Rogue Hunters. I wonder how that could be?" the wolf asked.

Serenity felt her cat prickle all over. "Just a minute, wolf man. I've been living here for a long time. I didn't just move in. Watch how you talk about my mates."

Shayne chuckled a little under his breath even though everyone in the area could hear him.

"Feisty kitten. Isn't she?" Alex the wolf said. "But I'm no wolf man to be trifled with. I'm Alpha of my pack and don't appreciate the attention that is being directed on shifters. You've been too long without a mate to keep you under control. Now that you finally have two, maybe this problem can be averted."

"Under control? I've done nothing to attract attention to either myself or other shifters. I rarely even leave my home. How dare you!" She could feel her nails lengthen with outrage.

"Settle down, Serenity. He's baiting you for some reason. Don't give him fuel for his fiery comments," Creed whispered for her ears only.

The fact that he'd leaned down to do it wasn't lost on her. It wouldn't have gone unnoticed by the others either and they'd assume he had brought her to heel like a dog. The resentment built, but she held it inside. She'd pick her battles. Allowing the wolf to dominate the conversation like this wasn't helping matters any. Still, she couldn't help but get one last growl out for good measure.

"So, again I ask, what do you mean by eliminate?" Alex asked again.

Creed narrowed his eyes, but talked as if he were ordering a meal. "They should be brought before the shifter alliance for incarceration. That way, they are no longer able to hunt us."

Alex lifted his eyebrows in obvious disbelief. "So you'd allow someone who was a threat to your mate to live."

Creed smiled, bearing teeth this time. "As long as he doesn't put up a fight when we track him down and capture him, there is no reason not to turn him over to the alliance for sentencing. But, if he doesn't cooperate and fights, we can't be responsible for our strength when blatantly attacked. I don't back down from a fight—ever."

Serenity could read the underlying warning in Creed's words easily enough that she was sure the wolf could as well. Why had Mojave invited this irritating shifter? This had nothing to do with him at the moment. She wanted to rake her nails down the wild dog's muzzle to show her displeasure, but didn't want to upset Wren. Instead, she shot him a look the first time his gaze landed on him. He took it without flinching. She had known he would since he was the pack's alpha.

Though Wren hadn't told them that, once he'd shown up at the motel, Serenity could feel the power in him. If he hadn't been alpha, she would have been very worried about the one who was.

"Why are you here, Alex?" Wren finally spoke up. "This doesn't concern you in the least."

"Oh, but it does, little pup. As your future mate, I get a say in anything that might affect you," he said with a great deal of satisfaction.

She narrowed her eyes after turning them on her brother. Serenity could tell she wasn't happy about that bit of news. Nor had she been privy to it before that moment. She turned her attention back to Alex who seemed to be preening in front of the crowd.

"Over my dead body. I'd rather announce myself to the Rogue Hunters and be killed before mating you," she hissed out, in a voice that being a feline, Serenity could appreciate.

"Now, Wren," her brother began. "This isn't the time for mating squabbles."

"Screw you, Mojave! You've been trying to push me at him for the last six months. I'm telling you and him in front of everyone that it's not happening." Her voice had gotten so growly that if you hadn't been a shifter you wouldn't have been able to understand all of it.

Since Serenity had been in her place before, she knew the struggle the other woman was going through. There was an innate need to please your leader and going against that not only hurt, but it weakened your trust and support in a way that could be dangerous for you as a member of the pack, chain, den, or sleuth. It had gone on for so long with her that leaving had been her only option. She no longer felt safe and secure within her den any longer.

She started to walk the two paces it would have required to reach Wren and offer her support, but became aware of a low, nearly imperceptible growling behind her. She looked over her shoulder and realized that Warren and Eason were bearing their teeth in the wolf alpha's direction. Evidently Creed noticed it, too. He didn't so much as turn to look at the other two, but Serenity felt something pass between the bear shifters through the hold both Creed and Shayne had on her hands. The growling stopped.

"We appreciate your offer of assistance in letting us keep the truck here, but if it is going to cause trouble, we can make other arrangements and leave," Creed said. His voice remained relaxed as if discussing the weather.

"No. You're welcome to leave it here for as long as you need to. We are all in this together. They somehow got information that there were shifters here and moved in to target us. Where there is one, there are others and they know this. Very few shifters live on their own. The need for other shifters around them is too great and they know this. Once this crisis has been resolved, I would like for us to all meet on neutral ground and discuss ways we can keep our separate groups safe from them." Mojave looked over at Alex expectantly.

"I agree. Keeping each other appraised of any information you find out is beneficial and I'm all for keeping my pack safe. I'd be willing to meet." He smiled broadly, the show of teeth an obvious show of power as far as Serenity was concerned.

"I will meet as well," Creed agreed. "My priority is in protecting my mate right now, but once this is over, I will be available."

"Good. If you need anything while we are searching for these men, just call the number on this card." Mojave handed a simple business card to Creed. "We will help in any way we can. While you are securing your mate, we will be trying to determine exactly who all is attached to the hunters and what they know."

"We appreciate the assistance, Alpha Mojave. I will contact you later to see if you've discovered anything." Creed turned to his brother and the other two bears at their bakes. "Let's go."

Serenity was surrounded by the overly tall and large males as they escorted her to the huge four-wheel drive truck. Creed lifted her as if she were as light as a child and settled her on the seat, easing her closer to the center of the back seat. Shayne climbed in on the opposite side and squeezed her knee. Once they were all inside, Eason backed the big truck out of the drive and onto the street.

"Better stay down until we're safe inside the garage, guys," Warren said from the front seat. "We don't know who is watching or where they are."

Creed growled but crouched down in the floorboard, pulling Serenity on his lap. Shayne scrunched down on the other side, taking her feet on his. She felt like a doll the way they moved her around as if she didn't weigh a thing. She'd never felt small before, but between these two hulking bears, Serenity could almost imagine herself as dainty.

"What's so amusing, kitten?" Creed asked in a gruff voice.

"Nothing. I was just thinking how uncomfortable you had to be all curled up so that you aren't seen. I would never have believed that you could make yourselves so small."

"We can do anything necessary to keep our mate safe, precious," Shayne assured her. He'd removed her shoes and started massaging her feet. As much as she was enjoying the decadence of it, she needed to be ready in case they had to make a run for it.

"Shayne, I need my shoes on in case something happens. It really feels wonderful but I don't want to be barefoot if I have to run," she told him.

"Good point. I needed to touch you and thought I'd sneak it in by giving you a foot massage," he admitted with a soft smile.

"I don't understand. Why do you need to touch me?" she asked. The males of her den hadn't been so demonstrative, dominant and protective, yes, but not touchy-feely like these bears seemed to be.

"You're our mate yet we haven't officially claimed you yet. It puts our bears on edge when you're around other unmated males. We need to touch you as much as possible to assure our bears that you are ours and not being wooed away from us," Creed explained.

"Somehow I don't think your other bears would dare try that," she mused.

"If they thought you were theirs, nothing would stop them from trying to claim you," Shayne told her in a quiet voice.

That made her stop and think. Was Wren Warren and Eason's mate? Was that why they'd been so angry at the way Alex had tried to stake a claim on her? And earlier, back at the motel, the little wild dog had taken one look at them and hid in the bathroom until her brother had arrived. It was something to consider, but not right then. She had enough going on in her life without adding matchmaking to it.

"So far there's no one following us," Warren said from the front seat.

"Contact the others when we're about five minutes out to see if they've noticed anyone watching the den," Creed told him.

"Yes, sir."

* * * *

Shayne needed to move. Every muscle in his body had been on alert since they'd left the store earlier that morning. Now, crouched in the back of the truck, cramping and multiple aches threatened to awaken his bear with the growing discomfort and outright pain. His left big toe had morphed into his bear form several times already in an effort to control the cramps. Much longer and he was going to lose it.

On top of that, Brother Bear was anxious to claim their mate, as well. He didn't like that she was around the others without his claiming mark on her and his scent blended with hers. As soon as they got to their den, they would take care of that issue. There was no way he could stay in control if she remained unmarked once they were within the walls of their home with other unmated males in the area. He just prayed that Serenity was in a receptive mood. He wasn't sure he had the patience to wait much longer and knew that gentle was out of the question.

Unease seeped into his blood at the thought of scaring her. Even a shifter female needed gentle handling at first. Not because she might be a virgin, which was highly unlikely as sexual as they tended to be. But because she would be unsure of them, having no history with him and his brother to know that they were good males who believed in respect and treating females well.

Every time she moved around between them her scent grew stronger. None of them were comfortable but knowing about and feeling her discomfort added to his anxiety. It was a good thing they weren't too far from the den now. He only prayed that both he and his brother would be able to control their bears until they could claim their mate. The other males would be anxious to meet their new Ursa and bond with her, but that couldn't happen until they'd satisfied their need to mark her and imprint their scents on her.

"You two have to be hurting all crouched down like you are. I'm much smaller and my legs and back are killing me," Serenity suddenly piped up with a groan.

"It won't be much longer," Warren told her from the front seat. "Maybe another eight or ten minutes, tops."

"I'll massage your back for you. Where is the pain worse?" his brother asked her.

"My low back, but I'll be fine. I know you have to be miserable. You and Shayne are so muscular. This has to be sheer torture."

Shayne winced as a bump jarred him so that his already sore ankles began to throb. He felt like a fucking pretzel.

"We'll be fine," he told her.

"Okay, coming up on the turn. Stay down. I'll let you know when the garage door is closed," Warren said.

"Hey, Locke. We're just about to turn on the street. Anything?" Eason's quiet voice as he talked on his cell had Serenity stiffening next to him.

"Shhh, baby. Everything's fine. Our sleuth is keeping watch for us." Shayne gently rubbed her shoulder.

"Wait until we've turned onto the drive before you open the garage," Eason was saying.

"How many of you are there again?" she asked.

"There are ten of us, honey," Creed told her. "They won't hurt you. We'd never allow them near you if we didn't know that for a fact."

"Small bump as we hit the drive, guys." Warren's voice was soft and sounded as if he was speaking through his teeth.

The bump was a little more than slight, but Shane was sure it was only because he'd been folded up like a lawn chair for the last thirty minutes. Twenty seconds later Eason gave the all clear.

"Door's down. You can get up now," he said.

"Untangle you mean," Serenity said with a groan as she tried to climb up on the seat. "I should have just laid across the back seat and left you guys the floorboard."

"Easy, baby. Let us help you down. You're legs are going to be stiff," Shayne told her as he reached for her.

"I'm okay." She still allowed him to help her to the ground. Despite the cramped space they'd shared, she didn't show any signs that she wasn't ready for anything. He admired her for not griping the entire ride or allowing anyone to see how it might have affected her.

"Status update," Creed growled as he walked around to where most of their bears stood in a semicircle around him and their mate.

"No one is in her house, but there are two men posted outside of it watching," Locke told him.

"One is on the other side of the house about even with the front corner of the house in some brush. Easy to see and even easier to smell," Seth added. "Stinks of Scent-A-Way fresh earth scent. I think he used baking soda to brush his teeth with, too."

"They treat us like forest prey. We are not prey for anyone," Otto muttered in his broken English.

"The other one is across the street between our house and hers like they suspect us, Ursus," Quill said.

"We haven't seen any other intruders within a thousand yards of our territory," Zeth told them.

While Zeth was the youngest and often needed to be reined in when his mischievousness got out of hand, he could always be counted on to do his job and do it well. If he said there were no others, they knew it was fact.

"Let's get our mate settled then we can make plans," Creed told them. He placed one hand on Serenity's back, leaving Shayne to follow them. He wasn't complaining. The sight of her ample ass swaying with her firm stride had his dick's attention.

As they entered the house through the garage entrance, Locke and Otto turned away from Creed's room, heading instead toward the basement door. Creed stopped and frowned at his Ruka.

"I think it is safer for our Ursa downstairs. We went ahead and moved you there while we waited on you. We will work around the clock to have the final suite completed as soon as possible," Locke said.

"She must be safe at all costs," Otto added, his face tight with determination.

"I approve of your decision. It is a wise choice," Creed acknowledged. "Give us a few hours to settle our mate. Then we will plan our next move."

"We'll unload the truck and have something to eat ready by then as well," Seth said from the back of the room.

"Thank you," Shayne told him as he followed his brother and their mate through the doorway that led down to the basement.

He nearly ran into poor Serenity as Creed stopped dead still at the bottom of the stairs after opening the door. He couldn't see around them in the narrow space to know what was wrong.

"Creed?"

"They've been busy, brother. Come, mate. See what your sleuth has accomplished for you this afternoon." He stepped into the small entry area and allowed first Serenity and then Shayne to pass.

Serenity's slight gasp did little to prepare him for what greeted them below.

Chapter Eight

The room in front of her was huge. A massive curved sectional sofa of brown leather with built-in mini tabletops to hold drinks and snacks flowed along one wall. Another smaller sectional sofa curved along the other side of the room with several comfortable looking lounge chairs between the two. They all faced the huge, theater-size flat-screen TV hanging on the wall in front of them. She'd never seen a more cozy or comfortable viewing room in her life. Along one wall behind the second sectional was a bar that looked to house a large fridge that would certainly hold their beverage needs.

"Wow!" It came out before she could stop it.

"They have been busy. This is the communal den area. Our final suite will be in that area once we've finished it. Right now, we'll take the one that already existed but isn't what I would like to live in for very long," Creed told her as he took her elbow and guided her across the room toward a closed door.

She noted that there was a small stove behind the bar as well as cabinets that would hold snacks and dishes. The door off to the side looked ordinary and simple, but when Creed opened it and stepped back for her to enter first, Serenity realized that nothing simple or mundane lay behind it.

Inside the room she found a massive bed that had to have been special ordered. She imagined the sheets for it would be several hundred dollars easy. On either side stood bedside tables of sturdy oak. A massive dresser with a full mirror took up on entire wall and two matching chest of drawers stood on either side of another door on another wall. All of the furniture looked well-made and overly large.

But then the two male shifters standing next to her were overly large bears.

"This is lovely," she finally managed to get out.

"It's too small for us, but we can make it work until our suite is ready," Creed told her.

"We aren't pompous or egotistical that we have to have the biggest and best just because we are the sleuth's leaders," Shayne said. "But we are big and need more room than this offers. When we move out, it will be enlarged."

"It's big to me, but then I'm not as big as the two of you and the furniture is larger than normal." Serenity figured she would need a stool to climb up on the bed as it was.

"If you don't like anything, we can change it. We want you to be comfortable and happy, Serenity," Shayne told her, his mouth not far from her ear at all. In fact, she could feel his hot breath fanning across her earlobe and neck.

"I love the furniture." Serenity didn't want them to think she was materialistic or anything. She wasn't.

"The bathroom is in here. We'll have a larger shower once our space is complete. There isn't enough room for large males in this house," Creed said as he showed her the bathroom.

To Serenity it was very nice, but would certainly be uncomfortable to a shifter the size of all the males she'd seen so far. She didn't blame them for wanting something bigger. Maybe she could talk them into letting her help with the bathroom design. She really wanted her spa.

"We don't have a very large closet in here, but that will change. I think we can make do until then," Creed was telling her as he led her back out of the bathroom to the only other door.

She didn't have that many clothes so she couldn't imagine needing much room. When he showed her the space she nearly laughed. It was the same size as her walk-in closet next door and she barely had anything in it. What size did they think she needed? Where they clothes horses?

"I know it's not large, but..." Shayne began, but she quickly stopped him with a finger to his lips.

"It's plenty big enough unless you and your brother have more clothes than I do. I can't fill up even half of it." Both of the shifters frowned at her.

"We will take you shopping as soon as things settle down. There's no need for you not to have enough clothes to be comfortable," Creed said.

A broad smile took over her face at the thought of the two shifters following her around from store to store as she shopped. Equally funny was the thought of her doing any marathon shopping in the first place. Serenity wasn't one to shop for no real reason.

"I can afford anything I want, guys. I make very good money with my business, but I don't need a lot." She didn't want to give them the impression that she didn't appreciate their offer, but neither did she want them to think she was poor and unable to keep herself in clothes either.

"Then you should use your money for things you want from now on. We will take care of you as is our privilege and duty," Creed said formally.

"Besides, we're going to enjoy spoiling you like you deserve," Shayne added with a mischievous wink.

"Um, if you want to spoil me, can I help design the bathroom? I really want a spa. I've been putting it off for years because I didn't want a lot of people in and out of my house. I have everything already planned out and even have some of it already bought, stored at my house."

Creed smiled, his face appearing more relaxed than she'd seen it so far. She liked the tiny laugh lines at the corners of his eyes. They didn't add age to his handsome face but character, making him seem much more approachable. Her heart fluttered at the way his smile brightened his entire face. She liked seeing this side of him and hoped to see it more once they became more familiar with each other.

"You can make whatever changes you want to, honey. Like Shayne said. We want you to be happy and feel safe here." Creed kissed the top of her head before pulling her closer to him, encircling her in his arms. "Maybe let us check the dimensions to be sure it is large enough for our big bodies if you don't mind."

She grinned up at him. "Of course. I'm sure we will need to add a foot or two so you won't feel claustrophobic, but I already had it quite large. I wanted to be able to spread my arms in it if I wanted to. Oh, and I wanted multiple shower heads, too."

"I'm already in love with it, and I haven't even seen the designs yet," Shayne chuckled.

"I'm in love with you, Serenity. You've made me and Brother Bear very happy. We've been searching for you for what seems like forever. I never dreamed we'd find you as soon as we moved in here. I've never felt so at peace before." Creed hugged her, barely squeezing her against his big body as if afraid of hurting her.

Serenity wrapped her arms around him to the best of her ability and squeezed him back, making no attempt at being careful not to hurt him. He was a big bear shifter. He could handle it. When he didn't even grunt, she pouted to herself. She wasn't in the same league when it came to his sort of brute strength. She'd have to work out more and build some strength. She was sure the guys would continue to treat her with kid gloves, but she wanted them to feel comfortable being themselves around her. That wouldn't happen if they perceived her to be weak.

"You smell sweet, like honey. I wonder if you'll taste like red clover or honeysuckle," Creed said with his nose buried against her neck. He licked her there, sending tingles along her skin. "Mmmm, even better. You taste like warm sunshine on a fresh honeycomb. I'm going to eat you alive, precious."

Another hot body pressed against her back and Shayne's tongue stroked the length of her neck without stopping until he reached her ear. There he sucked in her earlobe and nipped it before releasing it with an audible pop. She didn't even try to suppress the shivers it caused. The low moan she heard turned out to have come from her. How could they do this to her when she didn't even know them that well? It was too soon to be so attracted to them, wasn't it?

"She has on too many clothes, brother." Shayne's voice had sunk an octave at least. The effect that alone had on her seemed criminal.

"Clothes?" she managed to get out.

"Yes. Too many of them," Creed agreed. He started pulling her T-shirt up over her head and Serenity was too stunned to do anything other than lift her arms.

Shayne's warm hands wrapped around her waist over bare skin while Creed's massive hands cupped her still covered breasts in his. She hated that she was wearing plain cotton underwear, but she'd never worried that anyone would see her in them before. Of course she'd never expected to end up with a mate either. Now she had two of them.

Suddenly all of her long buried fears and insecurities surfaced to cut off her ability to breathe. She grabbed for her throat, certain that she would suffocate, but Creed seemed to understand what was going on. He lifted his hands to cup her face and stared into her eyes.

"Breathe, little kitten. It's okay. No one will ever hurt you. You're safe."

Well, he understood that she had panicked and lost her breathe though not the reason behind it. She wasn't afraid that they would harm her. She knew better. Neither brother would ever do anything to hurt her if they could help it. She also knew that they would sacrifice their very lives to keep her safe from any threat, but what she was afraid of couldn't be fought in one of the shifter's two forms. It had to be fought in her head and in her heart. She may end up fighting with them to keep her freedom, but it was something Serenity didn't think she could survive without. That worried her far more than any outside threat ever would.

* * * *

Creed's bear roared in his head. Their mate was afraid. It was their job to make her feel safe. The fact that she had just met them that morning didn't seem to matter to Brother Bear. He expected to be able to comfort and soothe her just by who he was to her. Creed didn't like her anxiety any more than his bear did. She'd been fine despite the threat earlier. Why did she suddenly close down?

He glanced over at his brother to find his face pale and a look of despair fighting to disrupt his normally easy going smile. It dawned on him then that it wasn't that she was afraid that they couldn't keep her safe. She was afraid of them for some reason. What had they done to spook her? Surely what they'd said over the last few minutes hadn't upset her. She'd seemed pretty turned on. Shifters were very sexual animals and his bear was about to die to make her theirs.

"Serenity," he began. "You know we'd never hurt you. No matter how badly we want you."

"Need you," Shayne interrupted him, taking a step back.

"We'd never hurt you. I thought you understood that, honey." Creed watched her face warm to a soft pink as her eyes widened for an instant before she dropped them to look at her feet.

"I'm not afraid of you. It's not that. I'm afraid of me. It's why I left my den in the first place. I need freedom and mating meant losing that freedom. My lynx is clawing at me to run as fast as we can, but we both know that it's too late. We've already started bonding and running away now would only send her into a tailspin."

Creed's stomach made a nosedive to his feet as his heart cramped at her words. Even knowing they were mates, she still would rather not be with them. It hurt far more than he'd thought it would. He'd always known that when they found their destined mate they would all have to adjust and grow into love with each other over time, but it had never occurred to him that their mate might not want that for herself. It was obvious she viewed it as something she had to learn to live with and not as something to anticipate as he and Shayne had for the last eight or ten years.

"What kind of freedom are you losing that scares you so much? Are you saying you don't want to settle down with just the two of us in your bed?" Shayne asked his voice gravely as his bear fought him. "I can handle a lot of things, Serenity, but I won't share with anyone but my brother."

Creed hadn't even thought of it in those terms before. They were very sexual beings with urges that were tied to every strong emotion from extreme anger to pure happiness. He would kill anyone who touched her. Even now, before they'd sealed their bond and joined their scents, Creed knew that he would destroy anyone who attempted to take her from them in any way.

"Ours!" he roared.

Serenity took a step back, her pupils dilating even as her fangs lengthened so that they showed between her parted lips. His brother had taken a step closer to her baring his teeth as he breathed in the air between them.

Fuck! This is going to end badly if I don't rein in my bear. Shayne asking if our mate wanted others in her bed has Brother Bear riled to the breaking point. I don't understand what she wants, though.

"That isssn't it," she hissed out. Her eyes shifted back and forth between them.

"Then what are you afraid you'll lose?" Creed demanded.

She drew in a deep breath and closed her eyes as if she were trying to put her fears into words. They came out stilted and choppy, but she managed to get them out without snarling any longer.

"I'm a cat. I don't like being confined or told what to do. I make my own decisions, and I have a very good business that I love. I'm not giving any of it up. It means we'll fight and there are two of you.

If you smother me, I'll go crazy and end up being dangerous. I can't live like that. The more you confine me, the worse I'll get," she said. When she opened her eyes, they shown and sparkled with tears instead of the merriment he would have preferred to see there. "I'm already drawn to both of you despite how hard I've fought this. I've been fighting to be free my entire life, Creed. You have no idea what it's like for a female to lose herself beneath a male's wishes and demands. I've seen it felt it to some extent outside of the mating bond. That small glimpse was enough to give me the strength to break the den bond and leave. I wasn't closed off from them. I tore away from them."

Creed knew exactly what she was saying. It floored him. Pulling loose from a bond, whether it was from a pack, a den, or a sleuth was almost unheard of. Normally when someone wanted to leave the Ursus, or a pack alpha would lift or cut the bond so the shifter could join another group or go off to form their own in the case of many strong shifters. It was essentially what had happened with him, Shayne, and the others. His father had dropped the preternatural tether that linked all members of a shifter group to the leader and Creed had easily latched on to the bears who'd chosen to come with him.

It had been simple for him and Shayne, but for most shifters, it was a little devastating even when they knew they were joining another group. To have actively broken that link, that phantom rope that secured her to her den for safety and balance had to have been extremely painful and frightening. And the little lynx had done it all alone.

And still he wasn't sure he completely understood why. She talked about freedom and independence as if she had none once she was mated, when in reality, she had even more with her mate's protection in place. She wouldn't need to ask permission from the leader just to leave their territory for mundane shopping trips or a quick visit with friends or family. With the mating bond in place, her mate would always know where she was and if there was trouble. It was a different type of bond than the one that connected her with a group's leader, stronger and more comprehensive.

"Are you saying you thought you would have even less freedom once you were mated? Why would you think that? Did someone tell you about the mating bond or did you just watch when someone bonded with their other half?" he asked.

His brother gently took her hand and led her over to the chair and pulled her down onto his lap, gently gliding his hands up and down her arms without holding her in place as if she were a prisoner. Shayne was giving her as much room as possible while still touching and offering her comfort. It was one of the things his sibling was good at and was one of the reasons sharing a mate would work so well for them. When Creed wasn't able to give their mate what she needed because of duties or the need to protect his sleuth, Shayne could without compromising his status in the sleuth.

"Both and more," she said so softly even his bear had to strain to hear her.

"What do you mean, baby?" Shayne asked.

"You really don't know how it is for the females in a shifter family, do you?" she asked, her mouth curling up into a sneer. "Once we reach the age to potentially mate, we're closely guarded. The males in the family won't allow any other males near us. We're watched all the time and never get to do anything outside of school. We can't even be a part of any of the usual activities like drama club or the debate team. I wanted to go to college, but that was out of the question."

"How old do they consider you old enough to mate?" Creed asked, his voice snarly, but he couldn't help it. Females in their sleuth weren't treated like this. Were they? He looked at his brother but Shayne wasn't looking at him.

"Fourteen unless we are small, then fifteen," she told him.

"They don't actually let a mate claim you at that age, do they?" he asked, astonished at how young it was.

"It's rare that a true mate is in the same den or a den close enough that they recognize each other at that age, but it does happen. In that case, if the female is under sixteen, the male will either return on her sixteenth birthday or move in with her family to be near her until she is sixteen. Then she is his to claim."

Creed shook his head. "That isn't how it is with the shifters I know. It certainly isn't like that in my home sleuth or how it will be in this one. Females need to develop and mature so that they are able to handle an adult male. We're aggressive and short tempered at times. It is through the mating bond that we are able to control ourselves better, siphoning off our female's calmer nature."

"It's all I know. My family was much more lenient than a lot of the ones in our den, but even they refused to allow me the freedom I craved. They did stand up to our leader and refuse to allow him to mate me off at a young age. If no true mate happened along to claim a female once they turned seventeen or eighteen, he started picking males for them and made them accept his choices. He wanted more cubs in the den since there were fewer than normal. I think it was because he forced matings when they didn't belong together." Her eyes glistened but still she didn't allow the tears to fall.

"Unless a female is too wild to control and her safety or the safety of the sleuth is at stake, we don't force matings and we never force them between couples who don't already care about each other," Creed told her with a shake of his head.

"He forced my best friend to mate with a relative of his from a different den. She wasn't far away from us at all, maybe an hour north, but she was never allowed to return to even visit her parents. When I left the den, I went to see her before I moved on. She wasn't herself. She'd lost so much weight she looked like a one of those starving kids you see on TV, and her eyes were so dull and lifeless looking. She'd had two miscarriages and her mate had beaten her when she'd lost the second kit. I begged her to go with me, but she was afraid of him and said he'd imprinted on her so closely that if she even thought about leaving he knew it. She didn't think she would survive more than a few days outside of the den without him. I don't want that. I don't want my life so closely tied to someone else's that I can't have my own thoughts."

Creed realized that he did understand some of what she was worried about. He'd often worried that once he found his mate and they'd bonded he wouldn't be able to keep his mind on the sleuth as he should with so much of her tied up in him. Then when he'd realized that he and Shayne would be sharing a mate he worried that instead of helping to diffuse the emotions and awareness of his mate in his head, he'd end up with his brother's presence there as well.

He sighed and looked down at the floor for a few seconds. It wasn't that he didn't want them there close to him, but concentrating on his sleuth was his job as the Ursus. The nagging thought that he had also worried that his mate would be able to sense his lack of intense feelings and emotions for her. It would hurt her to think that he wasn't happy with her. At the time, Creed had thought that keeping a tight control of his bear and the violence that was always so near the surface would dampen his emotions and make him appear cold to those around him. He had stopped worrying as much with Shayne on board, but now, with his true mate less than five feet away from him, he couldn't help but wonder if she would be offended or hurt once they sealed their mating bond only to find out that she still didn't have all of him like she would Shayne.

He became aware of his brother whispering softly in Serenity's ear. She'd relaxed slightly in his sibling's arms. No doubt Shayne was telling her that everything was going to be fine and that they would never treat her that way. Maybe his brother was speaking too soon. Already he felt the need to dominate her and keep her safe. He could already tell allowing her to go anywhere without his protection was going to be a challenge.

"Serenity, honey. Haven't you been around other shifter groups since you've been out on your own? They're not all like the ones you came from." Creed sighed as she shook her head even before he finished speaking.

"I've been around a few, but they've all been basically the same. There are just varying levels of control and imprisonment is all. Same rules, different type of bars on the windows and doors. A jail is still a jail no matter how much paint you throw on the walls or carpet you put on the floor," she said with a dry laugh.

Creed tried to hide his frustration. It wouldn't do them any good for their mate to sense how he felt in that moment. All they could do was show her. Actions always spoke stronger than words in the shifter world. Their Serenity would just have to see for herself that they weren't going to cage her in.

"Baby, we would never make you bend to our will. Your strength is part of who you are and what draws us to you," Shayne said.

"That's enough, brother. She isn't going to change her mind until she sees for herself that we won't subjugate her," Creed told him.

Shayne's expression looked anything but pleased by that realization, but he backed off of trying to convince her of it. Instead, he returned to seducing their mate. It was something Creed was in total agreement with.

Chapter Nine

Serenity felt anything but serene as Shayne buried his face in her neck and inhaled her scent. The feel of his rough tongue laving up her neck sent shivers down her spine. Just like that he managed to dissolve the fear and frustration of only seconds before. Mates could do that with each other. She just hadn't expected it when they had been talking about how mating meant she would lose her freedom, something she would fight every step of the way.

"You taste like vanilla and honey," Shayne said in a raw guttural voice. "Two things I love more than anything else."

The truth in his words was punctuated by the hard length of him against her ass as she sat on his lap. Her cat preened in the knowledge that he was hard, hot, and horny for her. She loved being lusted over.

Slut.

Then Creed joined in on the obvious plans to seduce her into their bed. Truth be told, they didn't have to work so hard if they didn't want to. Serenity was a realist besides being stubborn as the day was long. She knew it would only be a matter of time before she ended up there anyway. The pull between the three of them was strong, much stronger than anything she would have believed possible. Need ate at her resolve, turning her into a solid ball of anticipation.

Creed's mouth hovered just over hers as if waiting to see if she would move away or remain where she was. Instead, Serenity surprised them both by leaning forward to close the distance between them. Latching on to his plump, kissable lips, she kissed him with all of the building need inside of her.

"That's so fucking hot." Shayne's voice next to her ear reminded her that there were two of them. She reached back and curled her fingers in his hair, tugging on it as she did.

Serenity's cat stretched and purred, wanting to extend her claws and mark them, but she wasn't going to allow her to do that just yet. First, they needed them to satisfy the long denied needs she'd built a wall around for the last few years. It had been a while since she'd last taken a lover to her bed. Always before they had been human, since most shifters tended to get possessive at the drop of a hat. It had been a long time since she'd had sex with another shifter. The anticipation of what was to come curled her toes and made her insides quake with the possibilities.

Creed tore his mouth from hers. He licked along the seam of her lips before nipping at her bottom lip.

"Open up for me, kitten. I want to taste you. I need to taste you," he rasped out.

She relented and allowed him access to her whole mouth, his tongue slipping inside to torment her as he explored and claimed all of it as his own. When he'd conquered that to his satisfaction, Creed moved to kiss and lick the corners of her mouth down to her jaw where he nipped and licked over to her earlobe.

"Christ, you're sweet. Sweet and tangy all at the same time," he all but moaned.

Serenity responded with a moan of her own as Shayne's hands slowly unfastened her bra, slipping it from between her and Creed's bodies. The feel of his hot callused hands rubbing lightly over her mounds reawakened sensitive nipples. They peaked, straining to be touched as well.

"God, you're driving me insane," she said to no one in particular. They were both turning her into a puddle of need.

Serenity's clit, lubricated by her arousal, throbbed. They'd hardly touched her and already she wanted, no *needed* to be filled. Her pussy ached for something hard, thick, and long inside of it.

"We'll take care of you, honey. Relax and feel what we can do to you," Creed murmured in her ear.

All she could do was groan as Shayne rubbed his palm over her hardened nipples. Creed seemed to take that as acquiescence and knelt before her, his hands immediately going to the closure of her jeans. His hot knuckles brushed against the skin of her belly as he unfastened them. Her tummy fluttered at the contact.

"Lift her up, Shayne." As the big bear she sat on lifted her as if she weighed nothing, Creed pulled her jeans and underwear down all at the same time.

Once again, the reminder that she wore plain underwear dampened her mood. But the look of lust on Creed's face quickly chased away her soured mood. He wanted her as if just the thought of not having her would kill him. Sure, a lot of it was the mating heat riding him, but she knew enough about the big bear already to know that nothing, not even the heat could control him. If he hadn't already been attracted to her, it wouldn't have him almost salivating. It settled the worry that without the heat she wouldn't be as attractive to them somewhat.

"I've got to taste that sweet pussy, Serenity. I can't hold back." He looked up from where he'd been staring at her trimmed mound. "Put her on the bed, Shayne. Then get undressed."

It shouldn't have startled her to hear Creed telling Shayne what to do since Creed was the sleuth's leader, but it did. Shayne appeared just as powerful as his brother to her, but the other male didn't growl, flinch, or appear angered at his brother's order. And it was an order.

She quickly found herself transported back to the bed where a grinning Shayne tossed her so that she bounced twice before a now very naked Creed stilled her by covering her body with his. Her lynx charged for the surface at having the male on top of her like that, but Serenity kept her at bay, reminding her that this was their mate. The feline didn't care. She was a very dominant female and didn't like being attacked like that.

"Easy, kitten. I'm not going to hurt you. All I want to do is make you feel real good," Creed crooned to her before getting to his hands and knees above her. "I'm going to lick my way down your sweet body, tasting every inch of your silky skin. Then, when I get to the source of that intoxicating scent you're sending my way, I'm going to explore every inch of it as well. I bet you taste like spicy honey, don't you."

Her lynx whined at the promise in his voice. It had gone even deeper with his arousal. Oh it was very obvious just how aroused he was, too. The bear sported an enormous cock that bordered on too big, but just managed to stay on the right side of that line. His meaty cock stretched out hard and long, dipping down toward her. He had large balls that held no hair. They didn't even look as if he shaved them. The bulbous tip shown with a drop of pre-cum, making her mouth water at the sight.

Before she could say anything, Creed licked a circle around her belly button. She'd expected him to start with her breasts, but a second later, Shayne latched onto one of them while one hand captured the other. That explained Creed's focus lower.

Oh, God. I'm not about to complain either.

Even as Shayne sucked lightly on her nipple while plumping her other breast with his big hand, Creed had discovered that she had a sensitive spot just above the crease of her inner thigh. Every swipe of his tongue had her whimpering and struggling to move beneath the two males. Her pussy clenched, aching to be filled, sending her higher with every touch from the two bears above her.

"Oh, God," she moaned out.

Creed's tongue finally dipped lower to caress her wet slit. When he growled and spread her lower lips with his fingers, she almost panicked at the ravenous sounds he made as he buried his face in her wet folds. Then there was nothing but pleasure as both he and his brother drove her closer and closer to the edge of ecstasy. Each nip of their teeth and lick of their tongue had her squirming to both get closer and get away at the same time.

"Fuck, brother. She's addictive. She tastes like spicy vanilla honey," Creed said between devastating licks.

"Give me your finger, Serenity," Shayne demanded.

Confused, she lifted one of her hands from where she'd been digging into the covers to hold herself still and Shayne shackled it around the wrist, lowering it between her legs.

"I want a taste, baby. Give it to me," he told her.

She realized he wanted her to wet her fingers in her pussy juices so he could taste her. The thought turned her on even more than she already had been. Creed growled when she moved her hand down between her soaked pussy and his mouth. Instead of trying to push her out of the way though, the big bear shifter grabbed her wrist and moved her fingers up and down until they were drenched in her juices. Then he returned it to his brother who growled his approval and pulled her hand toward his mouth.

Shayne didn't take a finger into his mouth and suck like she expected him to. Using the tip of his tongue, he licked from her palm upward until he reached the tip of her finger. Then he licked back down the other side. The teasing touch made every hair on her arms lift. Even her clit seemed affected by that slight touch. Seconds later, he plunged three of her fingers all the way into his mouth and sucked hard, long drags, growling as he did.

Creed continued to torment her below with his talented tongue, lapping at her as if he'd never had anything so delicious. His tongue seemed to reach farther inside of her than was possible and he could move his mouth to nuzzle and suckle on her tender flesh in a way that a normal male wouldn't be able to do. God, he was going to kill her with that mouth.

"Please, Creed. I need to come. It's too much!"

He didn't respond, just continued eating her like a man starved. She had never begged in her life and the fact that she had without thinking should have upset her, but Serenity was beyond caring at this point. All she wanted to do was reach that pinnacle that promised to be mind-bending when she did. If Creed would just give her clit a hard swipe instead of the tiny nudges he was teasing her with.

The sudden invasion of a finger inside her cunt had her gasping, arching her back and neck in surprise. It almost gave her the push she needed to climax, but as if he knew just how much it would take, he gave her a tiny bit less to keep her on edge. Slowly, he fucked her with it, making sure to drag his digit along her sensitive tissue with each retreat. After a minute or two, he added a second finger and her body all but convulsed, leaving her gasping for breath and cursing him all at the same time.

"Fuck me, Creed! I can't stand it anymore!" she cried out.

Creed didn't say anything, but his clever lips latched on to her clit and sucked even as his fingers began to piston in and out of her pussy. Shayne pinched one nipple while rasping his sharp teeth over the other one adding fuel to the fire that had built into a roaring flame. It consumed her in a maelstrom of explosions that rocked her body to the core.

The two brothers stroked her down from the lofty high but despite closing her eyes to drift into sleep, she couldn't forget that they hadn't come yet, nor had they claimed her. Her eyes snapped open just in time to see Shayne stand up and step closer to the edge of the bed. Though not quite as long as his brother's, Shayne's rigid dick was thicker with a generous pair of balls that hung heavy between his legs. The sight of him standing completely naked in front of her had her mouthwatering.

"Don't worry, honey. You'll get to taste him. Now roll over on your hands and knees. I want to fuck you and my bear is going to tear us all apart if I don't mate you right now," Creed said in a husky voice with more violence than pleasure sounding in it.

Serenity wasn't afraid of him, only cautious. Males in the midst of a mating frenzy had been known to accidently harm their mate when the females unknowingly challenged them. She had no intentions of doing that. She wanted Creed just as much as she wanted Shayne. On hands and knees, she found her face at the perfect level to take Shayne's ruddy-colored cock inside her mouth and suck on it.

Shayne must have noticed how she stared at it with hunger because he fisted the base of it with one hand and shifted closer until the meaty length of him was within licking distance.

"I can't wait to see your lips wrapped around my dick, baby."

Without saying anything, Serenity swiped her tongue across the wet tip, scooping up the tiny drop of pre-cum that had appeared while she watched. His sharp hiss let her know that he hadn't expected that. His flavor exploded across her tongue, a heady mixture of bitter honey that wasn't unpleasant. She licked all around the crown before rasping over the slit once more and hummed her approval as more of his cum leaked for her.

"Aw, hell, baby. That feels good," Shayne crooned to her.

Raspy hairs brushed against the backs of Serenity's thighs letting her know that Creed had only waited long enough for her to get settled. His body heat soon enveloped her back as he bent over her, brushing her hair aside.

"Hold on, honey. I need you. I can't wait any longer," he whispered in her ear. Then his hands grasped her hips in a tight grip and the blunt head of his cock slid through her juices at her slit.

She moaned just as she took Shayne's cockhead into her mouth. It reverberated across the flesh she held there causing the other man to groan as she slowly swirled her tongue around the shaft. Creed's dick probed her opening then slowly pressed forward, filling her, stretching her sheath impossibly wide as he slowly, steadily filled her. She'd never felt so stuffed with cock before.

"Holy hell, you're tight," he groaned.

All Serenity could do was moan around the equally thick cock filling her mouth. She'd managed not to bite Shayne as his brother challenged her pussy to accept all of him. Instead, she'd stilled and concentrated on breathing through her nose and controlling the urge to scream. While she was certain it would have felt good to Shayne's throbbing penis, she wasn't certain that she wouldn't have choked trying.

When Creed's thighs touched the back of hers once again, signaling that he had managed to stuff all of that giant cock inside of her, he leaned his forehead against the middle of her back and grunted as if trying to calm down. She couldn't stop the slight smile that somehow managed to grow around Shayne's dick. As Shayne threaded his hands through her hair and fisted it, Serenity slowly backed off of his shaft, shiny with her saliva. He didn't try to stop her with his hands tangled in her hair, but he did groan. Serenity relished the sound of him losing some of his control.

She took more of him into her mouth and when the crown hit the back of her throat making her gag, she forced herself to relax and swallowed around it.

"Jesus! Do that again, babe. Just like that." He hissed with pleasure when she did. "Damn!"

Creed pulled slowly out of her burning cunt, dragging his dick through her tingling tissues. Then he pushed back inside of her as if unwilling to leave her hot, wet depths. She could totally agree with that. He felt so good inside of her. He stretched her just right. She loved the slight burning that all too soon changed into pure pleasure.

She moaned deep in her throat, then began growling when he increased his tempo, drawing more and more pleasure from her already quivering cunt. She'd never enjoyed sex so much before. Even though her cat was a very sexual animal, she'd lost interest in it once she'd secured her home and settled in. Maybe it wasn't that they were just good at this but that the mating heat had her in a frenzy. She'd never enjoyed sucking a male's cock before either, but she couldn't get enough of Shayne's taste or the feel of him in her mouth.

"So fucking tight," Creed groaned as he pressed deep inside her soaked pussy.

Pressure built inside of Serenity. Already her climax was close when before it had taken much more to stir her desire. The bond between the three of them tightened even as she sucked hard on Shayne's dick. His fingers massaged her scalp, the blunt nails stimulating her though they weren't sharp in his current form. She wanted him to come before she did, wanted to watch his face as he filled her mouth with his cum. Her cat stretched inside of her, pleased with the way her mates treated her. Serenity could agree, but right then all she could think about was the cock in her pussy and the dick in her mouth and her need to climax.

"Fuck! I'm going to come, baby. Your mouth is so damn hot." Shayne threw back his head and growled as every muscle in his body tightened in front of her.

Serenity rolled her eyes up to watch him as his cum filled her mouth in warm spurts. The way his face changed into a grimace as he growled, baring his teeth would have scared her had she not known it was pleasure that had him in that condition. His sharp teeth elongated and the roar that erupted from his mouth had the hairs on the back of her neck standing on end. The call of her mate triggered her own orgasm as she struggled to swallow the gift of his cum.

The muscles of her cunt quivered then spasmed and tightened down around the thick shaft as it pummeled her. Each thrust of his cock added to her blooming explosion until all Serenity could do was ride the waves of pleasure. Her belly tightened almost painfully and she screamed just as Shayne pulled free of her mouth.

"Aw, hell. So fucking tight, honey. You're strangling my cock," Creed said in a growly voice. His hands held tight to her hips, the tips of his fingers erupting into claws, but he didn't allow them to draw blood.

Serenity's entire body tightened until her muscles felt as if she'd turn into one huge cramp from all the pleasure that centered in her cunt. She was sure her eyes rolled up into her head as the first tendrils of the mating bond latched on to her, connecting her to her mates in a way that would bind them together forever.

Creed wasn't able to hold out against her orgasm as it milked his cock. She felt the heated jets of his release pulse inside of her even as his bear roared in pleasure behind her. He all but collapsed on top of her, driving her all the way to the bed where he curled around her as Shayne climbed on and buried his face in the side of her neck. It was at that moment that Serenity realized something else that had happened as the bond began to form. Her lynx was quiet inside of her. For the first time in over twenty years, her cat felt calm and settled. For the first time in longer than she could remember, Serenity's feline felt safe.

Chapter Ten

"Why didn't you mark me?" Serenity asked.

Creed slowly opened his eyes and yawned. What time was it? He looked at his mate's confused face with the dainty eyebrows squinched up above her equally expressive eyes. He could look into those gorgeous light green orbs for hours. They reminded him of new pine growth but full of intelligence that might have been intimidating if he and his brother weren't just as smart in their own areas of expertise.

"What? I'm sorry. What did you say?" he finally asked after remembering that she'd asked him a question.

"Why didn't you mark me? I thought we were mates," she said with a frown.

"We will mark you when we take you together. Since we share you as our mate, the final bonding mark must be made at the same time. I'll bite you on one shoulder and he'll bite the other one.

"You've already taken me together. I don't understand."

Creed hesitated. He hadn't considered that she might not have any knowledge of shared mates. Bears and even wolves shared sex between them in every way. He wasn't familiar with the feline shifters since they were rarer in nature and didn't often venture into colder territories. This wasn't going to be an easy conversation if she was adverse to the idea of anal sex. He glanced over to where his brother slept, oblivious to the serious conversation. Creed drew in a deep breath.

"When we both claim you, we will both be inside of you. Oral sex doesn't count. I'm not sure why it doesn't work that way except that it would be very difficult for us both to claim you at the same time."

Her eyes suddenly widened as realization of what he was suggestion hit her. A mirage of expressions flew across her face before they all disappeared as if a door had been shut against them. Her features no longer spoke of her inner thoughts. Creed worried that some of what he had seen before she'd managed to control herself were of fear and unease.

"You mean one of you would take my pussy and the other would take my ass?"

"Yes. Serenity, we would never hurt you, honey. You are our mate and the idea of causing you pain is abhorrent to us. You know this." He watched for any sign of what she was feeling, but she'd shut down so tightly that even their tenuous connection from the start of the mating bond wasn't helping him discern her feelings or fears.

"I'm going to take a bath. I didn't get mine before we went to sleep last night." She started to slip from between he and his brother. Creed stopped her with a hand to her shoulder.

"What are you thinking, Serenity? Don't run away when it's obvious that you aren't comfortable with something."

"I need a bath, Creed, and I need some time alone to process what this means. Felines don't share in anal sex. It's a form of dominance that few females will tolerate. I'm not so inflexible that I can't understand your way of things, but I need to think about it. I know that male wolves insist on it with their mates as a way to remind them of their dominance over them. I don't like that."

He sighed. "It is not like that with us. We don't wield dominance over our mates. We will only pull rank when it's a matter of your health or safety. We treasure our mates as the vital parts of our sleuth. You are our other half and help us secure and cement us all as a sleuth. I don't even know many wolves who practice that sort of mentality anymore."

She just shook her head and slid off the foot of the bed. "We come from different worlds, Creed. As a shifter, I would have thought we'd all be similar, but we're not. I need some time."

He watched her as she slipped out of their room into the in-suite bathroom and gently shut the door. He had no clue what to do about this. It had never occurred to him that their mate wouldn't understand or accept their way of bonding. Of course, he and his brother had always assumed their mate would be a bear shifter or wolf shifter. They'd seen so few other shifter types that any other possibility hadn't crossed his mind.

"What is it? Where's Serenity?" Shayne sat up in bed looking around.

"She's taking a bath," he told his brother.

"What is wrong? I could feel your anxiety as I slept. That's why I woke up."

"Serenity woke me up asking why we didn't bite her," Creed told his brother.

"Did you explain we would when we are both buried inside of her?"

"Of course, and that is why she is anxious, which is why I'm that way myself right now." Creed sighed. "She's feline and evidently felines don't do anal sex. It's a form of aggression, it sounds like."

Shayne rubbed his face and scooted back so that he could lean against the headboard. Creed could see his brother's worry etched on his face. He felt the same way. Getting her past the mindset that they were trying to dominate her was going to be tough. Until she accepted them both and they could mark her, their mate would be open to another's advances. It wasn't an option as far as he was concerned, but neither could he force her to accept them in their way. They would have to take it slow and keep her close to them. It would cut down on the chance that another would try and stake a claim on her while keeping her safe from the hunters.

"For now, we give her some room to think about it and continue to show her that she is our world and we would do nothing to harm her." Creed didn't like that idea much and could see that it didn't sit well with his sibling either, but they didn't have much choice.

"She's going to talk herself out of mating with us if we give her too much room," Shayne said.

"I didn't say we leave her alone. I said back off some. I have every intention of keeping our scent and touch all over her to keep the others away from her. Plus, this business with the Rogue Hunters will give us the time we need to bond with her and convince her to fully mate with us. She's stuck here until they are dealt with," Creed reminded his brother.

"True," Shayne smiled. "I have no problem with touching and rubbing on her all the time. I love the way she smells when she's aroused."

Creed smiled. "Keep her aroused all the time and when we take her to bed, she's wild with need. Eventually, she will relax enough to allow us to truly take her."

"My bear doesn't like that she isn't wearing our mark," Shayne said. "He's going to be difficult to control until she does."

"I understand. Mine isn't silent on the issue either. We'll have to keep her between us and away from the others as much as possible."

Shayne scowled at him. "You know she's not about to allow us to keep her sequestered in our suite. She's going to expect to have free rein of the house."

"I know. As long as she stays away from the windows and doesn't answer the door then she will be safe from the hunters. As for keeping her away from the others, that will be a little more difficult. We will take turns working with them on the master suite of rooms while the other one keeps an eye on her," Creed suggested.

"Okay. Besides, she did say she wanted to help with some of the design work. That will keep her down here some and help to keep her occupied."

Creed hoped it would be enough to stop any notions of refusing to finish the mating. Already his bear had covered himself in her scent and periodically played along the light tether connecting them. He could smell her from the bed. He could also feel some of the anxiety their earlier conversation had brought up.

"She's pretty anxious, Creed," Shayne said staring at the bathroom door as if he could see right through it.

"I know. I feel her, too. It's just going to take time. Remind your bear that the more you push her, the faster she'll run, and it won't be because she wants to get caught."

"I'll try and keep her occupied with designing the bathroom like she wants it. When she's tired of that I'll send her upstairs to your office so you can spend some time with her. Between the two of us, we'll keep her safe and occupied so she doesn't have time to think too much about running away," Shayne said. "I couldn't take it if she rejected us. My bear would go crazy."

"I know. It's not an option. We'll figure something out if she refuses to allow us to take her together. I don't know what, but there has to be another way." Creed would contact their father if it looked as if their mate was going to balk. He didn't want to do it yet, but if it became necessary, he'd do it. Securing Serenity as their other half was more important than his pride.

* * * *

Serenity stepped out of the tub after soaking for nearly an hour, having to add hot water twice in the process. The long soak had helped her relax enough that her lynx no longer fought her to run. It had also given her time to think about her entire situation. The only thing it hadn't done was provide the answers she needed that would satisfy her lynx and the bears just outside the bathroom door.

How was she supposed to convince her lynx that allowing them both to make love to her at the same time was a special part of the mating and not an attempt to dominate her into submission to them? Serenity actually believed that Creed was being truthful and they had no desire to humiliate or subjugate her. Where her cat didn't feel their honesty through the mating bond like she did, the wily lynx did feel their desire and need to complete the mate marks. It made her nervous. Learning they expected anal sex as part of that only stirred her up more.

"Crazy cat. You can't push me to bond with them then step back and refuse to finish it."

But, that was exactly what the bitch was doing. Now Serenity was stuck in limbo with a need to be near her mates and her other half wanting to run again. This wasn't supposed to happen. In fact, she wasn't supposed to ever find her mate in the first place. It was why she'd left her den. It was also why she'd come so far north, believing it would lower the chances that she'd find her mate if she lived somewhere most cats didn't want to. Fat lot of good that had done.

I guess all I did was play right into fate or destiny's hands by running. It was part of the big plan all along. Bitches!

As she dried off, it dawned on her that she hadn't thought ahead enough to bring something to wear into the bathroom with her. It didn't matter that she'd been naked when she'd entered an hour earlier. She really didn't want to walk back out there without clothes on. When she searched the little room she came up empty and settled for wrapping the bath towel around her torso. She'd dress in the closet.

With a solution in mind, Serenity checked to make sure she was adequately covered and opened the door to stroll into the bedroom as if she wasn't uncomfortable at the moment.

Never let them see you sweat.

Right.

She pulled open drawers in the dresser until she found the one with her underwear. When she walked toward the closet Shayne's voice startled her. She'd thought they were both still asleep.

"Come back to bed, baby. It's still early yet."

She didn't look in his direction but stopped with one hand on the closet door handle. "I'm awake now. I think I'll go get something to eat."

"Climb back into bed and I'll fix breakfast in bed for you," he said in a deeper voice.

She felt the weight of it slide down her spine, his voice a pick against the strands of her desire. No one had the right to be that sexy. She shivered but pushed down on the lever to open the door.

"Thanks, but I'm up now."

"So are we, kitten," Creed said in a raspy voice.

She rolled her eyes at his obvious suggestion and flipped the light switch before walking into the small closet. When she closed the door behind her, she breathed a sigh of relief and dropped the towel to pull on her plain-Jane cotton panties. As she pulled the straps of her bra on over the shoulders, the closet door opened behind her.

"Need help, babe?" Shayne asked.

"No thanks. I've got it. Go back to bed if you're still tired. I'll be fine," she said presenting him with her back.

Rough fingers took the ends of the bra away from her and hooked it for her. Hot breath feathered her bare shoulders. "I'll help you dress then make breakfast for you."

"Really. There's no need. I can fix my own meal."

"I know you can, Serenity, but I want to do it." Shayne's sincerity was obvious to her through their partially intact bond. How could she deny him something he seemed to need to do for her?

Instead of answering him, she pulled on a pair of jeans and reached for a T-shirt. Shayne took it from her. When she turned around to ask him what he was doing, he had replaced it on the hanger and held up a much larger one.

"Wear Creed's shirt, babe. It will make him feel better for you to have his scent on you until the mating is complete."

She blinked up at him. "What about you?"

A slow sexy smile spread across his face, making his light brown eyes twinkle. "Don't worry about me, baby. My scent is going to be all over you, too."

Before she could ask what he meant by that, he'd pulled the big T-shirt with a large grizzly bear standing on his hind legs over her head. Serenity blew her hair out of her face and punched her arms through the arm holes. Then Shayne opened the door of the closet once again and pulled her back into the bedroom by the hand.

Creed was no longer in the bed but the bathroom door was closed. Shayne drew her out of the bedroom into the main living area and up the stairs to the kitchen. The first thing she noticed as they emerged from the lower level was that all of the blinds and drapes had been closed around the house. She was sure that was to keep anyone from seeing her there.

"What are you hungry for, Serenity, eggs and bacon or pancakes or waffles?" Shayne asked.

"Waffles would be good," she admitted. "Do you have plenty of syrup?"

"Honey and syrup. You can take your pick," he said with a wink.

"Of course. Honey. That is so clichéd," she drawled.

"Are you telling me that if I threw a ball of yarn across the room you wouldn't go chase it?" he dared.

"Asshole." She couldn't help but smile though. Where Creed was mostly serious, Shayne's since of humor bordered on cheesy at times.

"I didn't see any yarn at her place when Quill and I snuck inside her place to pack some things for her." Zeth walked into the room grinning. "She does have a lot of milk, ice cream, and these."

The crazy bear held up a pair of her favorite house shoes that happened to have a mouse's face on the ends of them. Well, okay, she had several pair of them. She liked mice.

"Oh, and she also has these," Quill added from the doorway with an even wider grin.

The other bear held up some of her stuffed animals in his hands. And yes, they were all mice. She growled and stomped over to where the two males stood laughing with her prized possessions.

"Who gave you permission to go through my things?" she demanded with a snarl.

When she tried to snatch them from their hands, both bears held them out of her reach. She jumped up and managed to catch Zeth by surprise at her jumping ability, snagging her house shoes.

"Creed told us to gather some of your things and bring them over so you would feel more at home," Quill replied still holding her mice out of her reach.

"Give her the mice, Quill. Stop teasing her," Shayne said with laughter in his voice.

When Quill lowered his arms so that she could reach the stuffed rodents, Serenity hissed at him and sprang, knocking him backward so that they both hit the floor with her riding him down to the ground. The big bear cushioned her fall and that is how Creed found them when he walked into the kitchen. Serenity straddled poor Quill as he gasped to get air back into his lungs. Her fangs and claws were out as she hissed at him.

"What in the hell is going on?" Creed all but roared.

Serenity felt Quill freeze in midgasp. She retracted her claws and teeth to look up and see Zeth with his head down and a worried expression on his face. When she looked over at Creed, the big bear had fine fur sprouting across his bare chest and clawed hands. He looked furious.

Oh hell. What had she done?

Shayne stepped in front of his brother, blocking his view of her. Serenity scrambled off of Quill's body and snatched her beloved mice from his grasp as she did.

"Calm down, brother. The guys brought Serenity's things back and were teasing her about her obsession with mice. That's all. She jumped on Quill to get her stuffed mice from him. Nothing is going on." Shayne's normally calm voice had somehow grown even more tranquil.

Creed's bear slowly retreated, but his anger was still a palpable emotion. She stood in front of Quill, unwilling to allow the bear to be punished for something she'd done. Yes, he and Zeth had started it by teasing her, but she'd taken it farther.

The sleuth's Ursus slowly advanced toward her but his eyes were on the bear behind her. Serenity threw her hands up, still grasping the stuffed mice she'd taken from Quill.

"He brought me my stuffed animals," she said unnecessarily.

Creed stopped advancing and tore his eyes from the male behind her to stare at the various mice she held in front of his face. His eyes roved over her from head to foot then returned to stare at the ridiculous toys in her hands. A twitch at the corner of his snarling mouth sent a wave a relief through her body.

"Mice? Really? You've got to be kidding me," he finally said just before he all but jerked her into his arms.

"Hey! You have honey. I collect mice. Don't you dare say anything." She pretended to pout.

He squeezed her tight enough she squeaked before he slightly relaxed his arms around her. "Don't play games with the others while our bond isn't complete, kitten. I can't control my bear where you're concerned."

The whispered words next to her ear sobered her. She hadn't thought about how he would react to her being around the other bears of his sleuth. She was walking a tight rope by staying there with them. If she tried to leave though, Creed and Shayne would either try to keep her there or go with her. She just nodded her head to let him know she understood.

"Your waffle is almost ready, Serenity. Why don't you grab the syrup and honey out of the fridge? The bacon will be ready in a few minutes." Shayne continued cooking as if there wasn't a crazed bear lurking in the room with them.

She slowly slipped out of Creed's embrace and found the sweet stuff in the fridge to place on the huge table. Then she sat down when he pulled out a chair for her, scooting her closer to the table.

"What do you want to drink, kitten?" he asked in a voice that had lost some of the growly quality.

"Um, milk?" she said with a hopeful note.

Shayne and Zeth burst out laughing, but Quill remained quiet. She glared at both bears.

"I guess I should have known that," Creed chuckled, pulling glasses out of the cabinets and setting them on the counter. "Quill, grab the milk and the orange juice out of the fridge."

Serenity watched the other bear slowly lumber over to the refrigerator and pull out the milk and juice. He set the juice down on the counter and handed the milk to his Ursus without looking him in the eyes.

"I'm sorry, Quill. I overreacted. I know you weren't trying to take her from me, but my bear is on edge right now." Serenity was surprised that the big male would apologize to the other bear. It made her like him even more.

Quill nodded then smiled. "I know what to get her for her birthday now—cat toys."

Creed groaned and Serenity hissed across the table at the bear.

"Payback's hell, Quill. Don't forget that."

Quill just grinned and accepted the glass of milk from his leader to place in front of her before returning to take tall glasses of juice from off the counter as Creed poured them.

"Where is everyone else?" Creed asked.

Zeth spoke up from where he stood next to where Shayne was pouring more batter on the waffle iron. "They should all be here in a few minutes. Locke and Otto were making sure the cameras are working and will be a little longer."

"Cameras?" she asked, looking from Zeth to Creed.

"We're setting up our security system. One of the things we do is install and monitor security systems," Creed explained. "While they're working on setting the system up, they can keep an eye on the hunters then once it's all set up, we can watch from inside the house."

"Okay. After breakfast, I need to get back to work. I've got a program that I was supposed to have finished yesterday. I need to contact my client and explain that I've had an emergency and will have it ready by in the morning." Serenity wasn't going to let her business suffer just because she had hunters on her trail and a pair of mates clamoring for her attention.

"We'll set you up in the office with me, but save some time to help Shayne with designing the bathroom you wanted." Creed's knowing smirk irritated her but she wasn't going to pass up the chance to have her dream if there was a chance of it coming true.

"Spa. It's not a bathroom, it's a spa," she corrected him.

"Set up your workstation first while we finish clearing out the area so you have a good idea of the space you have to work with. Then I'll come get you and you can show me what you want," Shayne told her.

She couldn't stop a wide grin from exploding across her face. It was all she thought about while she finished two waffles and a handful of bacon. The bears ate a good deal more than she did and the thought of what their grocery bill must look like made her a little ill.

Shaking it off, Serenity offered to help with the dishes since Shayne had cooked, but he explained that it was Bane's turn to wash dishes. They all took turns with all of the chores. The only exception was that Otto wasn't allowed to cook at all. He took double shifts on guard duty instead.

"Yeah, after he nearly burned down his apartment three times trying to cook, his stove was pulled out and he had to live with a microwave and takeout after that," Zeth told her.

She couldn't imagine a shifter who didn't know how to cook. They needed such large quantities of food to fuel their bodies that it was almost ludicrous to imagine. Still, she didn't laugh. Instead, she followed Creed down the hall to his office. The room was quite large and they had already set up her precious equipment on a second desk that butted up against Creed's.

"Wow. When did they do this?" she asked as she sat down to check that everything was correctly hooked up.

"Last night after we went downstairs. Don't worry, everything should be right. Both Bane and Locke are computer experts and handle all of that part of our business."

She grinned over at Creed and promptly lost herself in her programming. She always felt most at home behind a computer where she understood the logic and processes much better than she did the world around her. It wasn't lost on her that as long as she was in her zone, creating programs for her clients, she didn't have to think about what she was going to do about her lynx, the two bears, and the anal sex issue, which was more than a pain in her ass at the moment.

Chapter Eleven

"Yes. That's exactly what I want. When the guys get back with my samples, you'll see how it will look," Serenity told Shayne.

"I hadn't thought about moving the door over. It gives more space to the vanity area. I like it," he said with a nod.

Excitement flowed through Serenity's bloodstream at the knowledge that she'd finally get her dream spa. She shoved the nagging reminder that her lynx still wasn't willing to allow the two bears to take her like they wanted to. She'd figure something out later. Right now, she had a dream to fulfill.

"Here you go." Seth and Warren returned carrying her dream box that held everything she needed to show Shayne her spa.

"Any trouble? Hunters?" Shayne asked as Seth set the box on the floor.

"No problem. In and out without detection," Warren said. "There's still one in the tree behind the house, but the one that had been in the bushes outside the back door is gone. We didn't see him anywhere else around the house."

"Do you think they are giving up?" she asked hopefully.

"I doubt it. They're probably regrouping and deciding what to do next," Shayne said.

"Great," she sighed. "Let's map out where I want everything and I'll show you my colors."

"As long as there isn't anything pink or lavender, I'm fine with the colors," he said.

"What do you have against pink?" she asked looking innocent. She had no intentions of putting pink anywhere. She'd always hated it since her parents had painted her room pink when she was twelve in an attempt to soften her tomboyish ways out of her.

"It's too girly. I can handle having your things strewn around the bathroom, but I'm not showering in a pink bathroom. I won't back down on that one, babe," Shayne said crossing his arms.

She poked out her lips in a pout and batted her eyelashes at him. "Maybe just a little pink?"

"Not even a stripe. No pink. End of story. Now what other colors do you have in there?" Shayne asked picking the box up off the floor to go through it. "I don't see anything pink in here. It's all stone colors and dark greens."

She grinned as he growled at her. She could see the playful glint in his eyes and hoped it would last long enough for her to convince him that the business part of the bathroom needed to have its own space, complete with a door.

For the next hour, she and the others worked on her plans and argued about logistics of how to put in heated tiles and the towel warming rods. She was having a ball. Shayne was so obviously frustrated that it was cute. He was trying to keep her happy while cutting down on some of the hard work creating the spa she so deeply wanted would create.

"Face it, Shayne," Seth said with a smirk. "You're already pussy whipped. Get it? Pussy whipped?"

Serenity couldn't take offense it was so funny, but she did have to step in between the two bears before they came to blows.

"That's enough, Seth. Shayne. You guys need a break. How about a sandwich to tide us over until dinner tonight? I know I could sure use something to eat." She smiled up at Shayne, one hand on his naked sweaty chest as she batted her eyes at him.

He visibly settled down and nodded, but growled one more time at the other bear before taking her hand and all but dragging her toward the door leading up to the main floor. She could hear the others behind them snickering and flashed a stern look at them over her shoulder. They immediately sobered up and looked down at their booted feet instead.

I could grow to enjoy this. Just wait until they meet their mates. The shoe will be on the other foot then, and I'll make sure they wallow in their meals of crow.

"We're going to clean up before eating. I feel like a pig that wallowed in drywall," Warren said.

"It will take a little while to make the sandwiches anyway. Take your time." Shayne waved them off as he escorted Serenity to the kitchen.

"I'll get the ingredients out of the fridge," she said. "What sort of meat?"

"Better grab it all," he said. "They're going to want three or four each. You worked them hard, baby. You're a slave driver."

She grinned but didn't say anything. Watching him reach for the chips in the top of the pantry made her drool. She quickly slipped back to the fridge and began pulling out the makings for sandwiches and set them on the bar where he'd already set two loaves of bread. Sheesh, how many sandwiches was he planning on making?

As Shayne put together sandwiches for them, she watched the play of muscles over his body. He had an amazing body. Even hot, dirty, and sweaty, she had the urge to lick the bead of sweat rolling languidly down his back, about to disappear behind the waistband of his jeans. God, the jeans! They encased his lower half as if they'd been shrunk wrapped on his body. His squeezable ass challenged the denim seams. It was all Serenity could do to resist going to her knees and taking a bite out of one juicy-looking butt cheek. She managed to convince herself and her lynx that it would be much more satisfying to wait until the jeans weren't an issue. Tender beefy flesh would taste oh so much better than nasty material.

"Serenity? Baby? Did you hear me?" Shayne was asking before turning around.

"I'm sorry. I was thinking about the shower. What did you say?" she asked in all innocence.

"Do you like regular mustard or spicy mustard? We have both."

"Spicy. I like things spicy," she purred up at him, licking her lips.

His eyes immediately widened then his lids lowered as his bear caught her meaning. She enjoyed seeing how quickly she could arouse him with just her words. Her lynx wanted to forget the snack and take that bite out of the bear instead. Serenity knew she needed the food or she wouldn't be worth anything later.

"Baby, you're hot enough to melt the sun, and I love hot things," he said as he slowly stalked her, backing her up to the fridge and pinning her against the door with his body.

The rumble coming from his chest pulled an answering growl from her cat. Serenity nearly moaned at the way his scent and the hard planes of his chest tightened things inside of her and made her pussy moisten in need. Dear God, she'd started something without really meaning to, but there was no way she going to put on the brakes. She wanted him just as much as he obviously wanted her. The impressive bulge blooming between them told her that loud and clear.

"Fuck, babe. You know how to play with fire, don't you," he said with a low growl.

"Like I said. I like things spicy, big guy." She slipped down to her knees and unfastened his jeans before he could say anything.

Serenity had his thick dick in her hands in seconds. She squeezed him at the base then lowered her head to tease the already dewed slit with the tip of her tongue.

"Hell, fire, damnation! The others will be here in a minute for that promised snack," he managed to rasp out as she sucked on just the crown of his cock. "It won't take them long to wash up."

"Then we'd better hurry." She punctuated that by taking him to the back of her throat and growling around him.

"You little minx!" Shayne pulled her to her feet then lifted her, turning to settle her on the end of the counter between the stove and the fridge.

He held her face between his hands and claimed her mouth in an almost bruising kiss. She could feel the barely restrained desperation in the way his muscles tensed beneath her hands on his chest. Serenity needed all of him. She wanted to see what she was in for when the bear lost control. With that in mind, she raked her nails across his chest, making sure to catch the brown discs of his nipples in their journey to his stomach.

* * * *

Shayne jerked his mouth from hers and growled deep in his chest. His bear was beside himself wanting to take her. The man wasn't arguing one bit, except that he was worried about harming her in the state his wild half was in. His hands ripped at the fastening of her jeans, nearly ripping the zipper out of the material in his haste to rid her of the covering.

"Shoes," she rasped out before he tangled the legs of her jeans up with them.

Cursing, Shayne stopped and took the time to pull off the shoes before jerking the jeans from her feet. All that stood in the way of his mouth now was the cotton scrap of cloth covering her pussy. He stared into her eyes and extended on clawed tip to rip through the offending material. When he jerked the torn edges from her body, she hissed at him. Instead of taking offense, Shayne sank to his knees and spread her legs wide before burying his face in the sweet nectar of her juices that coated the lips of her sex.

Nirvana. That's what she was to him. Every delicious inch of her sexy body was made for him and his brother. She completed him and they hadn't even sealed the mating bond yet. God only knew what it would feel like when they did. Right now, he was on fire for her and couldn't get enough of her sweet honey.

He growled around her as he thrust his tongue in deep. Her answering whimper was music to his ears. Shayne ran his tongue all around her clit, then sucked in each fleshy lip to clean every trace of juice from it before returning to claim her clit. He held her still with one hand on her hip and entered her cunt with one finger to test her readiness. As much as he needed to be inside of her, there was no way he'd hurt her if he could help it. She was his mate, the laughter in his world and the future mother of his cubs. She deserved nothing but pleasure.

When he could add a second finger to stroke in and out of her, Shayne knew she was ready. As much as he wanted to bring her to orgasm with his mouth first, his bear was just before taking over. He needed to be inside of her—now!

Jerking his mouth from her weeping slit, Shayne surged to his feet and gripping her hips, pulled her closer to the edge of the counter. Every muscle in his body strained in her direction. Still, he searched her eyes to be sure she was with him. The feisty little feline's mouth was open as she panted, her eyelids heavy with desire as if she didn't have the strength to open them any farther. Serenity's nails dug into his shoulders, pulling him toward her. Her legs wrapped around him, drawing her closer.

Shayne fisted his shaft in one hand and pumped it slowly, milking a drop of his cum to the slit before slowly pressing forward and breaching her pussy, slipping between the lips like an oiled piston. The sensation of hot, wet flesh rasping over his dick as he slowly slid deeper nearly snapped his control. Her cunt sucked at him even as the heels of her feet dug into his ass in an effort to urge him deeper. His cock felt as if a hundred burning mouths were sucking on him all at one time. Nothing had ever felt so good.

"Holy hell! You're killing me, babe. So freaking hot," he ground out.

"Fuck me, Shayne. Stop playing around and fuck me," she said in a loud, harsh whisper.

His cock finally made it all the way inside of her and he rested his forehead against hers for a second to catch his breath and clam the beast inside of him. Yep. This was going to be a quickie. Even if they weren't pressing their luck with the others, Shayne had no control left to draw it out any longer. She did that to him, took all of his control.

Pulling out as her flesh sucked at him, he thrust back in and nearly howled like a wolf at the pleasure that heated his blood. Her loud groan told him she enjoyed it as much as he did. With that, Shayne loosened some of the hold he had on his needs and hammered into her over and over. Each thrust sending white hot sensations straight to his balls. He could feel them boiling, tightening in readiness to erupt. Every nerve ending in his body strained toward that end.

The sudden tightening of his mate's cunt around his dick let him know that she was on the verge of coming, too. He released one hip and slipped his hand between their bodies to locate her clit with his thumb. Stroking it lightly, Shayne fought his climax with everything he had. He wanted her to come before him. She would come before him.

Serenity cried out as the orgasm took her. She buried her face against his chest and shook all over even as she sank her teeth into his flesh. The sharp pain burst through his veins and set off his climax in a hard, earth shattering explosion that had his legs shaking and his ass cheeks clenching to the point of cramping. He roared, or more accurately, his bear roared having taken control for a brief instant.

When the roaring in his ears finally lessened and he could hear around his own heavy panting, Serenity's purrs undid him. She nuzzled his chest, licking at the wound she'd caused and purred in pleasure. All was right in his world. He'd made his mate purr.

The heavy sound of running booted feet interrupted his satisfied lethargy.

"What in the hell have you done?"

Chapter Twelve

Serenity lifted her head from Shayne's chest to see Creed standing in the kitchen doorway, glowering at them, his eyes rich brown but rimmed by gold, meaning his bear was close to the surface. She didn't like the anger boiling just beneath the surface. What was wrong?

"Creed?" she said.

"Did you mate her?" Creed growled, his teeth lengthening as he spoke.

Shayne slowly backed away from her, pulling his cock from her body. He tucked himself back in and zipped up before turning all the way around. Evidently the sight of blood on her mouth and Shayne's chest bearing her teeth marks enraged the other bear. He threw back his head and roared in what sounded like anguish to Serenity.

"Easy, Creed. Calm down. I didn't mark her." Shayne stood in front of Serenity as if to protect her.

Unease crept into her veins at the possibility that Creed might lose control. The sight of his anger directed at his brother worried her. She'd done this. By playing around and seducing Shayne, she'd inadvertently caused a rift between the two brothers. She had to fix this somehow.

"She has your blood in her mouth. You bear her mark," he said in a low growl.

"I didn't mark her, Creed. I wouldn't do that. She belongs to both of us," Shayne said in a calm voice.

Serenity stared around desperate for something to wipe the blood from her mouth. She spotted a potholder by the stove and leaned over to grab it. She quickly wiped her mouth and face clean of the evidence of her misdeed then hopped down from the counter, very award that she was nude from the waist down with a combination of her juices and Shayne's seed sliding between her legs. This was so uncomfortable.

I have to stop them from fighting. This is all my fault. I never meant to mark him.

The two bears were growling and chuffing at each other like the wild animals they were. She pushed away from the cabinets at her back and stepped between the two males.

"Creed. Stop it. He didn't mate mark me. Don't do this. He's your brother. It's my fault. I lost control and marked him, but you're my mate, too." She pleaded with her eyes as she slowly moved closer to him.

In his present state, Serenity wasn't sure he was in control of his bear or not. She also didn't know if he would want to punish her for claim his brother without him present. This was so screwed up. What had gotten in to her?

"Please, Creed. Don't fight." She took another step closer and stopped when Shayne growled at her.

"Get back, Serenity. He's too angry to think rationally. If he hurt you by accident it would kill him," he said.

Creed roared loud enough the windows shook. "I'd never hurt a female, especially not my mate!"

"Calm down, Creed. Let's go sit down while Shayne finishes the sandwiches. I'm really hungry," she said, babbling in an attempt to calm the big male down.

She took another step closer and before she realized what he was going to do, Creed reached out, grabbing her by the wrist and jerked her into his arms. Despite the jarring to her shoulder, he was careful to not hold her too tightly as he enfolded her in his arms.

"Mine!" he snarled.

"She's ours, Creed. You know that. Calm down." Shayne looked worried but he didn't advance toward them. "She belongs to both of us and we're going to claim her together, just like is natural."

Now that she could see more of the room, it dawned on her that almost all of the others of the sleuth were crowded around the kitchen watching with wary eyes. No doubt they didn't understand why they were fighting.

"Creed. It's okay. Let's go take a nap together. Everything will be better once you calm down," she said, trying again to get him to back away from his brother.

She could feel him slowing his breathing. After a few seconds he felt a little less tense. She was afraid to breathe a sigh of relief until he said something. She watched the others around them. They all seemed to be relaxing some as well. They could see his expression and would know better than she how he was doing.

"Creed?"

"I'm okay, but we need to talk," Creed said in a more normal voice. "Shayne, fix her something to eat and let the others feed themselves. Bring it down to our rooms."

With that, he lifted her over his shoulder and turned away from the others to walk toward the stairs leading to the bottom level. Each step he took jarred her where her abdomen was draped over his hard muscular shoulder. She hoped he wouldn't jog down the stairs. If he did, she might end up bruised from it.

Creed took the stairs slowly then quickly strode across the open den area to their rooms. He closed the door behind him before tossing her on the bed. She bounced before managing to control the motion and scoot to the edge of the bed to stand up.

"Don't," he said in a harsh voice. "I need you to stay down right now. My bear is riding me hard right now to mark you before you bond with Shayne alone. Don't push me."

She nodded and remained sitting on the edge of the bed, watching as Creed paced the small area available to him between the door and the bed. Despite having reined in his bear, he was still battling to keep it under control. She understood that and remained still, waiting for either Shayne to show up or Creed to speak.

After what seemed like forever, the bedroom door opened and Shayne walked in carrying a large try with a plate full of sandwiches, two cans of beer, and a glass of milk. She couldn't help but tense until she was sure the two men weren't going to start snarling at each other all over again. Truthfully though, Shayne hadn't been the one doing the snarling. Creed had done all of that.

"I made enough for all of us since I doubt we're going to make it back upstairs for dinner tonight. I told the others to go out and eat but not to get into trouble," Shayne said. He held up his cell phone. "I brought both cells downstairs just in case they get into trouble. I warned them not to let their bears show or we'll have the damn hunters on us, too."

"As much as I don't want them out right now with so much on the line, they can take care of themselves, and we need to sort this out. Something isn't right with this mating. My bear shouldn't have gotten that riled up," Creed said.

Serenity hadn't moved since Shayne had walked in. She was afraid to draw their attention while they were talking without the growly thing going on. Shayne set the massive tray on the dresser then picked up a sandwich in a napkin and her glass of milk then walked over to hand it to her. She noticed that he watched Creed the entire time as if expecting him to freak out again. Thankfully he didn't.

Creed followed Shayne back to the dresser and opened a beer. The three of them ate in silence. Once they'd finished their first sandwich, Creed spoke up again.

"I keep trying to figure out what all is different about our mating than every other one I've witnessed."

"Besides the fact that there are two of us and she's feline, not bear or wolf?" Shayne asked with a snort.

Creed frowned at him. "Yeah, I guess you're right. Just the fact that she is one mate destined for both of us is reason enough for our bears to be on edge."

"The thing is," Shayne began. "Mine really isn't all that upset over it. He wants her and is chomping at the bit to claim her, but he isn't angry or out of sorts that he'll be sharing her with your bear. It's yours that seems more distressed by sharing. I don't get it. I was the one who thought it wouldn't work while you were adamant that it was our destiny."

Creed shook his head. "I don't understand it either. It was something we both knew was right as soon as we were told by Papa Bear. Now he's stressed out over it."

Serenity finished her second sandwich and drained the glass of milk before setting it on the bedside table. She couldn't stand the strained silence any longer.

"I don't want the two of you to fight over me. Maybe it's better if I just leave. I'll grab my stuff and find somewhere else to live. I can't stay here with the hunters after me, but I couldn't live this close to the two of you anyway. Once I'm gone, your bears will lose interest in me and find another mate who doesn't have my issues." She didn't wait to see their reactions. She stood up and walked over to where her bags were still sitting next to the dresser and pulled open a drawer.

Before she could grab the underwear and stuff it into her bag, large meaty hands grabbed her around the waist and picked her up, carrying her back toward the bed. Even without seeing Shayne standing in front of the closed bedroom door with his arms crossed, she had known it was Creed by his scent.

"Don't even think about it. What in the world makes you think our bears or your lynx would ever get over losing their mates? Mating is for life, Serenity. You know that." Creed glared down at her once he'd dropped her back on the bed.

"We aren't mated yet. As long as we haven't marked each other we can walk away. It's better if we do it now before the bond gets stronger," she said.

"You've marked Shayne. Do you think his bear is going to get over that?" Creed demanded.

She paled. He was right. She'd forgotten what had started entire mess in the first place. Her shoulders sagged as she looked down at her hands, wishing she'd just run when she'd first smelled them the day before. God! Had it only been a day?

"I don't know what to do, Creed. My lynx isn't going to willingly let you mount her the way you want to. She'll fight you. Even if I say go ahead and force her, she'll just fight until we're all worn out and she's traumatized. Then she'll never trust your bears again." She felt tears burn at the back of her eyes, but Serenity had no intentions of letting them fall and embarrass her any more than she already was.

"Kitten. Look at me," Creed said.

When she looked up it was to find that he had crouched down so that they were essentially at eye level now. There was strain in the lines on his face, but his eyes were tender.

"We would never force you or your cat into anything you didn't want to do unless it was to keep you safe. The bond is there. We have to be patient and look for another answer. I believe that if we weren't meant for each other, the bond never would have formed to begin with. There's another way and eventually we'll find it," he said with a tight smile.

"And what do we do in the meantime? I can't stand to see you and your brother at odds with one another. It's too much of a strain on your sleuth as well. You have to think of them." She didn't want them to give up on her, but Serenity didn't see any way around it.

"Shayne and I aren't going to do any more fighting. Now that we know this is a problem, we'll make an effort to remain calm. When you get ready, you can mark me as well, and the three of us will be on even ground again," Creed told her.

She drew in a deep breath to fight the dizziness that had suddenly slipped up on her. All of the emotions churning in her gut and blistering her skin was making her sick. She needed to relax and forget about it all for a little while. She swallowed past the nausea and nodded.

"I'm going to take a nap. I'm really tired." Before she could pull off her top, Creed was doing it for her. He also unhooked her bra then while Shayne pulled back the covers, he lifted her and eased her onto the mattress.

"Rest, baby. We'll be just down the hall working on your spa," Shayne said as he covered her with the sheet and top blanket.

She closed her eyes without saying anything. She didn't have the energy to even care about that right then. All she could think about was the need to clear her mind for a few hours. Then maybe she could face the problem they had with a fresh perspective.

* * * *

Creed watched as the little lynx almost instantly fell into a deep sleep. It worried him a bit that she had just sort of crumpled all of a sudden like that. She was a spitfire and didn't hide or curb her tongue when she had something to say. She'd thought to run from them as if they weren't already half-mated. It bothered him that they had somehow broken something inside of her with their near fight over her.

"Is she already asleep?" Shayne asked, a note of alarm obvious in his voice.

"Yeah, I don't think this is normal. We've got to control our emotions around her until the mating can be completed. The strain is too much for her." Creed ran a hand over his face. "I'm well aware that I'm the one who flipped out. I'm sorry."

He started toward the door, knowing they needed to leave her alone so she could rest without their emotional undertones rousing her cat. He stepped into the entrance area that led into the large open den and waited for his brother to softly close the door behind them.

"Was it the fact that she'd marked me or that we'd had sex without you present that upset your bear?" Shayne asked with a curious expression on his face.

Creed frowned, trying to remember what had first gotten his bear up in arms. It had been a scent. Try as he might, he couldn't recall the scent now to know what it had been.

"I'm not really sure, but I had been working on the taxes when I smelled something that had my bear perking up. I can't remember what it was now, but it drew me in the general direction of the kitchen. Before I reached you, I heard your roar and her scream. My bear instantly went into a rage, and I was just along for the ride for a few minutes."

"That's not good, Creed. We've got to figure this out and fully mate Serenity before something bad happens," Shayne said.

"I know, but until then, neither of us is alone with her without the other one. We can't take a chance that something like this happens again."

Shayne nodded. Creed could tell that his brother felt bad about what had happened. It hadn't been his fault, but Shayne had always been hard on himself when things went wrong.

"Let's go work on the bathroom while she's sleeping," Creed said.

"Spa. She calls it a spa," Shayne said with a weak smile. "Complete with message table and cabana boys."

"What?" Creed stopped walking and stared at his brother with his mouth open. "Are you fucking kidding me?"

Shayne grinned. "Yeah, about the message table, but not about the cabana boys. She expects us to wait on her hand and foot when we shower together."

Creed's frown turned into a wide grin. "I can't handle that. Pampering her isn't a hardship at all. I'll even paint her toenails if she wants me to."

Shayne shook his head and pushed the door open. "She hasn't seen you paint yet. I doubt that's going to be an issue once she does."

"Asshole."

"Buttface."

Chapter Thirteen

Serenity woke to the feel of a warm mouth suckling her breast. She hummed her approval and dug her fingers into Shayne's hair to hold him close to her. He nipped and sucked on her nipple while pinching and tugging on the other one. The electrical sensations his attentions created raced down some invisible line to stimulate her clit as if they really were connected somehow.

"Looks like our mate is awake now, Shayne." Creed's voice penetrated the sleepy aroused haze her mind was in.

Shayne removed his devilish mouth from her breast with a loud pop. "We thought you were going to sleep right through the sex, babe."

She groaned as she realized that Creed was nestled between her thighs and it was his heated breath she felt fanning the trimmed curls of her pussy. What was going on? Had they been messing with her while she'd been asleep? She couldn't even remember is she'd been dreaming or not.

"W–what are you doing?" she finally managed to rasp out. Her throat was dry and scratchy.

"Obviously we aren't doing it right if you can't tell, kitten," Creed said in a low rumble.

Before she could answer him, he'd buried his face in her pussy, running his tongue through her slit and rubbing the bridge of his nose against her clit. Immediately heat poured through her body in reaction.

"Oh," she moaned.

"I think you got her attention that time, Creed," Shayne chuckled.

Serenity groaned when the bear between her legs thrust his tongue deep into her cunt while continuing to rub her clit at the same time. She was going to come fast and hard if he kept that up. The sensations were stronger than she'd ever felt them before. Her pussy felt sodden as Creed fucked her with his tongue.

Shayne gave each nipple a sharp nip before dragging his tongue across them in a soothing stroke. Then he licked and kissed his way up her chest to her neck. She easily turned her head to give him better access, unbelieving her cat was allowing her to do so. In fact, the feline was purring from all of the attention. Serenity wasn't about to ask the cat to explain herself and risk losing her cooperation.

The feel of Shayne's teeth grazing across her neck sent a wave of shivers across her skin. He let the sharp points rake a line from her shoulder up her neck to her earlobe where he nipped it as well. Heat burned just below her skin like an electric blanket turned to low. When Shayne bit and licked across her jaw and up to the corner of her mouth, she didn't even try to muffle her whimpers. She needed them, wanted them to fuck her so badly it hurt. Serenity had no doubt she would be begging soon if they didn't act as if they were going to get in any hurry. She was in a hurry to douse the flames beginning to lick at her insides.

Oh, hell! Was that her making those raspy purring sounds?

I'm turning into a damn sex kitten or something.

Serenity nearly gasped when she started pumping her hips up into Creed's face, begging him to fuck her already. She wasn't like this. What was going on?

"Please, Creed. I need you inside of me," she whined.

Where was her cat now? The bitch would never allow her to beg that way.

But there she was, purring just below the surface as her human half lost all pride. Creed growled between her legs, the vibrations stimulating her clit so that she nearly climaxed right then.

"Fuck, you're hot, honey. I can't wait to bury my dick inside of you," he snarled, climbing up her body as Shayne moved out of the way.

"She's so beautiful with how her skin is shinny with sweat," Shayne said running his tongue across her shoulder before moving farther back.

When she opened her eyes to stare up into Creed's she felt as if she were staring through a smoky room. His features were slightly hazy as he lifted her legs over his shoulders and positioned the head of his cock at her slit. He rubbed the crown up and down, gathering her juices with each stroke. Then without warning, Creed slid inside of her with one thrust, stretching her vaginal walls to bursting.

"Yessss!" she hissed out as the slight burning turned into something much better.

Creed cursed as he held himself still inside of her. "So good. So tight and hot."

He pulled nearly all the way out before burying himself inside of her once again. The friction he created had her so close to coming that the need was killing her. He continued the slow pull out only to fill her once again in a long hard thrust before starting all over again.

"Oh, God, Creed. Fuck me! Harder!" she screamed out.

Serenity thrashed her head back and forth, expecting to explode at any second, but as if knowing she was on the verge of exploding, Creed would slow down and build it right back up again. She cursed him as she gripped the bed sheets with her fingers, barely able to keep from releasing her claws and shredding them. Instead, she dug her fingers into the backs of her thighs as the big bear above her had her nearly bent double while fucking her in that devastatingly slow pace.

It had to stop. She'd go crazy if he didn't let her climax soon. Serenity clamped down on his cock with every muscle and fiber of her lower body. Her cunt squeezed his dick in a viselike grip, in an attempt to drive him as insane with the need to come as she was.

"Fuck, Serenity! You're strangling my cock!" he snarled.

A heated slap to the back of one thigh drew a growl from her. She jerked her head in that direction to find a grinning Shayne fisting his cock with one hand while lifting the other to deliver another pop to her thigh. This one landed a little lower to sting the spot where her thigh met her ass cheek. She couldn't believe how it made her pussy gush around Creed's thick shaft buried inside her pussy.

Serenity couldn't take her eyes off of how roughly Shayne was pulling on his cock. He held it so tight in his fist that it had turned an angry red at the crown. He jerked on it slightly faster than Creed was hammering into her. With her ass in the air as the bear bent her legs almost until they nearly rested on her shoulders, she had no leverage to try and meet his thrusts. The inability to move was beginning to drive her insane. She needed him to pound into her harder and faster.

"Fuck me!" she finally screamed.

Creed gave a wheezy chuckle and released one of her legs. She quickly used it to help power her hips upward toward him. He used the extra maneuvering room to increase the pace of his thrusts and powered into her harder and faster. The frequency of Shayne's swats to her ass increased as well until her body felt like one giant nerve ending about to implode. Her orgasm struck like a viper, taking her by surprise despite how hard she'd been striving for it. She screamed in pleasure just as Shayne pinched her nipple and shot his seed all over her breasts. The heated ribbons of cum coated her skin.

Serenity didn't remember moving, nor did she think about what she was doing, but the next thing she knew, she'd bitten into Creed's chest just like she had Shayne's the afternoon before. His blood coated her tongue as she lapped at it before slowly releasing him and falling back to the bed. She smiled at the sight of her mark smeared with blood. When her eyes met his slightly glassy stare, she saw satisfaction there and sighed in relief.

"Mine," she purred and promptly fell asleep again.

* * * *

"Holy hell. That was intense," Shayne muttered as he collapsed back across the bed.

"You're telling me. I think I turned my balls inside out coming like I did," Creed grumbled good-naturedly.

"I can't believe how hot she is when she gets that way. My cock is already getting hard again." Shayne smiled up at the ceiling just thinking about burying his dick inside of her.

"Well you're going to have to wait and give her some recovery time. She's snoring like a little puppy dog over here."

"She'll cut your balls off if she hears you comparing her to a dog," Shayne warned with a laugh.

"Yeah. I know." Creed was silent for a few seconds and all that could be heard was their heavy breathing. "Have you noticed how she's gotten more and more demanding during sex each time we've been with her?"

"Yeah. I figured she's finally growing used to us," he said.

"Yeah. Maybe."

Shayne frowned at the question in his brother's voice. What did he mean by *maybe*, he wondered. Did Creed think there was something going on? He was almost afraid to ask. Then another thought hit him. She'd just woken up from sleeping for nearly nine hours straight and she was already sound asleep again. The sex had been hot, but it wasn't enough to knock her out.

"Why is she asleep again?" he asked without moving.

"We wore her out, I guess," Creed said, his voice sounding sleepy as well.

Shayne decided it was just that he hadn't really been all that active to be as worn out as Creed and Serenity were. He was making a big deal in his head out of nothing. He should feel relief that she'd marked his brother so Creed's bear wouldn't feel slighted anymore. They needed to remain as calm as possible until they could figure out how to claim her without angering her cat.

He heard the tell-tale sounds of the others getting up above them. Glancing over at the clock, he realized it was well after seven in the morning. Since their cell phones hadn't gone off during the night, he could assume that everyone was fine and accounted for upstairs. He needed to get up and shower. They had a lot to get done on the bathroom and he wanted to find out if the hunters were still hanging around Serenity's house or not. That was another problem they needed to solve and fast. She couldn't remain hidden for the rest of her life.

"What are you thinking so hard about over there? I can hear the wheels turning all the way up here," Creed asked in a husky voice.

"Just thinking about the Rouge Hunters and wondering how we're going to get them off her trail. Normally they don't bother shifters who aren't causing a problem unless they've broken a law somewhere else. It stinks to me," he said.

"Yeah. I think you're right. These guys are almost fanatical and seem intent on locating her since they haven't given up yet. I'm going to call our friend in Shifter Rights to see what he can find out for us."

"Good idea. I hope he can help with this. I don't like having them so close to her."

Shayne slowly sat up. He could smell their combined scent along with the obvious smell of sex. His hardening cock protested when he slowly threw his legs over the edge of the bed and stood up. As much as he would like nothing better than to crawl over on top of his mate, she needed rest and he needed to get busy.

"Whose turn is it to fix breakfast?" Creed asked.

Shayne frowned and tried to bring up the schedule in his fuzzy head. "Um, I think it's Bane's turn."

"Tell him to make a little more than normal. I think Serenity is going to be starved when she gets up. She missed dinner last night, and I can hear her belly growling already," his brother said with a soft chuckle.

"Got it. I'll tell him. Better wake her up soon or she'll just end up stiff from being in bed for so long." Shayne padded across the short distance to the bathroom and closed the door before flipping on the light.

When he turned around from turning on the shower he caught a glimpse of himself in the mirror. He noted that the bite mark on his chest appeared almost fresh, minus any active bleeding. He frowned. She hadn't bitten him again. He would have noticed that. It had damn near made him explode from the balls up when she'd done it the first time. He wouldn't have missed a second bite. So why did it look so fresh? They normally healed twice as fast as pure humans did.

Shayne shrugged and pulled out a towel and washcloth before stepping into the invigorating heat of the shower, wincing when it hit the bite. It was tender as if it had just happened, too. He would need to ask Creed about his to see what his brother's looked and felt like.

After cleaning up and drying off, Shayne slipped back into the bedroom to dress. Both his brother and their mate continued to sleep as if worn out. Well, they had been the ones doing all the work. Still, it bothered him. He placed Creed's cell phone on the bedside table closest to where he slept and made sure the ringer was all the way up. He'd call him in a few minutes to wake him up.

When Shayne entered the kitchen five minutes later, everyone except Quill was lounging, leaning, or sitting around the room talking. He nodded to them before grabbing a mug from the cabinet and pouring a cup of coffee.

"Everything okay?" he asked.

"Yeah. We all went to a steakhouse in town then stopped at that bar on the edge of town we'd talked about when we first rode in that night. It's pretty nice," Seth said.

"Where's Quill?" Shayne asked.

"He's doing a perimeter check," Locke told him. "He lost the draw."

Everyone chuckled. No one liked doing the first check of the morning because it meant missing that first cup of coffee since you didn't want to smell of food or coffee when you were trying to be stealthy.

"Is everything okay with you and Creed?" Locke asked in a carefully neutral tone.

"Creed's anger filled the house yesterday. Breathing became difficult," Otto pointed out.

"Everything's fine. Two males don't normally share a mate anymore so there are going to be some things to work out, but we're fine," he told the other man.

"Why is it happening now?" Eason asked. "I mean it's been hundreds of years without shared mates. What is happening now or what is going to happen?"

Shayne sighed. "Papa Bear only said it was a necessity to ensure our race continued. With the world knowing of our existence now and many not happy about it, he thought that it was nature's way of providing for our mate and future cub's safety if there were two males to keep them safe. One to hunt or work and one to watch."

"So does that mean that all bears will share a mate now?" Zeth asked.

"We don't know. He didn't exactly spell anything out to us, but Creed believes it's the beginning of the return to older ways again." Shayne looked at the others watching him.

"We were better off when no one knew of our existence. At least then the hunters couldn't go after us in public or in our human forms," Bane said with a look of disgust.

"I won't argue with you about that, but with so many advances in technology and forensics, it was becoming impossible to keep our existence a secret," he told them.

"What are we going to do about the Rogue Hunters?" Zeth asked. "They are going to figure out that we are keeping her here soon enough."

"Creed is calling a friend to find out why they are after her. They must have a reason to actually stake out her place. This isn't just a random group wanting to take out all shifters," Shayne pointed out.

"I didn't think so either," Warren agreed.

"Creed and Serenity will be up soon. Make sure you fix extra this morning, Bane. Serenity didn't get dinner last night."

The others all snickered, but Shayne ignored their good-natured teasing and walked toward the office. He wanted to check something that had been bothering him ever since their mate had told them about why she was living alone away from her den.

He sat behind Creed's desk and turned on the computer. The sight of her work space next to his brother's pleased him. He liked seeing something of hers among their things. He wanted more of her things there. Shaking his head, Shayne waited impatiently as the computer booted up and ran through the security program his brother had installed. As soon as he could, Shayne logged onto the Internet to do some searching.

He was still reading and pulling information together when Bane stuck his head in the door an hour later.

"Breakfast is ready. Creed and your mate have not come upstairs yet. Should I go down and knock on the door?"

Shayne checked the time on the computer and frowned. Creed wasn't one to lounge in bed like this. Of course if his mate was beside him, Shayne would be tempted to do the same thing. He grunted and shook his head.

"I'll call him. The cell is right next to him," he said as he reached for his own phone.

Bane nodded and disappeared out the door. Shayne had his brother's number on speed dial. The random thought hit him that they needed to program Serenity's number into their phones as well as theirs into hers.

The phone rang only once before Creed picked up with a whispered, "What?"

"Creed. Breakfast is ready."

"She's still sound asleep. Should I wake her?" he asked, a worried note apparent in his voice.

Shayne hesitated. "Yes. I don't think it's a good idea for her to sleep so much. Plus, she needs to eat."

"Okay. We'll be right up." Creed disconnected the call leaving Shayne worried about their mate.

He was standing up to meet them in the kitchen when he noticed that an e-mail had popped up on his account. He sat back down and opened it. It might be an answer to one of the inquiries he'd sent out. He really hadn't expected an answer this soon, though. Gathering information took time.

Five minutes later Shayne shut down the computer and sat back in the chair, stiff with anger at what he'd learned. Creed needed to contact their friend immediately. What in the hell were they going to do? He had no intentions of allowing anyone to take Serenity from them. He'd fight to the death for his mate. He had no doubt Creed would do the same, but how could they fight this?

Chapter Fourteen

Serenity couldn't ever remember being this hungry before. Not even when she'd first started shifting on her own without her mother's control. To add to that, she felt as if she'd slept for a month and every inch of her skin seemed to tingle. She couldn't figure out what was going on with her but didn't want to say anything to her mates. They had enough to worry about at the moment between her lynx's refusal to complete the made bond and the Rogue Hunters still hanging around her place.

"Um, would you like more bacon or toast?" Bane asked staring at her with amusement.

"Hmm?" Oh. No thanks. I'm full," she leaned back and realized that she was—finally.

"I don't think I've ever seen a female put away the food like that before," Zeth said with a grin. "Impressive."

"Shut up, Zeth," Creed said with a snarl. "Don't be rude."

"Hey! Just saying." The other bear jumped up from the table when Creed slowly stood up.

With a laugh, Bane slipped around the table. "My work here is done. Your turn to clean up, Qwill. I'm going to relieve Otto."

Creed sank slowly back into his chair and his warm arm rested along the back of her chair. Serenity enjoyed a feeling of safety there between her two males. She turned to look at Shayne who'd been quiet all during breakfast. She'd caught him staring at her several times with a worried expression that he quickly hid once he realized she was watching. Her lynx had been surprisingly quiet as well. That hadn't bothered her nearly as much since usually the cat was more trouble than help to Serenity when in her human form.

"Locke. I need you to stay with Serenity while Creed and I work on some things in his office. We'll probably be a couple of hours." Shayne turned to her and smiled, but it looked forced to her. "Why don't you work on your plans for the bathroom? Show Warren and Seth what you want so they will understand when they start working on the cabinetry. Creed and I need to take care of some business that we've let accumulate."

Serenity nodded, forcing her own smile. She didn't believe for an instant that there was some pressing need for them to address. Shayne was keeping something from her. Maybe he'd decided he no longer wanted her or to share a mate with his brother. Pain inched through her chest, alerting her lynx to there being a problem. She stretched and snarled at the scent of Serenity's pain.

She stood up when they did and turned to walk to the hall where the stairs were that led down to the basement level. Serenity forced herself to walk slowly when all she wanted to do was run. She had no desire to work on the bathroom any longer. Something was wrong, not only with her mates but also with her lynx. Something inside of her was building and it worried her. She'd slept far more than she'd ever been able to stay in bed. She was also eating more. Already her body was craving something sweet to eat. She ignored it.

As she descended the stairs, a cramp hit her abdomen that nearly doubled her over. She stumbled, but Locke's hand caught her shoulder before she started to fall.

"Careful, Ursa." He released her shoulder once it was obvious she'd regained her balance.

"Thank you. Call me Serenity. I'm not your Ursa yet."

Locke didn't say anything, but she could feel his curiosity as they walked across the large room toward the hall where Creed and Shayne's new suite would be. She no longer felt a part of things and her heart cracked a little more. The weak link she'd had with Creed and Shayne no longer felt as strong. She knew they were close, but couldn't tell what they were feeling. Before, she'd had a sense of their general disposition. Now there was only a vague awareness that they were there.

"Is something wrong?" Locke asked, his brows furrowing.

"No. I guess I'm a little distracted," she said.

She rubbed her arms, her skin beginning to itch some. Her clothes were irritating, but she couldn't remove them. Sure, shifters were causal about nudity, but not like this. She needed to distract herself until her mates returned and explained what was going on. There was something that involved her, she was sure of it. If she hadn't felt so odd and her lynx wasn't rattled by her pain, she would have demanded they be honest with her and talk, but she was afraid of what her cat would do if faced with the news that they no longer wanted her.

Freaking fickle feline.

She wanted them as her mates but wasn't willing to allow the mating to go forward because of the anal sex. And that was all it was, just anal sex, but the lynx saw it as humiliating and a darker form of domination. She was having no part of it.

Warren and Seth walked into the hallway behind her as she entered the large open space that was to be the spa of her dreams. She felt empty inside in that moment, realizing that because of her mistrust of both humans and shifters she never had been going to get her dream shower. She never would have allowed anyone into her home to remodel the bathroom because she was too suspicious of humans and leery of other shifters. The bears surrounding her didn't seem to bother her like they should have, but then she'd started thinking of them as hers. Bitter tears burned the back of her eyes. She hadn't even had time to get to know them and already she was losing them. It was the only conclusion she could come up with as to why Creed and Shayne would need to hide what they were doing from her. They were talking about how to dissolve their partial bonding.

Serenity knew in that moment that she had to leave. Once she was no longer around them, the partial bon would slowly dissolve and the males would be free to find a true mate. She was holding them back. The partial mating with no hope of completing it had to be tearing them up inside. She wasn't affected as they were since her Lynx considered them theirs without it. She was satisfied.

While she went through the motions of designing the spa with Warren and Seth, Serenity worked out a plan to disappear. As long as she was in the basement, there was no hope of escape, but once they returned topside, she could slip away. She wouldn't be able to take all of her computer equipment, but she could download everything on her external drive and send a back up copy to her personal cloud space.

Her laptop would have to do for now. There was no way she could run with the desktop. She was thankful the males had been slowly slipping some of her things over. They'd managed to pick out her most prized possessions which included a picture of her parents and the little jewelry box that held her grandmother's ring and the intertwined locks of hair she and her best friend had tied together, each keeping one as a promise to always remain best friends. Serenity missed her so much and wished she'd been there to help her figure out what was wrong.

While she had no idea where she could go, she knew the general direction. All that remained was finding the opportunity to carry out her plans.

* * * *

Creed ended the call and had to resist throwing the phone across the room. Shayne had been right. Her old Rufus was the one hunting her and had sent the Rouge Hunters after her, not to kill her or take her in to be judged. No, he wanted her as his own. Well, for his son. Why had the old lynx suddenly started looking for Serenity after all that time?

"He verified it?" Shayne asked.

Creed nodded. He was still attempting to control his anger and fear for his mate. When he looked up, Shayne had settled his bulk on the corner of the desk and was watching him closely.

"It's her old Rufus after her. He is behind the Rogue Hunters. They are acting as bounty hunters to drag her back to him. They aren't going to kill her or take her in for some infraction. He said that no kill orders have been handed down in the last six months. Unless a shifter is caught red-handed so to speak, killing someone, they have put a hold on all Rogue Hunters going after shifters while there is legislature in congress concerning us."

Shayne's brows furrowed. "What legislature? Why hasn't he notified us? Does Da know about it?"

Creed shook his head. "No one knows yet. They plan to notify all registered shifter leaders this week. There seems to be a move to appoint a shifter council to govern us. It will be made up of only our kind with two human advisors to help us make decisions. That was all he could tell me right now, but he said the hunters here were contracted by Serenity's Rufus to capture and return her to his den."

"Why? I mean it's been years now. Why would he be set on her?"

"I'm not sure. Since our friend said it is specifically for the Rufus's son, then there is more at stake than a future mating. Either Serenity knows more than she's told us or he found out something important about her and regrets allowing her to get away." Creed felt sure it was the latter. He didn't think she'd held anything back.

"Then we need to talk to her again," Shayne said and stood up.

"I want to make a few more phone calls first. The information you dug up alludes to some sort of special situation or position. We need more information before we approach her with this. It will scare her to know that her old den is still after her and it will upset her to know that we've been searching behind her back. We should have gone and gotten her before we made the call to my friend. Now it's too late to smooth things over so we might as well finish this and deal with her anger later." Creed worried that she would see this as too strong of a betrayal to ever fully forgive and trust them again. All he could do was hope and pray they could settle things so she had that right to be angry with them.

Shayne stomped across the room then returned and pulled over the chair from behind the desk that Serenity had been using so he could see what Creed was doing. He could tell his brother wasn't happy. Well neither was he. Creed had never expected there to be so much trouble with finding their mate. He remembered Papa Bear had told him once and almost laughed out loud.

"Son, nothing you receive free is as precious as something you worked hard to be worthy for. Remember that when you complain about your good fortune."

Yeah, I suppose that's true, old one, but the price may be too great this time.

He pulled up the yellow pages on the Internet and did a search, looking for Serenity's parents' phone number. He knew where they used to live according to her, but didn't know what her father's name was. Asking her now wasn't an option. Instead he searched for every Jones in her home town with the same prefix as her Rufus's number. She had said he made everyone live in the same community.

"Write these down, Shayne," he told his brother as he called out names and phone numbers.

"You're looking for her family?" The other bear asked.

"I want to talk to her parents to see if they know something. I wonder if they even know that their Rufus has Rogue Hunters looking for their daughter. She's called in occasionally to let them know she is alive. Maybe he got information of her whereabouts by tapping their phone lines." Creed didn't put anything past the bastard. He didn't deserve to be a leader of a shifter group.

"There are eight different numbers in that area. We don't even know if they have a landline. They may only have cell phones and that means that none of these will be related at all," Shayne pointed out.

"If this doesn't work, we'll get Locke in here to do some hacking to locate cell numbers if need be. I would rather not involve him if we don't have to. The fewer of our den who knows about this until we have the answers, the better it will go."

They spent the next hour making phone calls but came up empty handed. They had one number that no one ever picked up on, but Creed didn't hold out much hope with it being the one they needed. It was time to ask Locke for his expertise. He knew the Ruka of their den would be able to find what they needed, but hated to involve him. It bothered him that he and Shayne couldn't keep their mate safe and provide what she needed without help.

"Want me to go get Locke?" Shayne asked with a frown.

"No. He'll want to use his own equipment. I'm sure he's got it set up behind even more firewalls than what he provided for this computer. I refused to allow him to make it so that I couldn't easily navigate without providing proof of who I was every five seconds."

One side of his brother's mouth curved up. "He's a paranoid bear that's for sure. You know he's going to give us shit for not involving him in the first place."

"I know. I'll deal with him later. Right now, we need to talk to Serenity's parents and find out what her old Rufus is up to."

"I'll go find Serenity and make sure she is okay. I'll tell Locke you want to talk to him since he's with her." Shayne stood up and stretched, groaning when he did.

As his sibling closed the door to the office behind him, Creed felt like stretching as well. It had only been a couple of days since he'd run in his bear form, but it felt like weeks. All the stress and strain of the last two days was eating at him, keeping his body on alert to the point that he felt wound tighter than a coil. Much more and he would explode.

As he waited for his Ruka, Creed went over everything he knew once again. Their mate had run off from her old den because her Rufus wanted her to mate someone she hadn't wanted to. Had it been his son even then? Or, had that come later? Forced matings in the bear shifters rarely produced offspring. A couple didn't have to be true mates, but they had to want to be with each other before the female would breed cubs.

He sighed. Evidently it wasn't like that for cats, or at least the lynxes. She said that kits were born in her den. Of course she hadn't said how many survived to adulthood. What possible reason could they have to want Serenity? What was special about her other than the fact that she was their mate and a gorgeous female? Why had they waited all this time to come after her? Creed couldn't believe that she'd managed to stay hidden from them all this time only to be discovered just when they moved there. How old was she, he wondered? What would age have to do with it anyway? He was thinking in circles and learning nothing new in the process.

A knock on the door interrupted his useless musings. "Come in."

Locke walked in and closed the door behind him with a soft click. His expression as always appeared perfectly calm and slightly bored if anything. Creed wondered how he would change when he found his mate. Creed had been the same way up until the night he'd scented his mate's presence, then most of his staunchness had begun to melt.

"I need your hacking skills, Locke," Creed said by way of greeting.

A slow satisfied smile tugged on the big bear's mouth. "FBI, CIA, Shifter Agency?"

"Cell phone records," Creed said concealing his smile. "I need some phone numbers."

Locke's smile fell and he screened his expression once again. Not before Creed saw the bear's disappointment.

"It could lead to some higher hacking, but let's start with phone numbers first."

To his friend's credit, Locke didn't pout. Instead he cracked his knuckles and stretched his fingers before accepting the sheet of paper Creed handed him.

"Here is what I need and it's urgent that we get these numbers immediately."

"These are relatives of your mate, aren't they?"

"Yes. Her brothers and parents. The landlines we called were a bust. That means they only have cell phones. This plays into the reason behind the Rogue Hunters on her tail." Creed hesitated before sighing and realizing Locke needed to know more in order to cover all the possible bases. "Her old Rufus of the den she's from is the one who hired the hunters to capture her and take her back there. He wants her as a mate for his son. We don't know why but we need to find out and put a stop to this immediately."

Locke's brows shot up. "I don't understand why you don't complete the mating bond. Once you do that, he can't mate with her anyway. It would be stupid to continue to try and capture her."

"There are issues that have to be resolved before we can go farther with the bonding. We have reason to believe that even if she is completely mated to us, he will still want her. There is something special surrounding her or being mated to her. We've got to figure it out." Creed had stood and was watching the other bear closely.

"I take it you are doing this without involving your mate's input," Locke said with a sigh.

"She's already upset about the hunters. If she finds out who is behind it, I'm afraid she'll run. The only way I could prevent that would be to lock her in our suite, and I don't want to hold her prisoner."

Locke nodded. "I need my own computers for this. I'll be upstairs if you need me. I'll call you the second I have the information you need."

"Thank you, Locke."

The other bear just nodded and left without making a sound. For a huge bear, the shifter was light on his feet. Now that he'd put that into motion, Creed wasn't sure what to do next. There wasn't anything more he could look into and he didn't have the patience to deal with business right then. He wanted to be near Serenity. No, he needed to be near her. She was in danger and despite knowing that every bear in the den would fight to protect her, Creed needed to touch her and know she was okay.

Just as he reached the door to his office a loud knock sounded. He smiled. It had to be Serenity since the knock had been louder than was necessary and lower on the door panel than any of his bears would have knocked.

"Come in," he called out and leaned back against the front of his desk.

His mate hurried into the room and closed the door behind her. When she looked up at him, unease shot the hairs at the back of his neck straight into the air.

"Hi. I need to work on the computer some. Do you mind? I can't get behind on my contracts," she said looking at his chin and not into his eyes.

He narrowed his eyes. "You're keeping something from me, what is it?" he demanded.

The way her eyes jumped from his chin to stare into his before lowering once again confirmed his assessment. She was holding back. What was she hiding? Anger began to boil in his gut. With everything he and his den were trying to do to keep her safe, it was an insult to him that she'd try to conceal something. That thought jumped up and bit him right back. He was the one doing the concealing. It must be his own guilt eating at him.

"I don't understand why you and Shayne still want me when we can't complete the bond. Having only half a mate isn't good for you or your den. I'm worried. That's all," she said.

Creed studied her face then nodded. Guilt had gotten a tooth into him and was holding on for dear life. Once it began gnawing in earnest it would be difficult to keep his silence around her. Already the need to tell her everything rode him hard. He resisted though. First he would try finding her family and finding out what they had to say, then he'd re-evaluate telling her what was going on. Until then...

"Go ahead and work some, Serenity. I'm sure you're behind since you haven't been able to do much. I'm just clearing off some things anyway. You won't bother me." Creed walked back around to his desk and sat down, watching from the corner of his eye as his mate did the same.

He could feel her nervousness as if it were his own, part of the mating bond at work. He could tell she didn't want him in there with her and that made him worry that she was hiding something after all. Why else would she be uncomfortable around him? He'd given her no reason to be scared of him and had done everything in his power to make her feel safe. The more he thought about it, the angrier he got.

When she started squirming and a slight whine escaped her mouth, he realized she was feeling his emotions and worked to calm down, trying to tamp down on the tenuous link they shared. It seemed to work because she stopped fidgeting in the chair.

Creed couldn't handle the pressure any longer and was just about to open up and talk to her when his cell phone rang. He cursed but relaxed when he saw that it was Locke. The big bear had already found something.

"Hello?"

"Creed? Find Shayne." Creed fought not to look over at Serenity at the sound of worry in his Ruka's voice.

"You both need to see this."

Chapter Fifteen

The instant Creed walked out of the office, Serenity stuck the USB cord into the computer tower and started downloading all of her files and programs. Then she began reviewing her anonymous e-mail to see if her parents or one of her brothers had contacted her lately. Maybe they knew some reason why Rogue Hunters would be after her. If she'd been more active in the human's world, Serenity might have thought it was possible that someone thought she'd done something, but she rarely left her home.

No, something wasn't right and she couldn't stay holed up with Creed and Shayne for the rest of her life. Plus, something was up with them as well. Shayne had been a little more himself when he'd come downstairs earlier to take over her bodyguard duties from Locke, but she still felt that they weren't as convinced that she was who they wanted as they'd been before finding out her lynx was going to be stubborn.

She sighed. It was just as well. She needed to leave before someone got hurt. The memory of her two males fighting over her before still bothered her. Then there was the risk that someone could get hurt by the hunters trying to keep her safe. No, it was better for her to leave.

She spotted an e-mail from Evil Eye, her youngest brother's online name. He was the only one still living at home with their parents. The others had moved out to a different den. Being males and strong ones, they weren't refused when they requested to break the den bonds and go off on their own.

Serenity opened the e-mail after scanning it for spyware or viruses and finding none. It was nearly a week old. She hadn't realized that she'd neglected to check for that long, but when she was in the middle of working on a project, time got away from her.

Hey, tiger. I'm worried about you. Something's going on here. The Rufus has been here talking with our parents a lot lately. They are never happy when he leaves. I've tried getting them to tell me what is going on, but they just say it's nothing for me to worry about. Mom especially, is upset. She doesn't leave the house much at all now, and Dad makes me promise to call often when I'm gone. Somehow, I'm afraid this has something to do with you.

Serenity wondered why the Rufus would be visiting her parents. He'd never been one to just visit anyone unless he wanted something from them. What could they possibly have that he would want?

He stopped me yesterday and asked me a lot of stupid questions about the family like where was our grandma from and had I heard from you since you'd run off. Why would he care about where our grandma came from? Hell, I don't even know if he meant the one on Mom's side or Dad's. Just let me know that you are okay. I'm worried. If I don't hear from you in a reasonable amount of time, I'm going to come looking for you. Something just isn't right.

She read through the last lines then reread the entire e-mail before destroying it by sending it through her secondary shredder software. She sent a quick e-mail back to him, telling him that she was fine and was going to be moving and would tell him where she settled once she got there. She prayed it reached him before he decided to come looking for her. That's all she needed, her youngest brother showing up to demand to know what was going on.

Serenity pulled her external drive from the tower then set up the program to transfer everything to her cloud storage before leaving a program to wipe some sensitive files off the hard drive in case someone went through her computer. It would leave the non-sensitive programs there and her browser history would remain intact. She had nothing to hide, only private files that belonged to the companies she did work for. She couldn't in good consciousness leave them wide open.

Once everything was finished and she had her external drive packed away in the computer backpack she'd also stuffed with clothes, her parent's pictures, and her jewelry box, Serenity stood up and looked around the room. She hadn't been there long enough to become attached to any of it.

God! Has it only been two days?

No, what she was going to miss was her mates, and the mistaken promise of belonging to a family again. No matter how much she told herself that with the mating bond being incomplete and so weak she would soon forget about them, Serenity knew that she would never forget them. True mates were a once in a lifetime experience. All others were potential mates that you could imprint on if there was mutual attraction.

She fought back tears, slid her arms through the straps of her backpack, and picked up a bag she'd packed to get her through the coming days. Hunger pains hit her and she groaned. She'd grabbed a couple of sandwiches left over from lunch and eaten them before coming to the office. Why was she so freaking hungry?

It was enough to drive off the tears but not enough to keep her from leaving. She walked over to the widows and located the alarm wire. After tracing it to the junction where it joined the one from the other window, Serenity quickly spliced it into that one as well. It would make the connection think the window was still closed when she opened it since the other window would still be closed. She wasn't real sure it would work, but when nothing happened once she'd unlocked the window and shoved it up, she relaxed.

Dropping the bag out the window she crawled through the open space then closed it behind her. It wouldn't be locked, but with it closed, they wouldn't realize she'd left that way for quite a while. Hopefully it would be long enough she would have time to reach town so she could buy a bus ticket out of there. She'd get off earlier than planned and buy another ticket to her destination.

Guilt ate at her along with the empty gnawing in her stomach. This wasn't how things were supposed to be. Hadn't she suffered enough over the years? She thought about her best friend and knew she hadn't nearly suffered what the others had. She felt ashamed and kept going. As much as she wanted to shift, she couldn't carry the backpack and the bag in that form. She wasn't as fast in her human form, but if she kept to the woods, she could travel much faster without detection. The fact that she'd made it that far without a hunter dropping her in her tracks gave her hope that she was going to make it.

She would check in with her brother as soon as she stopped for the night. Her only worry at that moment was that there wouldn't be a bus out of town before the next day. If that happened, she'd have to find somewhere to hold up other than a hotel. They'd find her in one of only three in the little community. One of those was a bed-and-breakfast and there was no way she could stay there. It was run by one of the families of wolf shifters in the area.

Nearly an hour later, she strode into the drug store that sold bus tickets and asked when the next bus out was leaving. To her surprise, they had one leaving in fifteen minutes. It was getting diesel at the station and would be back soon. She bought a ticket to Seattle, Washington, pleased that it would be in the opposite direction she planned to go. While she waited for the bus to return, Serenity bought all the snacks she could stuff into her backpack and bag. As soon as the bus returned, she climbed on board, refusing to give up her pack or bag. They would fit over head and under the seat. She couldn't afford to be separated from either one if she was going to get off at a station somewhere along the way.

After studying the map, she decided to ride until they reached Coeur d'Alene, Idaho. She'd change busses and eventually make her way to Carson City, Nevada. Her old roommate from college lived there now. She'd let her stay there for a few days until she got a place to live.

With that thought, Serenity settled down to rest. Her stomach growled and cramped. She cursed under her breath and pulled out some peanut butter nabs to eat. Thankfully there was no one sitting next to her, so she was able to spread out, leaving her backpack on the seat next to her. She wrapped the strap around her wrist and turned it so that the zippers were face down before leaning back in her seat and closing her eyes to rest. It was a long way to Coeur d'Alene.

* * * *

"What do you mean she's gone?" Shayne snarled softly.

Locke and Otto both stood their ground but did wince at Shayne's glare in their direction.

"We've searched everywhere but can't find her. Creed said he left her in the office when he came upstairs with you to see what I'd found. After he left to meet with Mojave, I returned to the office to watch her, but she wasn't there. Her computer is there, but she isn't. I called Locke and we've searched the entire house without a sign of her. We wanted to tell you before we started outside," Locke said.

"She may have returned to her home for something. We'll check there first," Otto said.

"Did you check to see if her things are still here?" Shayne asked already heading in that direction.

"Yes. Her clothes are still where we unpacked them," Lock said.

Shayne didn't stop until he'd reached their rooms and started looking around. Sure enough, her clothes seemed to still be in the same place, but something was different. He looked around, checked the closet and then the dresser again. He couldn't put his finger on it, but something was different.

"Find Quill and Zeth. Something is different, and they'll know if something they brought over for her is missing. I wasn't paying attention to what they brought back with them to know if something of hers is missing or not," he told Locke.

The other bear stepped off to the side to call the two bears. Shayne stared at Otto. The Russian bear's emotions were all over the place from the vibes he was putting off, but nothing showed on his face.

"We must find her before the Ursus has to be told she is missing," Otto said.

"I'm not looking forward to telling him either," Shayne agreed. "But I'm going to have to call him if we don't find her soon."

Locke walked back over. "They are on their way."

"No one could have come in and taken her. We would smell them, plus the alarm system should have gone off," Otto pointed out.

"It should have gone off if she left the house on her own as well. I checked and it hadn't been inactivated except when I turned it off for Creed to leave. I reset it as soon as the garage door had closed," Locke said.

The sound of booted feet hurrying down the stairs snagged their attention. Qwill and Zeth both hurried into the room. Their faces showed that Locke had apprised them of the situation. Neither bear looked at Shayne. Instead they started looking around the room as well as the bathroom and closet.

"Her laptop, the backpack it was in, and a few odds and ends are missing," Zeth said.

"She had a picture of her parents and a little cheap jewelry box that are gone as well," Qwill added.

"She took a change of clothes and a few of her toiletries, but left the majority of it, moving it around so that it looked like it was all still there," Zeth explained.

"I can smell her strongest in the bathroom, so that was probably the last place she was before she left the suite. It's been a good four hours though since she was down here," Quill told them.

"Fuck! She can't have been gone that long. I know she was in the office with Creed until about two hours ago. He's been gone for an hour so we can assume she left just before or just after he did," Shayne said.

"We're going to check her house," Locke said.

"We'll take the back and surrounding woods," Quill said. "Maybe we can pick up her scent to tell what direction she went."

Shayne ran his hands over his face before giving in to the need to roar. It echoed throughout the downstairs. The temptation to change and go hunting for her himself was strong, but Shayne knew it was his duty to talk to Creed and direct things. Locke would coordinate the search while he handled his brother.

He walked over to the bed and picked up the pillow she'd slept on and held it to his nose. Her scent both comforted him and enraged him. She wasn't there and if they didn't find her soon, they could lose her forever. Why had she left? What had happened to cause her to change her mind about them? Had she overheard some of what they had found out?

It wasn't as if he could blame her for wanting nothing to do with any of it, but running away from them tore a piece of his soul away. Surely she didn't think they would force her into anything. Hadn't they already proved that when they hadn't forced the mating issue? No, he didn't think she'd overheard anything. She'd been acting odd since she and Creed had come up to breakfast. Everything had been fine up until then.

The fact that she'd been unusually tired, hungry, and irritable would have made him think she had been carrying their cub, but she'd never smelled as if she had been in her breeding cycle. Of course they weren't familiar with a cat's cycle. Maybe they smelled different than bears or wolves.

He stomped up the stairs to the main level. He wasn't looking forward to calling Creed with the news that their mate was missing. While they had been upstairs learning more about her, she'd been sneaking away. He still couldn't believe that she didn't know more than what she'd told them, but Creed was convinced that she was as much in the dark as they had been.

Locke had uncovered more about their mate than just her parent's phone numbers. He'd found out that she was the only female decedent left of the royals who'd once been in charge of justice for all shifters before The Awakening, the revelation to humankind of the existence of shifters. That of itself wouldn't have been such a big deal in the world they lived in today that didn't care about royalty or ancestral importance if it hadn't been for the prophecy made by the last advisor for the royal ruling family over all shifters. The last family had been wolf in nature, as had the advisor, a very old female wolf known for her prophecy. She had predicted The Awakening nearly a hundred years before it happened.

Lock sighed. Did he believe the prophecy? Papa Bear had often said that it took people believing in them for them to come true. Without the power of their belief, they couldn't come to fruition. Who was left in their modern world to believe in the prophecy enough to make it real?

The Rufus of her den did. Did his son believe as well? Whether it came true or not, the fact remained that Serenity was their mate, and she was missing. As soon as he heard back from Locke and Otto, he would call Creed. Regardless of the future, they had to find her before the hunters did.

* * * *

Serenity woke with a blinding headache and what felt like a blow torch on her skin. When she jerked upright, it was to find that there was no one standing over her with one. In fact, there were only two other passengers anywhere near her, an older human female snoring three seats up and a middle aged human male at the very front talking with the bus driver about sports. Why did it feel as if someone had set fire to her skin? Just as suddenly, the feeling went away but was replaced by abdominal cramps so bad she wasn't sure she could keep quiet. What was happening to her?

She curled up on the seat and rocked back and forth in an effort to comfort herself. The pain nearly blinded her for what felt like hours but turned out to be about twenty minutes. She lay panting on the seat, too tired to move but her belly began grumbling for food once again. How could she go from being in excruciating pain one moment to being ravenously hungry the next?

Serenity didn't understand what was happening to her. She'd never felt this way before. Digging in her pack, she pulled out another pack of nabs and a candy bar. When she went into her heat cycle, she sometimes got overly hungry and her belly was uncomfortable until it passed. She would be horny as hell and no amount of self-pleasure came close to relieving the symptoms, but this was different. Not only was it so much more extreme, but she burned all over.

The only thing she could think of was that having not finished the mating bond with Creed and Shayne, she'd somehow messed up her system's natural rhythms. Whatever it was, she just had to get through the next few days and she'd be fine. It usually only lasted about five days and she'd started feeling odd the night before.

Once she'd finished eating, Serenity tried to find a comfortable position, but the rough material of the bus seats bothered her skin. She tried pulling on a long-sleeve blouse to keep her skin away from the seats, but she got too hot and had to remove it. There wasn't a position on earth that allowed her to relax for long. As a result, she was constantly shifting in her seat. Even the bus driver noticed and asked her what was wrong. She'd mumbled something about hemorrhoids and he shut up, concentrating on the road ahead and the football team the man sitting up front kept bringing up.

After over an hour of misery, her body began to settle down again and exhausted she fell asleep once more only to be jarred awake after what felt like five minutes.

"Hey, lady. This is Coeur d'Alene. We're stopping here for dinner. Be back on the bus in two hours if you want to ride with me." He loomed over her as he spoke, but as soon as he'd finished, the bus driver scooted sideways down the aisle, his overly wide hips too large to fit between the seats.

Serenity checked the time on her cell and sighed. It was almost six. The bus would travel on to Seattle after this. She needed to find out how to get to Nevada next. She doubted there would be a bus back this way before the next day, but she wanted to know her options before locating a place to spend the night.

The Greyhound bus station wasn't huge, but it was better than the drug store back home. She walked over to the window but it was shut tight. There was a bus schedule taped to one side so she studied it, trying to make sense of some of the abbreviations. She finally admitted defeat at figuring it out. She would come back early in the morning when they opened.

Once outside again, she located the direction with the most lights and noise and started walking that way. It didn't take long to find the main drag of the town. She located a dinner and ordered a steak, baked potato, and an order of fries. Before she had finished eating that, she ordered a couple of burgers to go, figuring they would think they were for someone at home. She didn't need to call attention to herself by eating it all right there in one sitting with so many people around. So far she hadn't scented another shifter in the area, so Serenity felt fairly safe.

The food had been good and she felt much better than she had after getting off the bus. After paying her tab, she carried the burgers to the little motel the waitress at the diner had told her about. She'd said it was clean but short on amenities.

The clerk at the front desk hadn't batted an eye at her backpack and bag, nor had he protested cash instead of a credit card. She paid for one night and walked around to room 115. The waitress had been right. It was clean and even smelled decent despite the outdated style.

An old TV sat on a stand that didn't look strong enough to hold it up. She checked the bathroom and was pleased to see that it was clean with complimentary soap, shampoo, and conditioner.

Serenity had decided not to take her toothbrush and toothpaste since that would have tipped them off faster if that had been missing. She would have to make do with her finger and water for the night. She checked the bed and was satisfied that it was just as clean as it looked since the sheets still smelled of laundry detergent.

After finishing off the two burgers, she took a quick shower, wedged a chair under the door handle, and unplugged the TV to move it in front of the window. It would alert her when it crashed to the floor if someone tried to get in that way. Satisfied that she'd protected herself as best she could, she changed into her lynx form and crawled under the covers in the makeshift den she'd created with the pillows and blanket. It didn't take her long to fall into an exhausted sleep once more.

Chapter Sixteen

Creed had broken every speed limit on his way back to the house after his brother had called him. They'd essentially finished their business but had been talking about how to handle future threats like the hunters when he'd received the call.

Before he'd even turned off the engine, both Locke and his sibling were at the truck, opening the door. The grim expressions on their faces said that there had been no luck in locating her.

"They lost her scent once she made it to town. They're checking with the female wild dog now and will call back as soon as they have," Locke told him.

"You're sure she was alone?" Creed asked as they walked into the house.

"Yes. They found no other scents anywhere close to hers," Shayne said.

"How long do you think she's been gone?" he asked.

Shayne opened his office door. "We had figured that she'd left sometime within an hour of you leaving her in the office."

Locke walked over to the window. "But when I found this, I knew she left exactly when you did. She had tried to rig the window so that when she opened it the alarm wouldn't beep and alert us that a window had been opened. It was a good try and would have worked with just about any other system, but when she tried to keep the circuit closed by switching it to this one, she still opened the circuit since I didn't wire it that way. Each window is on a separate circuit and this is just a dummy case for show."

"So she had to leave exactly when I did because otherwise the alarm would have beeped anyway. She lucked out that you had shut off the alarm long enough for me to get out the door and down the drive. Son of a bitch!" Creed pounded his fist against the window facing.

"At least we know she didn't overhear our conversation. She was too busy setting things up to sneak out to have made it up the stairs then down before you left," Shayne said.

"What about the Rogue Hunters?" Locke asked. "Are they gone?"

"They were escorted out of town by over half of the wolf and wild dog packs. It was explained to them what would happen if they ever showed their faces there again. They will be clearing out the few stragglers if they are still here in the morning," Creed said absently.

"What did you tell the others that convinced them to help you get rid of them?" Locke asked.

"I alerted them to the fact that they weren't acting on official business anymore and that with the new legislature being introduced in the next day or so, they would no longer have jobs which left them open to continuing their bounty hunter plans if we didn't put a stop to it before it got started."

"They believed you about the government angle without you having to give them some sort of proof?" Locke pushed. "I don't understand. Wolves never cooperate with anyone unless it will benefit them, and then they have to have something tangible to sink their fangs into."

Creed smiled. "They probably wouldn't have but Mojave backed me and even confirmed what I had to say. It seems one of their uncles is part of the group working with the political group on the bill. The wolf knew him and agreed that if the old guard was changing, the hunters had to be shown that they would no longer be tolerated."

"None of this gets us closer to Serenity though," Shayne snarled.

Locke's cell shrilled. He answered it on the first ring. "What did you find out?"

Despite their keen hearing, Creed couldn't hear what was being said on the other end with all the static on the line.

"Get back here then." Locke ended the call and slapped the cell back on the holder on his belt.

"What?" Creed demanded.

"The female wild dog hasn't heard from her since we left the meeting the other day. They didn't scent her anywhere around the apartment or her car. Neither did they scent her around the garage. What they did find was that she had been at the drug store. Someone overheard them asking Wren about her. The older woman was worried that she was missing and started talking about hunters and how she'd warned her to stay clear of them. She said she saw her in the drug store purchasing a bus ticket," Locke told them.

"They need to find out where she was headed," Creed shouted.

"They did. She bought a ticket to Seattle, Washington," Locke said taking a step back.

"Shayne, pack for a couple of nights. Locke, you and Otto are in charge while we're gone." Creed started to walk out of the office, but Locke stopped him.

"Ursus, wait. I don't think she'll go all the way to Seattle. She's smart. She'll get off at another stop and buy a different ticket to where she's really going. Wait and let's look at a map with the route the bus takes to figure out where she might have gotten off to snag a different bus. They will be here by the time you finish packing," Locke said without looking him in the eyes.

He could tell he'd shed power since Locke had called him by his title and wasn't looking at him. He regretted it, but there was nothing he could do about it now. Drawing in a deep breath to settle his raw nerves, he nodded.

"We'll be downstairs packing if they return before we come back upstairs." He nodded at his brother to follow him.

"I'm sorry it took us so long to realize she was gone," Shayne said quietly as they crossed the house to the stairs that led down.

"I'm as much to blame as anyone. I never should have started the search without including her. At least then she would have been with at least one of us while we worked on a solution to the problem," he said.

"I was the one who started digging in the first place," his brother said.

They both grabbed a duffle bag and started throwing clothes in it. By the time they'd returned upstairs, Zeth and Quill had returned and were dressing since they'd shed their clothes to shift into their bear forms.

Zeth handed the bus schedule to Shayne. "Sorry it's a little wet. I had to carry it in my mouth."

"Let's go to the kitchen," Locke said. "Otto has a couple of maps spread out on the table for us."

They followed the big bear to where Otto had pulled the chairs out away from the table to give them all room. Creed watched as Locke took the schedule from Shayne and laid it on the map. Otto handed him a red marker.

"Okay, here we are here." He put a red *X* over the community. "This is the route the bus is taking to Seattle." He drew a red line along the road between them and the bus's destination.

Creed studied all the potential towns along the route and cringed. There were way too many to have a hope of finding her soon.

"The dots are the towns they usually make stops at to exchange passengers and the *X*s are where they stop for longer periods of time such as for meals or fuel stops." Locke continued making marks on the map. When he'd finished, there were a lot fewer towns to have to worry about.

"Looks like, five, six potential places she could have gotten off," Shayne said with a low growl in his throat.

"She wouldn't have wasted the ticket by getting off at the first few stops. She would have wanted to put some distance between her and us," Locke said. "My vote is either here"—he pointed at Coeur d'Alene, ID—"or here." He indicated Moses Lake.

"Why not Spokane? It's a much large city and she could easily disappear there," Creed asked.

"She doesn't want to disappear yet. She just wants to put some space between us and her until she can locate a bus or train going directly to her actual destination," Locke told him.

"How do you know that's what she'd do? You haven't known her any longer than we have," Shayne said.

Locke sighed. "I don't know for sure, but I know strategy and she's a strategist. I'd bet my truck on it after looking at her computer setup and how she took only what she thought we wouldn't miss. She made sure to leave things that would obviously be missed, like her toiletries."

"So where do you think she got off that bus at?" Creed finally asked.

"I'd bet on Coeur d'Alene. It's far enough away from here to give her a measure of comfort without forcing her to ride all the way to Moses Lake on a possibly full bus of humans. Plus, it looks like they were planning on eating here since the stop is for two hours."

"Let's go, Shayne." Creed stooped to pick up his bag, but Locke beat him to it. He also had another one that looked an awful lot like his Steelers bag.

"Locke…" he began but the other bear stopped him.

"I'm your Ruka. I can't protect you and Shayne from here. Otto will handle the sleuth until we return. I'm not leaving your side," he said, showing his chin.

"Stubborn bastard," Shayne muttered under his breath.

Lock grinned but quickly sobered when Creed growled at him.

"You can drive then." Creed snarled and stomped out of the kitchen.

* * * *

Serenity woke at some point during the night hurting so badly she had returned to her human form and was all tangled in the covers. She fought the pain and the covers until she finally rolled out of the bed, hitting the floor with a loud thump, her head banging against the side of the bed frame. More pain exploded along her cheekbone as it made contact with the unforgiving floor.

Tears welled in her eyes as she untangled herself and attempted to crawl back onto the mattress. She didn't bother with picking up the blankets. She didn't think she could stand for anything to touch her skin right then. Even the bottom sheet felt rough against her overly sensitive flesh. Sizzling heat scalded her as if she'd stepped into an oven. The combination of glowing heat and tender skin made it feel as if instead of walking into an oven she'd walked into a windstorm in the middle of a desert where sand blasted her skin from her body.

Serenity stuffed the corner of a pillow into her mouth to muffle her screams of pain as her lower abdomen seemed to be eating itself. Why was this happening to her? What was wrong with her?

After a while, the pain and heat subsided leaving the gnawing hunger she'd had before. It took her two tries to get up from the bed and dig through her pack for the last of the nabs and candy bars she'd bought at the drug store. When she felt better she was going to have to go shopping or she'd starve to death.

Her cell phone said it was nearly ten. She hadn't slept all that long. As soon as she felt up to moving again, she would look for somewhere close to load up on something to eat. If she was going to do this every few hours, she wasn't going to be able to get on a bus full of people yet. It looked like her one night was going to turn into at least two.

Almost an hour later, Serenity felt able to walk some. She needed to find a store before they all closed. Most convenience stores only stayed up as late as ten or eleven if they weren't open all night. Her first stop was the motel office. She said she decided that since the place was so clean she would stay another day and rest up. The male didn't even blink, just took her money and marked her down for another night.

After that, she located a twenty-four-hour store and stocked up on food that wouldn't spoil and bottled water. Then she returned to her room and arranged everything within reaching distance before arming her make shift security system once more.

Another wave of sizzling heat seared her skin making her cry out before she could stop herself. Serenity quickly stripped out of her clothes and curled into a ball on the bed, wishing she would die as pain tore through her belly once more. This time, instead of lingering or growing worse, it turned into arousal unlike anything she'd ever known before. Her body ached to be filled. Her lynx whined, feeling the effects for the first time. Where before she knew her human side was in pain and uncomfortable but hadn't felt any of it herself, not even the raw hunger. Always ready for a nap, the exhaustion hadn't seemed a problem to her, but this need was different.

Oh, God. I can't take this much longer.

She'd never felt this overwhelming need to be fucked before. Even when she'd had her breeding heat in the past, it had never been like this. She'd always been able to ride it out alone, preferring not to risk accidently finding her mate or ending up pregnant. The chances of creating kits when in heat were almost ninety percent in favor of receiving a visit from the stork.

This wasn't something she could handle on her own. If she'd had her mate's numbers in her cell phone, Serenity would have broken down and called them. That was how bad the need was pulsing inside her cunt. As it was, she was seriously considering kidnapping the man at the front desk for a few hours. He looked to be at least twenty-five or so. He would be able to handle her heat—maybe.

"Please! I can't take this. Please stop," she sobbed as another roll of heated desperation washed over her.

After an hour of rolling around on the bed wishing for a vibrator or even a damn cucumber, the need slowly receded to a bearable level. It didn't go away completely this time though. Instead, it felt as if someone had taken mercy on her and turned it down to give her time to rest. She had no doubt it would be back though.

While she was able, Serenity ate again and drank two complete bottles of water before slowing down. Her mouth felt as if she'd swallowed her pillow and her skin felt brittle. She contemplated taking another shower, but exhaustion poured over her once again and it took all of her remaining energy to climb back into the bed and find a fairly comfortable position before she slept.

* * * *

They'd arrived in the little town Locke was certain she'd stopped in to find most places already closed for the night. The bus station was dark as were most of the stores they saw. Creed felt as if it was a sign that they would never found her. He wasn't usually this negative, but just the fact that she'd run away from them depressed him and his bear. She didn't want them. If it wasn't for the danger she was in, he'd have let her go and suffered through the pain it would cause to lose her, but he couldn't let her go while there was a danger to her out there.

Shayne pointed out a convenience store that remained open, so they pulled in to fill up the truck's tank and grab something to eat. They had no idea how far they'd have to drive the next day.

All three of them climbed out of the truck and stretched before walking into the building. He and Shayne took turns in the bathroom then started grabbing food. They'd have to find a hotel and spend the night to find out anything at the bus station. When they walked back up to the counter to pay for their goods, it was to find Locke talking with the young male behind the counter.

Locke turned with a smile on his usually neutral face. "There's a motel just one block over. It's very clean and reasonably priced."

He and Shayne exchanged confused expressions. Why would Locke be so pleased about that? He started to ask the bear what his problem was, but he told them he'd be waiting for them in the truck and hurried outside.

They paid the man who looked just as confused as they felt then took their bags out to the truck. As soon as they climbed in, Locke took off.

"What in the hell is wrong with you?" Creed asked.

"I thought you were going to fill up while we were here," Shayne added with a frown.

"The kid back there saw your mate. She's staying at the motel around the corner where we're headed. Evidently she walked here around ten tonight to get some food and water. He asked if she needed a bag since she was carrying a backpack. She said yes, that she was going to have to carry it to where she was staying at the little motel around the corner."

"What made him tell you about her?" Shayne asked.

"I asked him if there was a clean cheap place to stay close by. I figured she'd want to conserve her funds. We don't know how much cash she had with her. He told me that a woman who'd been in around ten mentioned that the motel around the corner was clean and cheap. He remembered her because he worried about her since she looked sick."

"There it is," Shayne pointed out even though it wasn't necessary. It was the only building that still had lights on in it.

As soon as Locke pulled into the parking lot, Creed was out of the truck heading for the office. Locke stopped him but lowered his eyes.

"Please let me do the talking, Ursus. You're worried about your mate. You'll scare the human and he'll clam up on us or call the police. Let me try to learn something first," the bear pleaded.

Creed drew in a deep breath knowing Locke was right. He could feel Shayne's anxiety and something else. He stilled and quieted the normal feelings in his head. A faint link to his mate remained and through it he could feel her exhaustion and discomfort, but that was all. He nodded at Locke.

"See what you can find out. We'll be quiet while you talk."

His Ruka sighed before leading the way inside the little office. A young male of about twenty-five or so stood up from where he'd been sitting on a chair at with a laptop on his lap. He set it on the seat cushion before approaching the desk with a bored expression.

"Can I help you?"

Locke smiled and leaned on the counter. "We need a couple of adjoining rooms. Decided we were too tired to keep driving tonight."

"Um, I've got a couple of rooms with two double beds each around back," he said.

"Is it quiet?" Locke asked. "Don't want some crying kid waking us up in the middle of the night or a couple of teenagers partying next to us."

"Oh, the only other person on that side is a lady and she won't be bothering you I don't think. She wasn't feeling too well. She's right next to you, but like I said, I doubt she'll bother you," he said.

"Sounds good. We'll take them," Locke said turning a triumphant smile in their direction.

Creed had to admit the male was good. He wouldn't protest anytime the other bear wanted to tag along on a trip like this. He just hoped there wouldn't be another one anytime in their future.

As they filled out the required information and paid for the rooms, all he could think about was that both the store owner and the motel manager mentioned that she had looked ill. It worried him. Knowing that she'd been running while sick bothered him. Since shifters rarely got sick unless poison was involved, Creed hated waiting around while the manager performed his job and checked all the paperwork before handing them their keys.

"Wow, real keys. I didn't realize anyone still used actual keys anymore," Locke mumbled as they climbed back into the truck to drive around the building.

"Okay, we've got rooms 116 and 117. She's going to either be in 115 or 118," Shayne said as they pulled up in front of their rooms.

"We should be able to scent which room she's in," Creed said, climbing out of the truck.

"She's going to know we're here the minute our scent reaches her," Locke reminded them.

The three bears advanced on room one eighteen, nostrils flaring as they worked to find a hint of her behind the door. Creed figured they looked like drug-crazed idiots if anyone saw them sniffing at the door. Locke seemed to have the same thought since he started looking around them while he and Shayne walked down to one fifteen having failed to pick up their mate's scent at the first room.

Even before they stood in front of the poorly painted door they knew she was there. Her lynx's distinct aroma had Creed's bear flexing his claws to tear down the door. Retaining control was becoming increasingly more difficult.

"I take it from the looks of your claws that she's inside," Locke said with a pointed look at Creed's paws and extended claws.

"Knock on the door for me," he said in a growly voice. "My fucking paws are useless and until I can see her and touch her, I'm not going to be able to control this."

Locke wisely didn't say anything to him about it. Instead, he knocked on the door then stepped back. They waited for a few seconds, then Shayne stepped up and banged with his fist. Even with their enhanced hearing, they couldn't hear a single noise from the other side of the door. Shayne beat on the door again, this time louder. Still no sounds of anyone moving around.

"Something's wrong. Even if she didn't want to answer the door, there would be some type of noise for us to hear. If she was asleep,

Shayne's knocking should have woken her up. Hell, I'm surprised the damn kid from the office hasn't shown up."

"I agree," Shayne said. "We need inside. Stand back and I'll kick the door in."

Locke stepped in front of him. "I'll pick the lock. If she has the chain on, we can break that without doing as much damage to the door. Someone will call the police if we break in like that."

"He's right," Creed said, looking at his brother. Then he turned back to Locke. "Hurry, or I'm going to kick it in myself."

He watched as Locke hurried back to the truck then returned a few seconds later with a small black case. He opened it and started to work on the lock as Creed and Shayne stood over him, blocking what he was doing from anyone who passed by on the street behind them. As much as he hated waiting even one minute, Locke was right. They couldn't afford to attract the attention of anyone.

Just let her be okay. I won't be able to handle it if something's wrong with her.

After what felt like an eternity he heard Locke's triumphant grunt and then the pop of him breaking the chain holding the door closed.

"Okay, we're in." Locke stepped aside to allow him and his brother to rush inside. A broken chair lay on its side next to the door, but his attention was snagged by the sight of their mate and his brother's tortured cry.

"Serenity!"

Chapter Seventeen

Shayne's breath caught in his throat at the sight of their mate curled into a fetal position on the bed and unmoving. He could barely discern her chest rising and falling as she breathed. Even as he listened for her heartbeat, it was so soft and slow that he worried it would cease to thump in her chest.

Creed's growl warned him that his brother, already on the edge, was about to lose it. He turned and growled back at him to get his attention.

"Hold it together, Creed. We've got to get her help and if you lose it, we'll lose her." Shayne turned from his brother and climbed up on the bed.

He felt the bed dip behind him and the next second, his brother, back in control brushed Serenity's hair from her face. Pale skin accented by dark circles beneath her eyes gave her a haunted look. What little hope he had almost left him. What was wrong with her? Had someone poisoned her? Shifters didn't get sick. They didn't even have allergies or cold sores.

"What's wrong with her, Creed?" Locke asked from the doorway where he stood guarding the door.

Creed looked up, worry lining his face. "I don't know. I've never seen anything like it. She's comatose and barely breathing. We need to get her home and find a healer."

"I have her bags. Bring her out whenever you're ready," Locke said crossing the room to pick up Serenity's bag and pack.

"I'll carry her," Shayne said. "You need to find a healer. The wild dogs should know or have one."

Creed nodded but helped Shayne settle their mate in his arms before leading the way for him as he carried her to the truck. His brother opened the door and helped him climb into the back with her in his lap.

"What about the chain on the door?" Locke asked. "Do you think they'll notice it when they go to clean the room?"

"I doubt it, but if they do, they won't do anything about it. There's no evidence of a struggle or anything. We'll handle deal with the fallout later if anything comes of it," Creed told him.

Shayne kept Serenity close to his chest. He inhaled her sweet scent and prayed she would be okay. So far she continued to breathe and heart kept a steady though slow beat. She appeared uncomfortable to him. She didn't seem to be relaxed in the least despite being unconscious.

While he looked down at her pale features, he could hear his brother talking to someone on the phone. He hoped they had access to a healer and would be able to help their mate. He remembered part of the conversation they'd had with her family concerning her heritage and what it might mean.

The prophecy said she would bear the sons of her mates who would one day rule over all shifters to assure their continued existence in the new world around them. Her sons would create the new ruling family and put an end to the need for human hunters.

They had speculated on what that meant, but in the end, it hadn't really mattered. All that mattered was how they felt about her and how she felt about them. She meant everything to them no matter who she was to the rest of the shifter community. As the last surviving female relative of that family, she would be in great danger from both the shifters and the humans who didn't like shifters. They would have to make keeping her safe at all times their number-one priority.

Something had triggered the prophecy. Had it been their meeting and beginning the mating process? He felt like that had something to do with it, but the hunters had already been there for several weeks before that. Plus they hadn't officially met when the hunters first approached her in the parking lot of the grocery store.

"The wolves have a healer that will help us," Creed said a few minutes later. "Locke, we're going home. The healer will meet us there. I'm calling the others to let them know what is going on so they let the wolf into the den."

"I don't like the alpha, Creed. You know he's going to be there with his healer when we get back." Shayne was fairly sure Wren didn't want to have anything to do with that wolf and if he wasn't mistaken, two of their bears were fighting their instincts when it came to the wild dog female.

"Neither do I, but our mate comes first. We can tolerate him for as long as it takes for his healer to help Serenity," Creed reminded him.

"How much longer, Locke?" Shayne asked instead of saying anything more on the subject.

"We're still three hours out," Locke said, "and I'm pushing ninety as it is. If we get pulled over, they're going to know something is wrong with your mate like she is."

"They know what we are, Locke. I'll explain what is wrong and pay any fine." Creed's temper was flaring again.

"Don't go any faster, Locke. If we tell them what we are, they might decide to detain us and separate us from our mate. You and I both know what will happen if they try that," Shayne met their Ruka's eyes in the rearview mirror.

Nothing was said for the next thirty minutes but the tension in the truck was suffocating to Shayne. Creed's bear was so close to the surface now that Shayne was having trouble keeping his bear under control. The possibility of losing a mate would turn any male crazy. Their being alphas increased the possibilities of disaster exponentially.

Without warning, Serenity's body bucked in his arms as a low moan filled the cab of the truck. Shayne struggled to keep her sequestered in his arms so she wouldn't hurt herself as she jerked in his arms as if she was convulsing.

Fuck! She's been poisoned. That's the only explanation.

"Creed! We need help now," he yelled.

His brother had his cell phone at his ear before Shayne had even finished speaking. Heat wrenching whimpers had his bear ready to tear something or someone apart for causing his mate such pain. His hands burned and itched as pain sliced at the tips of his fingers with the need to change. He willed them to remain human, reminding his bear in an almost chant that he couldn't take care of her with paws and claws. That would come later when they had someone to focus on.

"Locke, how far are we from Missoula?" Creed demanded.

"Um, maybe twenty minutes. Where do I go?" he asked.

"Mojave said there is a wild dog pack there he knows. He's calling them and will call us back." Creed put the phone back to his ear after scrolling through the numbers.

Serenity finally settled some in his arms, but her body was soaked with sweat and she whimpered with almost every breath she took. He could no longer feel her as he'd been able to before. Shayne could hear Creed telling someone that they appreciated it but they no longer needed them. That would be the alpha's healer. They couldn't afford to wait until they made it all the way back home. Secretly he was relieved. He didn't think it was a good idea to trust the wolf's leader.

A few seconds later, Creed's phone rang. His brother answered it on the first ring. He could tell by the slight relaxing of the other bear's shoulders that it was good news. The wild dogs were going to help them, help their mate.

"Okay, as soon as you reach the city limits, start looking for county road 1452 on your left," Creed told Locke.

Shayne breathed a sigh of relief. He kissed Serenity's forehead and whispered that she was going to be fine next to her ear in hopes she could hear him. In that moment, he would have given his own life to know that she was going to be fine.

* * * *

Serenity felt as if she'd gone over Niagara Falls in a barrel. Every single inch of her body ached. What had happened to her and why couldn't she get her eyes to open?

Slowly she became aware of the strange scents surrounding her. When she identified those of her mates and what smelled canine, she relaxed slightly, believing she was back at Creed and Shayne's home and the dogs had come to visit.

That's not right. I left. They didn't need me and my cat's problems. I don't think they were even real certain about mating my any longer. I left. Why can I smell them so strongly?

Serenity forced her eyes to open to mere slits. She felt swollen for some reason. When she finally focused it was to find herself in a small bedroom she didn't recognize. How had she gotten here and where *was* here anyway?

When she tried to sit up, it was to find that her body was sluggish. The slightest movement irritated her skin. It felt as if she were rubbing it across sandpaper. Then it all came back in a warm rush of heat. She'd been going through her heat—a crazy supped-up version of it, but she was sure it had been her heat. Serenity had decided during one of her reprieves from the pain and burning sensations that having started the mating process and not finished it she'd screwed up and was paying for it. Was she over it now? How long had she been out?

As much as she wanted to get up and find out where she was, Serenity couldn't make her body obey her. She was just about ready to call out when the door suddenly burst open and both Creed and Shayne raced inside.

"Serenity?" Creed's voice almost broke.

"Thank God," Shayne said as climbed on the bed near her feet. "How do you feel, baby?"

"What happened? Where am I?" she asked instead.

"We're at the home of the Missoula wild dog pack's healer. She's been kind enough to help you when it was obvious you weren't doing well enough to make it all the way back home," Creed told her.

"You came after me? How did you find me?" she asked.

"Of course we came after you. You're our mate!" Shayne all but snarled.

"Locke is good at finding people, honey. There was no way were going to just let you run out like that." Creed had pulled back from her some once he'd been assured she was okay. It worried her.

This was one of the reasons she'd left. They'd seemed so different after it became obvious that her cat wasn't about to submit to their mating needs. Nothing had changed so why had they still come after her?

"Why did you go?" Shayne asked her.

"Because it would be easier now for me to leave before we imprint then if I waited until you'd gotten tired of trying to deal with my lynx. She isn't going to change her mind about this," she told them, closing her eyes to keep the tears inside.

"We aren't going to get tired of you or your cat, honey. You're our mate. Nothing will ever change that. For us it was instant and there's no going back." Creed ran a hand through his hair. She'd noticed that he did that when he was agitated.

Her lower belly began to cramp again. She swallowed a moan but the two males seemed aware of her discomfort. They both tensed then looked at one another before returning their heavy stares to her.

"What?" she asked as she fought the burning sensation beginning in her skin all over again. Hunger bloomed in her gut as if she hadn't eaten in days.

"Serenity, the reason you were unconscious was because your body couldn't take the pain and stress you've been going through any longer. If you continue denying what you need, it will happen again." Creed stepped closer to the bed once more.

She stared at him. He must know she was in heat. "What do you mean?"

"You're in heat, honey. The healer believes that we've messed up your normal cycle by starting the mating process but not completing it. She thinks that we need to finish it or you're just going to get worse."

"Are you listening to me? My lynx isn't going to allow it. I'm all for forcing her, but you and I both know if we do she'll reject you for good and I'll have to fight her all the time," she said on the verge of crying. "I don't know what to do."

"We can mate your lynx the way she expects, Serenity. Bite her but without the anal sex," Creed told her.

"That won't complete the bond for you though." She didn't see how they could do that and it be enough for her lynx and the heat if they weren't tied to her.

"It's the only option we have right now. From the way you're sweating again, I don't think we have much time left to come up with a different plan." Creed looked over at his brother. "Here or do we find a hotel close by?"

"Here. I'll go tell them we'll take care of any damage." Shayne stood up and walked back to the door and opened it.

"W–what are you talking about?" Serenity was pretty sure she knew.

"You're going to start hurting again and you and both know our bears aren't going to be able to stand your heat. We're going to have to fuck you, honey. It's the only thing that will stop the pain and discomfort." Creed began to slowly remove his clothes. "From what the healer has told us, it's a good thing there are two of us since she says cats are nymphos when they are in heat."

Serenity groaned. Between the growing tightness in her breasts and the look in Creed's eyes, she was sure she was going to embarrass herself with them. The healer was right, female cats in heat proved to be wild and a mated feline would go at it with her mate until she was pregnant. It was the only thing that stopped the heat.

Shayne returned, locking the door behind him. "They're fine with it and are going to stay at their son's house for the night. They gave me the number in case there were any problems."

"Good. Undress. We have a mate to satisfy and I have a feeling it's going to take both of us in the state she's been in," Creed said with a deep rumble in his chest.

Shayne didn't argue. With smooth movements, he soon had his clothes off and was climbing up the foot of the bed. The sight of his shoulder length light brown hair loose around his head made her want to grab handfuls of it and hold on while he licked her pussy. God, she had turned into a horny bitch overnight.

"Let's get your clothes off of you, kitten. I think you'll feel a lot better with nothing but us touching your soft skin." Creed carefully pulled back the covers, handing them to Shayne to discard from the bed.

She didn't appear to have on anything other than a large T-shirt beneath the covers. Evidently they'd already undressed her or she'd not had anything on when they'd found her and hadn't bothered to fully dress her when they carted her away. The touch of his hand didn't hurt like she had expected it to. It seemed that everything else irritated her when it touched her.

"Easy, honey. Let us take care of you. We'll do all the work," Creed said as he carefully pulled the shirt over her head.

"I'm so hot. My skin feels like it is on fire," she said with a groan.

Shayne crawled up the bed, his corded muscles straining with each move. Her eyes were drawn to his massive erection straining forward as if it had a mind of its own of where it wanted to be. The thick shaft looked heavy with the large bulbous head swollen and ruddy, a drop of pre-cum pearled at the slit. She licked her lips and Shayne groaned as his eyes followed her tongue across her bottom lip.

"Hell, baby. You're going to make me come just from the way you're looking at my cock like you could swallow it whole." Shayne finished the slow sensuous crawl up the bed to lie on his side next to her.

She whimpered as his fingers toyed with one nipple. The bed dipped and Creed climbed on to the other side wasting no time before he'd covered her other nipple with his mouth. The sudden wet heat surrounding the overly sensitive nub sent sharp pinpricks of arousal straight to her clit. Already it felt swollen and seemed to pulse with need.

Shayne replaced his fingers that had been playing with her breast with his mouth and the feel of both of them sucking and nipping at her swollen nipples was almost more than she could take. She dug the fingers of both hands in their hair, kneading and scratching their scalps in time to the rhythmic pull of their mouths on her breasts. Every tug at her nipples had her clit throbbing to the point of pain.

"Oh, God! So good," she moaned, arching her back and holding their heads tight against her chest.

Both males growled as they tormented her mounds, the vibrations tickling her flesh to the point she was sure she was going to come. How could she climax when they weren't doing anything but playing with her breasts?

Without warning, both of them bit down lightly and pulled her nipples at the same time and Serenity flew. Her cunt convulsed with the orgasm despite having nothing to squeeze. It just made her ache for more.

"Damn! That was fucking amazing!" Shayne said, male satisfaction gleaming in his eyes.

Before she could say anything, her abdomen began cramping again. She cried out, clutching her belly with both hands.

"Shayne. She can't handle the foreplay. Fuck her, man. She's in pain," Creed said, smoothing her hair from her face. "We'll stop the pain, kitten. Just hold on."

Tears burned in the back of her eyes. She hated this need that gnawed at her. What if their plan to bite her didn't work? She couldn't live like this. It was too much. Every instinct inside of he screamed for them to take her and make her theirs, but her lynx wasn't responding to them at all right then. Why? The finicky cat hadn't stirred since she'd woken up. Panic had her mouth drying out. What if her lynx was lost to her now?

"I can't feel her!" she nearly screamed.

"What?" Creed asked as Shayne covered her with his body.

"My lynx. She's not responding to me. Something's wrong."

Shayne lowered his head and nuzzled her neck, sniffing and licking along her shoulder and up around her jaw. He pulled back, a worried expression on his face.

"I don't feel her either. Creed?"

Creed began growling and calling to the cat as her Ursus and mate. Serenity felt her lift her head but she didn't respond in any other way. What was wrong? Why wasn't she responding to her or to them?

"Creed," she pleaded.

"I know, honey. We're going to take care of you. Just hold on for us." Creed nodded at his brother.

Shayne sat up on his knees and spread her legs farther apart so he could fit between them. The sight of him grasping the base of his dick did things to her insides. She could feel her juices slickening her pussy lips. She wanted him inside of her so much it hurt. She wasn't above begging right then, but didn't have to. The big bear between her legs growled deep in his chest before fitting the head of his cock to her slit and pushing inside of her.

She almost sighed with relief as he slowly filled her aching cunt with his thick, hard cock. The sight of his lips curled back in a snarl should have scared her. Instead, it turned her on. It wasn't the expression of an angry male but one of a male fighting to remain in control while he fucked his female. It thrilled her and the lynx sniffed the air.

"Fuck! You're so damn swollen and tight, baby. It's like sliding my dick into a warm wet glove." Shayne's words meant little to her. It was the growly quality of his voice that appealed to her and her lynx. The she cat finally seemed interested and cocked her head, nostrils flaring at the scent of sex in the air.

Shayne's shaft delved inside of her swollen pussy, rubbing sensitive tissues with every thrust and retreat. The stimulation of his course pubic hair against her clit when he bottomed out inside of her, bumping her cervix in the process, had fire racing up her spine and electricity tingling along her clit. She was going to explode when she came. Her lynx whined but still didn't stand. It worried her that the cat wasn't responding as she should.

"Creed," she gasped. "Take me. Please, Creed." If both of them taking her didn't stir her cat, Serenity was afraid she would slip away and be lost to her forever.

"Serenity, honey. I don't..."

"Fuck my ass, Creed. I'm losing her. I need you to make her fight!" she all but screamed in desperation.

He growled at her. She could see the uncertainty in his eyes. He was afraid that even if they managed to stir her to action, their forcing her would send her over the edge or worse, she'd refuse them as mates. She knew the moment he made the decision to take the chance. His eyes closed in resignation and he lowered his head as if in defeat. Serenity felt as if she'd broken him somehow and wanted to tell him to forget what she'd asked of him, but couldn't do it. She couldn't lose her lynx. It would leave her only half-alive and no good to her mates.

"Shayne," Creed snarled. "Roll over with her on top of you."

Shayne did as his brother said but flashed a worried look toward him. It was clear from the look that he was just as worried about what they were going to do as his sibling. Looking down into Shayne's sturdy face with the light brown of his eyes that were a shade short of being odd, she knew he would do anything for her. Just like his older brother, they would save her at the risk of losing her cat's favor.

Serenity loved them. In that moment it was crystal clear that she loved them despite only having known them a short time. They had accepted her lynx's quirk without arguing or trying to cajole her into trying. They had bent over backward to keep her safe, and were creating her dream spa just like she had always wanted. Even when she'd left them, they'd come after her and were even now risking the wrath of her lynx to save her from losing the persnickety cat.

She lowered her body to Shayne's and kissed him. Their tongues met and slid together in a mating that had her gasping for breath long seconds later. She was well aware of Creed moving around behind her and of the heat of his body just inches from her ass and thighs. Instead of acknowledging his presence behind her, she concentrated on Shayne and the taste of him against her tongue. She licked along his bottom lip then sucked it into her mouth and bit it. Enjoying the way Shayne's cock twitched inside of her when she did it, she sucked harder on it then let go.

The big bear beneath her shafted in and out of her pussy in long slow movements that kept her on the edge and aching for more. She wanted him to pound his thick dick deeper into her cunt to alleviate some of the burning need that ate at her sanity. Instead, he slowly pushed inside only to drag his hard rod back out across sensitive areas she hadn't known existed till right then.

The feel of Creed's tongue rasping over her ass cheeks sent shivers along her skin. His hot tongue left a trail of saliva that instantly cooled and made her super aware of her ass. The big bear nipped one buttock before squeezing both cheeks in his burly hands.

"Your ass is so pretty, honey. I can't wait to sink my dick into it. You're going to be so hot and tight. Aren't you, kitten?"

"Yes!" she hissed out as Shayne licked up her neck.

Something warm and slippery dropped at the top of her buttocks right at the crack. It slowly slid down her ass, reaching her back hole where it was stopped by Creed's finger. He rubbed slow sensuous circles around the little hole, pushing inward a little bit each time. The slight pressure didn't bother her in the least and it looked like her cat wasn't worried about it either.

"Creed," she whispered hoarsely. "She's not reacting."

"Give it time, Serenity. I'm not going to hurt you just to wake up that bitch inside of you. She'll get the picture soon enough," he said in a strained voice.

"Look at me, babe. I want to watch your face as he prepares that sweet ass of yours. I bet your pretty green eyes are going to grow so wide before they start flashing fire at me when he sticks his cock in that tight ass." Shayne grinned up at her as he moved his hips just right to hit her cervix and send tiny pulses of pain that had her clit aching for more.

Over and over Creed added the warmed lube to her little hole pushing it deeper inside of her with the tip of his finger. It wasn't until he sank one finger all the way to the knuckle out of the blue that she felt the first twinges of excitement lick at her spine. That sudden thrust gave her a glimpse of what was to come but in a much bigger package. Serenity screamed as her lynx finally lifted her head and extended her claws.

Chapter Eighteen

Creed didn't want to do this. He didn't like risking their future by alienating her lynx. If the lynx refused to acknowledge them as her mates, it could make their bears go crazy. Having Serenity without her lynx was a far better outcome than losing both of them or Serenity losing her lynx and always feeling half-alive. He would risk anything to have her whole and by his side. She was their heart now and that made risking anything hard to handle.

He stared down at her perfectly rounded ass and moaned at the thought of filling her there with his cock. She'd be so sweet there, hot, tight, and amazing. As he prepared her for his thick cock, Creed couldn't help but watch his brother's dick sliding in and out of her precious pussy. It had his own shaft jerking in reaction, pre-cum sliding over the crown.

Over and over he added more of the lubricant he'd found in the attached bathroom. He wanted to be sure he didn't harm her in anyway. She was his mate and the future of his sleuth. Nothing was too difficult or too good for her, his Ursa.

The way her little rosette reacted to his finger was fascinating to him. He loved seeing it flare wide when he pressed against it with the tip of his finger. It was as if it knew he would never hurt it. All he wanted to do was give his mate pleasure and bind her to him and his brother for the rest of their lives.

When she was taking one of his fingers to the webbing of his hand, he added more lube and a second finger. He slowly entered the dark hole with slow shallow thrusts until she was moaning and pushing back against him in order to take more. It amazed him that she was already so pliant but then her mating heat was riding her hard. Maybe the heat would ease the way for all of them.

Soon the two fingers sank easily into her tight virgin ass with her shoving back each time she sank down on Shayne's shaft. He had to quell the urge to pump his on throbbing dick against her thigh just watching the way her body took everything they gave it.

Pulling his fingers slowly from her tight hole, he ignored her whimper of protest and added more lube. His fingers were thick enough that he felt confident that she was as ready as he could make her. Creed added lube to his cock and positioned the crown at her back hole. He grasped her hip with one hand and the base of his shaft with the other.

"Shayne, hold her still until I get inside of her. I don't want to accidently hurt her."

His brother wrapped his arms around her back and held her against his chest while watching what Creed was doing. Anticipation shown in the other bear's eyes. He knew exactly what his brother was feeling. It wouldn't be long now before they claimed her once and for all. He prayed that it worked and that Serenity's lynx didn't freak out.

"She's burning up, Creed. Hurry. Even her eyes are glazed now."

Their mate's moans and whimpers were driving their bears crazy. Her pain was more than they could take and twice Creed had to will his change back as his hands had begun to morph into clawed paws. He couldn't risk tearing her up inside.

Creed flexed his ass and pushed at the winking hole with the head of his dick. At first she resisted his probing, but suddenly she relaxed and his cock entered her moist, hot depths. Her body tensed around him before relaxing once more. He pulled out just enough to move then pressed deeper and entered her another inch. His cock throbbed at the hot tight sheath surrounding it. He wanted more but was determined to take it slow so he didn't hurt her.

Pulling back out until only the mushroom head remained inside her delicious heat, Creed waited for Shayne to pull back out before he slid in a little more this time. Each time he retreated and returned, he gained another inch inside her tight hot heat. He ached to pound into her as hard and deep as he could get, but she wasn't ready for that. Soon enough he'd be able to dive into her balls deep.

Bending over her back he grabbed a handful of her glorious golden brown hair and pulled her head back with it so he could whisper in her ear.

"You are so fucking sexy, honey. I want to lick your body from head to toe. My cock is having to fight its way inside this tight ass. Can you feel me, kitten? Do you feel your mates filling your body with their cocks?" Creed smiled when she hissed out a loud *yes*.

He slowly sank his cock all the way inside her dark heat, thrilling at the knowledge he was fucking his mate's ass and was about to mate mark her. His balls burned with the need to empty inside of her. The way his mate's ass tightened around him each time his brother's cock sank into her nearly made him shoot his load before he was ready.

He whispered dirty suggestions into her ear then relaxed his hold on her hair so she could rest her neck. Every quiver of her body vibrated along his shaft taking more of his control. Several times he had to concentrate to make his claws recede so he wouldn't scratch her skin. She was hell on his control and having her lynx so close to the surface trying to fight only added to his bear's anxiety. He wanted to subdue his mate not understanding that it was only the lynx who was fighting them. Serenity's human side wasn't protesting their dominance at all.

"Oh, God! Fuck me! Please. I need to come so bad!" Serenity's hoarse voice was all the prompting he needed to turn his concentration back to pleasing her by pulling out and sinking deep inside her again and again.

He and his brother took turns tunneling in and out of her perfect body as she bucked and moaned between them. Her lynx had not only stirred to life but was fighting to get out. He could feel her anger and arousal. The dual emotions were confusing her. He took advantage of her confusion and worked harder to make her come, pouring every ounce of energy into giving her what she needed without losing control and spilling his seed much too soon. She came first, always.

* * * *

Serenity was on fire and stuffed full of cock. When Shayne pulled back from the depths of her cunt, Creed tunneled deep into her ass. She swore she could feel them in her throat. They touched her in places no one had ever reached. Every nerve ending in her body seemed alive. The ones in her ass she'd not even known she had. How could her lynx not want this? It felt so damn good—too good. She could become addicted to having both of them connected to her like this.

The spring deep inside of her wound tighter and tighter with each thrust of their dicks and every touch of their mouth on her skin. They kissed and licked everywhere they could touch. The feel of their sharp teeth raking over her skin had her tightening every muscle in anticipation of their bite. She wanted them to bite her. She wanted to bite them again.

"Harder!" she screamed as her need to come and the pressure building made it more difficult for her to draw in a full breath.

Both males growled and pounded into her hard and fast just as she demanded. They wanted only to please her and give her what she needed. She instinctively knew that once she finally climaxes, they would follow her into their own. Then they would bite her and claim her as theirs once and for all.

"Baby, you're killing me." Shayne gasped as she tightened around his hard shaft. "I swear you've got muscles in that sweet pussy of yours. My dick is strangling inside of you."

She nearly laughed out loud at his words. Shayne would always make her smile, even when she was made about something. Serenity purposely contracted her inner walls around his thrusting cock and smiled at the almost painful look he gave her.

"Holly, hell!" Creed yelled. Her squeezing on Shayne had affected her other mate as he tried to pull out of her ass.

Creed jerked on her hair once more, causing her head to fall back. He leaned over her, his body caging her in, making her feel safe and loved. She enjoyed knowing that he would never let her go. She had ached for that sort of feeling for years. Deep down, she'd always known she needed someone to master her, but hadn't wanted to have her life dictated so she'd run. With Creed and Shayne, she knew they would never try and run her business or tell her how to dress, but they would set limits to keep her safe. That she could live with.

Her lynx snarled at her and swiped at her with her claws. Serenity expected to feel the pain of that swipe but instead, all she felt was the security of her males surrounding her. It felt good, right.

She felt one of them slip a hand down along her belly until they reached her pussy. A large callused finger located her clit and applied pressure in a tight circle over it. Lights exploded behind her eyes, blinding her as she squeezed them shut in a silent scream. A low roar filled her head, growing until all she could hear was the noise and her heart beat. She finally managed a gasp before she screamed out loud this time, bucking between them as her body convulsed with the sheer ecstasy of her climax. Nothing could ever compare to this. No one could ever give her what her mates gave her as they too shouted out then roared and each sank their teeth into her shoulders.

The swift change from pain to pleasure left her dizzy and triggered yet another orgasm from her already weak body. She barely had the energy to react as spasms of bliss filled her head and burned along her bloodstream. If drugs would work on them, she was sure this was how it felt to be on a high. She had no words, but her lynx sure did.

Claws exploded from her hands as she struggled to regain control of the she cat. The she cat was pissed and excited all at the same time.

Creed and Shayne reacted fast despite having just climaxed. While Creed shackled her wrists to the bed with his hands, Shayne held her face gently in his hands before leaning in and kissing her, mindful of the much larger sharp teeth protruding from her mouth. He licked at her lips then ran the tip of his tongue over one long tooth. Her cat shuddered.

"Easy, kitten. No one is going to hurt you. Relax for me," Creed crooned to the anxious lynx.

Serenity closed her eyes and tried to reason with the female. She needed her to back down, but didn't want to make demands in the state the cat was in. Instead, she tried to reason with her.

They are our mates. Don't hurt them. They would die for us and will provide for us.

The lynx didn't respond at first, but after another full minute of pleading with her while the men uttered soothing words and petted her with their mouths and hands, she retreated. Serenity's hands returned as did her normal teeth. Heaving out an exhausted sigh, she collapsed on Shayne's muscular chest and fell into an exhausted sleep.

* * * *

Even before she opened her eyes, Serenity's stomach growled like a mountain lion instead of the smaller lynx that she was. The soft chuckle next to her let her know that Shayne was awake and lying next to her. She slowly opened her eyes and found that Creed was on his side on the other side of her, one hand propping his head up as he watched her.

Her belly issued another threatening roar making Creed's normally quiet face brighten with mirth. It gave him an entirely different look. She liked seeing him smile or at least seem to smile. His eyes lightened a little and the normally tense lines around his eyes and mouth smoothed out some.

"I think that was a warning that if we didn't feed you there would be hell to pay," Creed said.

"My bear agrees that it's time to eat," Shayne said, more than making up for Creed's less jovial attitude. "Do we look for something here or give them our thanks and head out?"

Both males turned and looked at her as if she held the answer to the decision. Serenity didn't know what to think. They were leaving it up to her. She hadn't expected that.

"Um, maybe it would be a good idea to find our own place while I'm relaxed," she told them.

Creed frowned. "Are you saying it isn't over with?"

She winced inwardly. At least she hoped it was inwardly. "Ah, no. My heat normally lasts a week. Five days at the least. It's only been two or maybe three days, right?"

"Probably three since you seemed to have been off the day before as well. You were so hungry and slept a lot," Shayne pointed out.

"Okay. Let's get dressed and locate Locke. We'll find a place to eat then a hotel to hold up in for a few more days," Creed said as he rolled off the other side of the bed.

"I'll take a shower. I'm sure I need one," Serenity said feeling her face heat at the thought of what she must look like by then.

"Only if you want to take one, baby. We cleaned you up last night though, so you're nice and clean." Shayne smiled at her before he too sat up and began pulling on his jeans.

"I–I don't remember bathing," she said.

"Honey, you were dead to the world. Nothing short of a nuclear disaster would have woken you up. I'm not even sure if that would have," Creed teased, that hint of a smile still evident at the corner of his mouth.

"Oh."

"Come on babe. Let's get you dressed." Shayne reached out with on hand to help her slide over to the edge of the bed.

While a fully dressed Creed used his cell to contact Locke, Shayne helped her dress. She chose sweats since most everything else felt scratchy on her skin now. That would go away once her heat had passed. She didn't bother with underwear. It would have irritated her and made her squirm. She tolerated the sandals on her feet but wanted them off as soon as they found a place to stay.

"Okay, Locke is securing a place for us for a few days and will pick us up in thirty minutes. Abba and her mate Leon are back and have prepared a meal for us. I thought it might tide you over until Locke gets here," Creed told them.

Serenity couldn't help but feel uncomfortable about meeting the two wild dogs who'd taken them in then left their own house to give them privacy. It was more than generous of them when not only where they strangers, but also not wild dogs. She would make sure to send them a nice gift once they returned home.

Home. She stopped dead in her tracks before they made it through the door. She realized that her home had officially changed locations now. Her cat swished her tail in irritation.

"What's wrong?" Creed asked when she stopped in front of him.

"I was just realizing that everything has changed for me. I guess it's just now sinking in."

"Don't think about it right now, honey. We've got plenty of time for you to worry about it. I know you're going to. Females worry about everything," he said.

"Creed," Shayne sighed. "That's not the best way to help her relax."

Serenity drew in a deep breath and put it all away for the moment. Despite Shayne's comment, Creed was right. There was plenty of time to worry about her future after they got past this meal and maybe even after her heat was past.

"How are you feeling?" a warm throaty voice interrupted her musings. The voice was attached to a tall female of about fifty with long, flowing black and gray hair that reached her waist.

"I'm fine. Starving but doing well, thank you. I can't thank you enough for helping us," she said smiling at the other female.

"It is fine. We were happy to help. I've only seen something like what had happened to you once before and knew immediately the trouble. I'm glad it is working out for you," the wild dog said with a smile. "Now. I have a meal on the table. My mate is putting the finishing touches on the meat now."

They followed her through the living are into a large eat-in kitchen with plenty of room for everyone and some left over. The table had to seat twelve at the very least, Serenity thought. She wondered if she had a large family and if they visited often. It would be such a waste and a sad reminder to have such a huge table and it never was filled.

"Meat's ready. Let's eat. I'm starved." A male wild dog who stood maybe an inch shorter than his mate stepped into the kitchen from another door that seemed to lead outside. He had a huge serving platter piled high with steaks.

"Have a seat, everyone. We don't want the food to get cold," Abba said with a broad smile.

Once they'd all taken their seats, the wild dogs began passing around the food. Serenity felt more like a hog than a lynx with the amount of food she ate, but it was obviously a symptom of her heat. Before, she'd get hungry more often and seem to sleep a little more, but this had been a thousand times worse than before. Abba had told her it was because her mating claim had not been completed when she'd gone into heat. The fact that she had two mates instead of one played into it as well, she had said.

Locke had shown up not long after they'd begun eating and as soon as they were finished, they helped clean up then thanked them once again for their generosity and help before climbing back into the truck.

"The hotel isn't far from here. I got a suite with adjoining rooms," Locke informed them. "I also made sure they had the fridge stocked with plenty of snack foods. Otto says everything is well back at the den. They've had no problems with hunters and none have been seen since you left."

"Do you think he's given up now that he knows she's already mated to us?" Shayne asked Lock.

"Who?" she asked, looking from Creed to Shayne and up to Lock's gaze in the rearview mirror. "What are you talking about?"

"We need to talk about the hunters and why they've been after you, honey. As soon as we've gotten settled in at the hotel, we'll talk," Creed promised her.

She felt the growing heat between her legs again and wasn't so sure they would get around to talking just yet. Her clit throbbed and her pussy lips felt swollen and achy. A few warning tremors began in her low belly, telling her she wasn't finished with it yet.

"I don't know. It's possible he will back off, but I doubt it. I think there's too much at stake for him to let her go if there's even a chance he can get her to produce his heirs through his son," Lock told them grimly.

"I–I don't think I like the sound of that. You're talking about my old Rufus, aren't you?" she said.

"Yes, but let us tell it all to you at one time. Just giving you bits and pieces will only be confusing." Creed's face had returned to his normal stoic look.

They pulled into a nicer end motel chain and parked only a few spots from the front door. When they all got out, each of the three males grabbed luggage then she was surrounded as they entered the front doors. Locke led them directly to the elevator which took them to the fifth floor. Their rooms were less than twenty feet from the lift. She'd been fighting her heat in earnest for the last ten minutes. She knew the males could tell by the way all three of them kept scenting the air with straining nostrils.

The knowledge that Locke smelled her need as well only ramped up her nervousness and that gave the mating heat ride her stronger.

Gritting her teeth, Serenity forced herself to keep a relaxed expression on her face as they entered the main door to the suite.

"We'll take the left side," Creed said ushering her in that direction.

"I'll be in my room if you need me," Locke said. "Don't go anywhere outside of the room without letting me know. I'm fairly sure we haven't been followed, but I'd feel better if we all stuck together."

"I agree. We'll let you know if we plan to go downstairs for any reason," Creed told him.

The second they were inside their room with the door closed and locked, Creed and Shayne began undressing while their eyes never left her. She knew they were reacting to her scent and the need her cat was projecting.

"I thought we were going to talk," she said without moving from where she stood just inside the room.

Creed stalked toward her completely nude and obviously comfortable that way. Her eyes were drawn to the jutting erection between his legs. Serenity couldn't help licking her lips as she watched it bob as he strutted toward her.

"We'll talk once you're sated. I can feel your need, kitten. You're in pain and as long as you're uncomfortable, my bear is going to insist on taking care of you first. Get used to it," he said.

Before she realized what he planned to do, Creed had her shirt over her head and was bending over to suck on her nipple. Large hands tugged on her sweatpants from behind, startling her so that she lost her balance. Creed quickly grabbed her upper arms in an easy hold, keeping her from falling.

With his mouth sucking on her nipple, she couldn't think. The pleasure shot straight to her clit where it built into something almost frightening in its intensity. When he nipped her she screamed then bit into her fist to keep from doing it again as Shayne nipped an ass cheek before licking over it with his raspy tongue.

They're going to kill me. I can't take both of them doing things to me at the same time.

But they weren't giving her much choice. When she tried to wiggle away from them to climb on the bed, both males held her still as they continued to attack her with their tongues and teeth. Pleasure had never been so nerve-wracking before. Serenity wanted to scream for them to stop at the same time she wanted to beg them to never stop.

"I can't get enough of your sweet breasts, kitten. You taste warm and sweet. I could make a meal off of you. And your cream, it's like a tart desert right out of the oven, all warm and tasty." Creed went to his knees and buried his face in her belly

Shayne growled and pulled her from Creed's embrace, picking her up and carrying her to the king-size bed. He gently laid her down before kneeling on the bed and positioning himself between her legs.

"I've got to taste you, baby. I need to taste your sweet pussy now," Shayne said. "I can smell you and it's driving me and my bear crazy."

Before she had time to answer him, he'd shimmed his shoulders between her thighs and was kissing all around her pussy. The first swipe of his tongue drew a soft squeal from her. He continued to lap at her as if he couldn't get enough. Every time he circled her clit without touching it she tried to move her hips to drag him across the tingling bud. Shayne just chuckled, sending more sparks to her clit in the process.

"Stop teasing me!" she screamed.

Her body was already on fire and she was beginning to cramp in her belly now. She wasn't going to be able to tolerate foreplay with the way her heat was riding her. Right now she needed them to fuck her, not play with her.

Creed crawled onto the bed and knelt next to her head, his big hand fisting the base of his shaft in a tight grip. She watched as he slowly pulled up the long, thick stalk before pulling back down again.

"Do you want to suck my dick, honey?" he asked with a heavy-lidded gaze.

"Please, Creed. I want to taste you."

"Open wide, Serenity." He lowered his hand and let the crown settle lightly on her tongue.

Serenity instantly closed her lips around it and sucked, rubbing her tongue over the slit to taste his essence. Tart and tangy, she licked, hoping for more.

"That's it, kitten. That feels so good."

She took more of him as he slowly fed his cock to her. When he bumped the back of her throat, she relaxed it and forced herself to take a little more. When she swallowed around the thick head, he cursed and fisted her hair in one of his hands.

"So fucking good, Serenity. One more time. Just once more, honey." He pulled back then thrust back into her as she wrapped her tongue around the shaft then swallowed when he nudged the back of her throat.

His hoarse cry let her know he liked it, but he pulled out and gripped the base tightly. His harsh pants proved he was having trouble remaining in control. Her heat was affecting them as much as it affected her. Shayne wasn't slowing down as he sucked on her pussy lips before thrusting a thick finger deep into her hot, wet pussy.

"Move, Shayne. I need to be inside of her. She's just about taken all of my control," Creed said with a low growl.

Shayne gave one last lick up her pussy before moving over to let his brother take his place. Serenity was almost beyond reasoning with the need to be filled. Her lynx was clawing at her insides for more. She wanted to mark her mates again, and she'd start with Creed.

She watched through slitted eyes as he rubbed the head of his dick up and down her pussy slit, wetting it with her juices. When he slowly began to enter her, relief seemed to seep through her skin and into her bones. His thick cock pushed through swollen tissues, scratching the itch that had begun all over again.

"Yes. Please, Creed. I need more," she cried out.

He pulled out then surged back in, going deep and bumping her cervix. The pleasure-pain was perfect. She moaned and reached up to hold on to his shoulders as he slowly increased his pace, pumping into her harder and faster until Serenity wasn't sure she would live through the climax he'd set into place. She had no doubt it would be massive. Every nerve ending in her body seemed to light up as he thrust deep over and over.

Shayne hadn't been able to resist playing with her breasts as Creed shafted in and out of her making the rounded globes bounce with each thrust. Shayne held them while he moved from one to the other, sucking and nipping at her nipples, leaving reddened marks on the sides where he sucked and bit them.

"Holy hell, Shayne. I can't hold on much longer. She's so damn tight," Creed snarled.

Shayne reached between them and fingered her clit, rubbing a callused finger over it then pinching it so that she exploded into a million pieces. Her scream was muffled by Shayne's mouth as he took her scream and kissed her. She pulled away from him and lifted up to grab at Creed as he began to empty his seed into her with his climax. Serenity stared up at him then sank her teeth into his shoulder, making sure it would show to anyone who questioned that he belonged to her.

Chapter Nineteen

Shayne growled deep in his chest as their mate marked his brother again. His bear wanted her to mark him as well and was pushing for Shayne to shove the other bear out of the way. He barely managed to restrain himself as his bear snapped his teeth and growled inside. He'd get his turn. Right now their mate needed rest.

Creed kissed and cuddled their mate before rolling off of her and lying next to the little lynx. It hit him again that she was so small compared to their bears. They needed to be more careful of her, but she stole his concentration when he was inside of her. There was just something about their little cat that sent every good intention out the door.

"Shayne. I need you," Serenity said, turning to stare up at him. "Please."

God she knotted his heart up when she did that. He wanted to kiss her senseless when she looked at him with such longing like she was now. Not five minutes ago, she had he fangs deep in his brother's shoulder yet now she wanted him there with her.

"Rest, baby. We've got plenty of time," he said kissing her lightly on the forehead.

"My cat's still horny and the heat hasn't receded yet. Please, Shayne. I need you."

He smiled and rolled her over on top of him. He wasn't going to make her suffer and his dick was hard as steel from tasting her honeyed cream earlier. The promise left unsaid in the air that she would claim him again as she had his brother had him and his bear restless and needy.

"Whatever you need then, sweetness. I'll do anything to make you happy," he promised her as he stared up into her gorgeous green eyes.

She shifted over him so that her blazing hot pussy rasped over his shaft as she slowly moved back and forth, spreading her juices across his dick. The friction was almost more than he could take, but he resisted the urge to grab her and thrust up into her hot, wet cunt. This was for her, and he'd let her take him anyway she wanted him.

Right now, it seemed she wanted to torture him by rubbing that perfect pussy all over his aching cock. It twitched with each pass of her clit across the rim of the bulbous head. The more she rubbed and stimulated herself on him the more he had to fight to keep his hands from grabbing her. He wanted to play with her breasts, but was too worried that he'd screw up and take back the control he'd allowed her.

"Fuck, baby. You're killing me. Have mercy and sheath my dick in your tight pussy. I'm begging you," he said, only half joking.

She laughed and the sound had his heart pumping with joy. His bear panted to hear that wonderful sound again. She completed him and completed their sleuth. She'd be the bridge between him and his brother, her calming balance soothing his brother's need to dominate all and his constant battle to get his brother to relax some and allow him to help. He was sure she would lure Creed into giving her more of his time which would let Shayne do more of his own job.

Her strong independence was a blessing as well. She didn't need them to keep her entertained while they created their home and strengthened their sleuth. She would have her work to keep her occupied while interrupting them to make sure they followed her preferences for the den and took breaks.

I can already feel myself falling in love with her. How could anyone resist someone so strong and fierce? I bet Creed is fighting the need to tell her as well.

"Oh, God, you feel so good. You're so thick and hard, Shayne. I want you inside of me."

Her words couldn't have come at a better time. He was ready to plead with his mate. He helped her lift up while she positioned his straining cock at her entrance. When she slowly sank down to suck him inside of her, Shayne snarled and growled, throwing his head back as he did. Thank God it didn't scare her. Instead, she did the same, wiggling her ass as she slowly slipped down his already slick shaft, surrounding him with her wet heat. Nothing had ever felt this good. He was certain of it.

Serenity moved up and down as she struggled to engulf him with her swollen cunt. It made her so much tighter than he remembered and worried he wouldn't be able to last long enough for her to reach her climax.

Every time she moved on him, Shayne had to grit his teeth to keep from yelling out. It felt that damn good.

The second she finally made it all the way down his dick to rest against his pelvis and thighs, they both breathed out a sigh of relief. He wasn't sure he could handle much more of her sensuous torture. The gentle massage of her inner walls was enough to have him on the edge of blowing his wad right then and there.

"I'm so close," she whispered out in a husky voice. "I don't want to come yet. I want it to last."

"Let it go, babe. We've got all the time in the world. We'll fuck you till you can't walk if you'll let us," he told her with a strained chuckle.

Please put me out of my misery.

As if she'd heard his silent plea, Serenity pulled up off of him, nearly allowing him to slip completely out of her, before dropping fast and hard back down his rod.

"Holy hell!" he rasped out.

She did it over and over until Shayne couldn't stand it any longer. He would make it up to her later. He promised he would. But this was too much for him or his bear to stand. He rolled them over and immediately she wrapped her legs around his waist as he shafted in and out of her in desperation. His balls had long sense drawn up in anticipation of emptying his seed deep inside of her.

Every time his cock disappeared inside her hot cunt, he felt as if his eyes were going to roll out of his head. How could this little female lynx completely tie him up inside this way? No female had ever had this effect on him and he was sure that he'd never seen his brother even half this obsessed with one.

"Harder, Shayne. Fuck me hard and fast. I'm so close," she whimpered.

Shayne didn't hesitate one second. She was shifter just like him. She could handle all of him. He powered in and out of her, hitting her cervix with nearly ever piston of his shaft. When he didn't think he'd last one more stroke, she exploded around him, screaming and snarling, milking his dick with her orgasm. When she sank her elongated teeth into his shoulder, Shayne was positive he saw stars as he erupted in jets of semen deep within her cunt. Nothing had ever felt so right to him. He felt the three way bond completely cerement even though they'd already completed the mating earlier. This felt tighter than steel-encased concrete.

"What in the hell was that?" Creed snarled climbing closer to them to look at their mate.

"I–I don't know. It felt like you both tugged on something inside my chest. It was really weird feeling," Serenity said in a hoarse voice as she panted in an effort to catch her breath again.

"That's what if felt like to me, too," Shayne agreed. "Like something strummed a string between us so that it vibrated."

"Are you okay, honey?" Creed asked her, brushing a strand of hair from her cheek.

Shayne loved seeing the broad smile that brightened her entire face. "Yes. I'm better than okay."

Creed's face lit up as well. Shayne had never been this happy in his entire life. They had a mate and she made them both very happy.

* * * *

Serenity stretched and rolled to her stomach. Her males had gone out to the shared living area to raid the fridge for something to eat. She was ravenous and needed to eat. Then she wanted a nap. It was a cycle she was familiar with from her previous heats, but this one had been much stronger, something she hadn't been prepared for.

Then it hit her, they needed to talk. Her mates had something important she needed to know. It dampened her mood some since she knew it wouldn't be good. Now that they were mated, she could feel them inside of her like two very distinct message boards that alerted her to their moods and feelings. She knew if she pushed, she could feel more than that, but she didn't want them pushing at her that way so she refrained.

What was going on that they needed to talk to her about it? It had to involve her so it must be about the hunters after her. If they knew why and still wanted to be mated to her, then it couldn't be something she'd done wrong without realizing it. What could be so important that they would come after her in such a remote location? It was why she'd chosen the little community in the first place.

She thought about the e-mail from her brother and wondered if it had something to do with his fears or not. Could it all be connected? She wanted to check her e-mail again and see if he'd written her back, but would have to wait on that. First she wanted to find out what her two males had learned.

When they returned a few minutes later with their hands full, she laughed and jumped up from the bed to help them with it. Creed closed the door with his foot then let her take the large carton of chocolate milk from him before he dropped it.

"Mmmm, milk! Locke ordered all of this, didn't he? I have to remember to give him a hug and thank him for remembering my milk," she said with a wink at Shayne.

"You don't need to hug him," Creed snarled.

"Sure I do. He's part of my sleuth. I'm going to hug all of my bears every chance I get."

"Serenity! Where did you get that name anyway? You are anything but serene or serene inspiring," Creed snapped with a low growl to his voice.

She laughed and threw her arms around him. "My dad asked my mom why she named me that nearly every day I lived at home."

"I bet we could talk a long time about you," Shayne teased.

"I'm not that bad," she said with a sniff, throwing her nose in the air.

"Yes, you are," both bears said at the same time.

"You create chaos wherever you go, baby. But we love you anyway," Shayne told her.

"You do?" She stilled, realizing what he'd said. Had it been a figure of speech or did he truly love her? What of Creed?

Shayne seemed to have realized what he'd said and froze as well. Creed looked anywhere but at her. Had she jumped the gun and put them on the spot when they weren't ready? Why had she said anything?

Because I can't stop my big mouth from getting me into trouble. My cat has to know everything and know it immediately.

Shayne was the first to recover. He walked around the edge of the bed where she'd sat down with her carton of chocolate milk. Kneeling in front of her he took her face in his hands, staring into her eyes.

"I love you, Serenity. I hadn't expected it to happen so fast, but I guess I couldn't resist your quirky attitude and the way you insist that you can do it all yourself. You complete us and you make me very happy. My bear is happier than if he had an entire jar full of honey all to himself." Shayne bent forward and kissed her gently on the lips.

Before he could stand back up, Creed had walked over and stood over him. His normally serious face seemed even more so in that moment. She was afraid he was going to tell her it was too soon for him.

"Honey, I've loved you from the moment I smelled your enticing scent our first night at the house. I haven't even tried to fight it because I knew you were the one for us. I just haven't wanted to show it so much since I knew you could still refuse us and walk away. Now that we've mated, I don't mind telling the world that you're the love of my life."

She snapped her mouth closed. It had fallen open at his very first words. *I've loved you from the moment I smelled your enticing scent*...It was too much. She felt tears trail from her eyes to her cheeks. What had she done to deserve two such wonderful mates?.

"I think this is the place where you tell us that you love us, too, babe. How about putting us out of our misery, here," Shayne drawled.

She chuckled and wiped at the wetness on her face. "I love you both. I think I've loved you since I laid eyes on you, but I was so scared of losing my independence. I'm still scared of that, but I know you'll work with me on it. I'm not giving up my business though so get that out of your heads!"

She could tell by their indulgent smiles that they weren't planning on taking that away from her, but would still keep her close to them any way they had to. She sure hoped it involved sex. Her tummy growled loud and long making all of them chuckle.

"Let's feed you before you eat us," Creed said. "We can talk while we eat."

And just like that, her good mood soured a bit again. Still, nothing would take away the fact that Creed and Shayne loved her. She believed them, too. They had looked so solemn when they'd said it then grinned like it was the best thing since honey-covered chocolate cake. Well, she'd made that up but figured honey-covered anything would be good to them. In that instant a naughty idea came to her, one she'd have to plan on trying in the near future. Honey-covered cock sounded so delicious.

"Here you go, babe. Dig in." Shayne handed her an opened roast beef sandwich. He emptied a large bag of chips in a bowl on the bed and the three of them began eating.

"There's plenty more sandwiches here when you get ready for another one, honey," Creed told her.

"What is it we need to talk about?" she asked as she nodded at him.

Creed took a deep breath and set what was left of the sandwich down on the wrapper it came in. He let the air out with a heavy whoosh before wiping his hands on a napkin. His face had returned to its normally tense expression and his eyes seemed so much colder again. She mourned the loss of lightness that had been in the air less than a second earlier.

"The hunters were hired by your old Rufus to track you down and take you back to him. They aren't on a sanctioned hunt. They're acting as bounty hunters now," he told her.

"What? But why now? I'm much more off the radar now than I've ever been. I mean while I was in school, he could have found me so much easier." She couldn't wrap her head around this. It didn't make sense. Her brother had been right. It was all about her.

"Somehow he found out about an old prophesy that involves you, Serenity. If you were mated to his son as he planned, you would be under his control and therefore, he would have ended up a very powerful lynx." He hesitated. "In theory."

"What does the prophecy say and why would anyone think I was part of it?" she asked looking from Shayne back to Creed, still unconvinced.

"You are the last female descendent left of the royals who were once in charge of dispensing justice for all shifters whether wolf, bear, or feline before The Awakening. The prophecy was given by the last advisor for the last ruling family before they dispersed."

"The last family was wolf shifters, and their advisor was a wolf shifter as well," Serenity said absently. She still couldn't understand how she, a lynx, would be mixed up in this.

"That's right. They knew there would come a time when a ruling family would once again be needed. Evidently that time is close at hand," Shayne said.

"I don't understand. What do you mean?" she asked.

"Eat, Serenity. You need to keep up your strength. You're already getting sleepy. If you fall asleep without eating enough, you'll just end up sick again," Creed said. "I won't continue until you finish that sandwich."

"Stop it. I'm not some wayward child!" she snapped back at him then instantly regretted it.

"Shhh, honey. I know that, but you're too worried about what we're telling you to pay attention to what your body needs right now. As your mate, it is one of my duties to protect you," Creed said.

"From starving myself?" she asked with a weak smile.

He grinned back at her. "Yes, even from that. Now eat up."

Serenity sighed and took another bite of the sandwich. In truth, it was very good. She wasn't much for sandwiches, but the meat for these hadn't come from a processed deli pack. It was freshly carved rare beef that all but melted in her mouth. In less than a minute she'd devoured the remainder of the sandwich.

Shayne grinned and unwrapped another one for her. "Here you go."

"I'm eating, keep talking," she said, taking a bite for emphasis.

"The prophecy says that the last living female of the royal house would bear the sons of her mates, and they would one day rule over all shifters to assure their continued. In other words," Creed finished. "Her sons would create the new ruling family and put an end to the need for human hunters."

Shaking her head she just looked at them. How did any of this affect her? Why would her old Rufus need her? It wasn't lost on her that the prophecy said *her mates,* meaning more than one. That was a coincidence since she had just met them at the same time the hunters had shown up. That of itself was a huge coincidence as well.

"The prophecy said mates, as in more than one. If I mated his son, the prophecy wouldn't come true since there would only be him."

"He evidently planned to mate you with another of his choosing as well," Creed snarled.

"I still don't get it. What has this got to do with me? I'm a lynx, not a wolf. I wouldn't be a descendent, much less the last one. Why is the Rufus after me when I'm obviously not related to the ruling family?" she asked again.

"But you are," Shayne said. "Your mother's mother was the daughter of the last remaining royal of the family. That royal was a lynx."

Chapter Twenty

Shock poured through Serenity's bloodstream. Nothing they might have suggested or revealed could have possibly prepared her for this.

"I–I don't understand. The last royal family was made up entirely of wolves. I remember the old stories. My parents told them to all of us many times."

"From what we've been able to piece together by talking to your parents," Creed began.

Serenity gasped. "You've talked to my parents? When?"

Unease replaced the shock with a cold oozing pain that they'd gone behind her back to talk with her family. Had her Rufus not already known where she was, their contacting her family would have instantly alerted him of her location. They were under a compulsion by him as their Rufus to report her whereabouts anytime they found out. It was why she didn't tell her brother where she was, only that she was okay and what was going on in her life.

"I'm sorry, precious," Shayne said. "We found out that it was your old Rufus who'd sent the hunters after you and needed to find out how best to protect you."

"Why didn't you tell me you were going to talk to them?" she demanded. "I would have loved to talk to them."

"I'm sorry, honey. At the time we were so upset and shocked that a shifter would send hunters after one of their own that we panicked and started trying to find out what we could before we realized it would hurt you to go behind your back." Creed looked genuinely sorry and distressed over what they'd done, but at that moment she couldn't think straight. All she knew was that it hurt.

"Once we'd found out about the prophecy, we planned to tell you all about it, but you were gone," Shayne said.

"That's not entirely true," Creed said looking over at his brother.

She looked from one to the other again. She realized that Creed planned to be completely honest with her even if it looked poorly on him. Shayne sighed.

"I decided to talk to the other shifter leaders to find out what they knew about the prophecy. I'd never heard of it before, but I haven't been a leader long. My father hadn't passed it down to me, so I don't know if he didn't know about it or if he just didn't believe it. Either way, it was something I didn't feel comfortable asking about over the phone. I went to talk to them before I came to look for you." Creed's expression appeared contrite and worried.

"Once we realized you were missing, it hit home that we should have told you from the beginning and allowed you to be right there with us as we learned everything that we did," Shayne said.

"Why didn't you?" she asked.

"I think we were subconsciously protecting you, kitten. To begin with, we weren't sure if your parents were in on it or not. We had no idea what your relationship was with your parents at the time. Plus, we didn't know if having you back home wouldn't make them feel better knowing you were safe from other, outside forces. This prophecy will bring down not only other shifters, but the humans as well. Without the need for hunters, their legalized sport of hunting shifters will no longer be allowed or tolerated," Creed said.

"Regardless of the reason, baby, we were wrong to keep it from you and are sorry. We never meant to hurt you. We only wanted to protect you. It's part of who we are as bears and as your mates," Shayne told her.

She watched both males knowing they truly hadn't meant to hurt her and were only looking out for her best interests. Still, it bothered her that they would do something like this again. She wanted to be sure they knew it wouldn't be a good idea to keep things from her.

"I have to be able to trust the two of you not to keep things from me. I can't be in a relationship where I am always wondering if you're telling me the truth or hiding something from me. I'm not a child or a fragile human. Don't do this again or we're going to have a problem with our mating," she said in a quiet voice. From the look on their faces, she didn't think it would be a problem in the future.

"Never again, mate. I promise you we will never hide anything from you again," Creed said.

"Except for maybe birthday parties or gifts," Shayne said in all seriousness.

Creed popped him over the head and growled.

"What?" he asked rubbing his head. "I don't want there to be any questions. I'm going to get her surprises and so are you."

"Shayne, you are certifiable," she said laughing. Then she sobered and turned back to Creed. "How am I related? I don't remember there being any felines in the royal family except in the beginning. After a few hundred years, only wolves ruled."

"That's true, but right after the royals stepped down and the throne was disassembled, so to speak, the young prince met his true mate, your great, great, great grandmother, and a lynx. The story is that she was actually a descendant of the last original member of the last lynx in the royal family, but we don't know that for certain," Creed explained. "What we do know is that you are the result through your mother."

"Why wasn't mom considered to be the one?" she asked.

"She only has one mate," Shayne reminded her.

"But she could end up with another mate at some point in the future," she argued.

"True, but our thoughts are that she is no longer able to have kits and that is what triggered the prophecy to be revealed. Without asking your mother that question, we won't know for certain if that is why or not, but we think it might be." Shayne watched her closely.

"She had a lot of trouble when she had me and I'm the youngest. My youngest brother is less than a year older than I am. I was a surprise," she admitted. "So, it is a possibility. But how did my old Rufus find out about it? Why would he have even put me into the equation in the first place?"

"We don't know. It's one of the mysteries we need to clear up. Our first priority though is taking care of you through your heat and keeping you safe. That is why Locke will never leave us. If not him, then Otto. One of them will always be close at hand," Creed told her. "So get used to it. They are your guard, though the entire sleuth will protect you with their lives."

"I don't want anyone to get hurt protecting me. I can fight for myself," she said, narrowing her eyes.

Shayne spoke up before his brother could. She had a feeling she wouldn't have liked what Creed had to say anyway.

"We know you can, but remember, you will have cubs to watch out for. You're priority is to stay alive and take care of them," he said.

Her eyes few open. Cubs? Kits? What?

"Um, honey. You do realize that there is almost a hundred percent chance that you will become pregnant during your heat, right?" Creed asked with a half-hidden smile.

"Um, yes. I guess I just hadn't really thought about it," she said.

She yawned and stretched, her back arching as she did. Suddenly she was exhausted and with everything she'd just learned, her mind was just as tired.

"Looks like nap time, baby." Shayne began picking up the trash and leftover food from the bed.

Creed scooped her up in his arms and shoved back the blankets before depositing her in the middle and covering her back up again. She pried her eyes open to frown up at him.

"Shhh, we'll be right back. Shayne's putting up the food and I'm going to check in with Locke to be sure everything is okay back at the den. We'll both be right back, kitten. Sleep." Creed kissed her cheek then her nose before standing up to look down at her. It was the last thing she remembered before she slipped into sleep.

* * * *

By the time her heat had passed, Serenity was ready to climb the walls. They had spent three entire days and nights at the hotel in the bedroom. She'd rarely even made it out of the bed, taking long relaxing baths and eating being her only reprieves from either fucking or sleeping. Now, she felt much better, more herself without the heat riding her nonstop. She prayed she didn't have to deal with it again for several more years.

Then she thought about the fact that she was probably pregnant and wondered how she was going to adjust to that. In that moment, she desperately wanted to see her mother. It pulled at her so hard that she turned to Shayne as they descended in the elevator of the hotel with tears in her eyes.

"What is it, baby?" he asked pulling her into his arms.

Lock stepped closer to the door, blocking it in case they stopped somewhere before reaching the ground floor.

"I want to see my mother," she confessed.

"Shhh, baby. We'll get you to see her. Relax and let's get home first. Then we can make plans for that." Shayne hugged her tight.

When the doors slid open, they all got off after Locke checked around them. The quick trip outside and across the parking lot was made without incident. Yet Serenity had a feeling that there was someone there watching them. She started to say something to her mates, but the feeling disappeared and they were rushing her into the truck. With Shayne kissing her as he buckled her in, she quickly forgot that she had anything to say.

While Creed rode up front with Locke to discuss security changes, Shayne cuddled with her in the back. Despite all the rest she'd gotten, Serenity was still tired. She suspected it had more to do with the heavy burden she felt resting on her shoulders than having just come off her heat cycle.

The fact that she was going to bear the sons who would one day restart the royal ruling families scared her a bit. Maybe most shifters would celebrate the fact that they would produce the ruling family, but all Serenity could see was the constant worry and fear for her children's safety and happiness. How could they grow up content and normally if they were always going to be at risk? All she had ever wanted in her life was to be normal and have a normal family like any other shifter.

From the very beginning she'd known the way they lived hadn't been right. She just hadn't known how it was wrong. Now, she had found her mates and had a chance at a family of her own and the past had come back to bite her. Instead of the overbearing cruel Rufus of her den dictating every part of her life, she was going to have two mates who were bears trying to keep her and her children safe in a world where both shifters and humans might want them dead.

"What are you thinking so hard about?" Shayne asked her sometime later.

She sighed and closed her eyes for a few seconds. "I just can't believe that after everything in my past, I'm still going to have to look over my shoulder to be sure no one is waiting to grab me or our offspring. I'd hoped for some semblance of a quiet life."

Shayne grinned. "Quiet? With you? Never. You're full of fire, baby. You would never have been able to lead a quiet life if you wanted to."

"Shayne's right, honey. You're a fighter. With me as one of your mates, there would have always been fireworks in our den."

"I'm looking forward to the makeup sex," Shayne admitted without shame.

"You don't get to participate in makeup sex if you didn't participate in the fight, little brother," Creed said with a twinkle in his eye.

There was a choking sound from the driver's seat. "Did you just tease Shayne?"

Creed frowned at Locke. "What?"

"It's just that I've never heard you tease like that before. It caught me off guard," he said.

"Get used to it, Locke, our Ursus has learned to relax a bit, thanks to our Ursa," Shayne told him.

"I can't wait for the others to hear this," Locke said with a snort.

"Just as long as you don't forget that I'm still in charge," Creed rumbled loud enough that the hair on the back of Serenity's neck stood up.

"Hey! Tone it down some, bro. You're upsetting our mate," Shayne protested, shaking himself.

Creed didn't look the least bit apologetic to his brother, but he looked over at Serenity and grinned before returning to his earlier conversation with Locke. It touched her that he had wanted her to know it wasn't aimed at her so much as it was for the others' benefit.

She began to recognize some of the landscape thinking that it felt as if she'd been gone forever and not less than a week. Creed had been on the phone almost nonstop since they'd left the hotel, actually needing to plug in his charger about an hour ago. She felt guilty that they'd gotten so far behind with whatever businesses they had because of her running away.

I just didn't think I had an option though. I never dreamed my lynx would back down with the help of my heat. Of course my heat had never been as intense as that before either.

"Looks like we're almost home, baby," Shayne said pulling her close to him once more.

"Shouldn't we duck down or something so they won't know that I'm staying with you?" she asked, looking around as they entered the main part of town. She remembered the feeling she'd had earlier and worried that she should have said something to the men.

Creed looked back at them, holding the phone over his chest to mute his words. "Don't worry about that anymore, honey. I sent a message to your old Rufus that you were mated and protected by us and that any further attempt at taking you would be met with force all the way back to his territory."

She gasped, her eyes, as well as her mouth, flying wide open at that. "What do you mean? When did you do that?"

He smiled. "I mean just what I said. We'll kill anyone who threatens you and if necessary, we'll go to the source of the danger and take care of him as well. I don't think anyone in your old den would mourn his loss. Do you?"

She just stared at him as he returned to the phone. He hadn't answered her question of when he had contacted the Rufus of her old den. Had it been before or after they'd talked? She turned her narrowed gaze to Shayne and lifted one brow.

"Well?" she asked.

Shayne looked puzzled for a second then understanding dawned and he sighed. It was obvious that she wasn't going to like the answer one damn bit. Where had their promises gone to not make decisions that concerned her without talking them over with her first?

"While you were soaking and we were catching up with Locke. He wanted to be sure there was no danger when we went back home again. You have to understand, Serenity, that if it involves your safety, we're not going to delay something to talk to you first," Shayne said.

"You didn't even talk to me afterward!" she snarled back.

"Serenity. That's enough, honey. You're bleeding all over poor Locke while he's trying to drive," Creed said with an indulgent appearing smile.

"What?" she asked, having no idea what he was talking about.

"Your power, babe. You're making it hard for him to concentrate because you're upset and all he wants to do is make it okay again," Shayne explained.

"I don't have any power," she protested.

"Yes, you do," Shayne and Creed said at the same time.

"You've always been a very strong alpha female, but now that you're our mate, you have the power of being Ursa of the sleuth as well," Creed told her, then nodded at Shayne to finish as he returned to his call.

"It will take you a while to learn to temper it so you don't bleed power into everyone every time you get upset or excited or anything. It's how the others will know that you need them and how you can control them if or when they get unruly or are going to do something you don't think they need to do," Shayne explained.

She sat still for a few moments thinking about what Shayne had said and what it meant. Then she just concentrated on feeling and being aware of everything around her. She hadn't felt any different since their mating was complete, but now that she was concentrating and searching, she could feel the other bears as if they were right there in the truck with them. She couldn't hear their thoughts or anything like that, but she felt their energies and some of their feelings as well. Each of them had a different energy signature so that once she got to know them, she'd know who was who just like that. It was a little disconcerting.

"Okay. We can talk more about that later. Right now, I want to know what is going on with my old den and we've got to come to an understanding about anything concerning me. I won't just lie down and let you control my life, Shayne," she said making a great effort to keep her tone and emotions as even as possible.

The big goofball grinned widely at her. "Very good! You barely sent out power at all that time. Keep practicing."

She popped him on the back of the head and growled, focusing her *power* solely on him. "Don't patronize me or ignore what I'm talking about."

He chuckled, but winced, obviously feeling her ire. "I'm sorry, baby. You're just so cute. Wait!" He threw up his hand to stop her from focusing on him again. "You're right. We should have talked to you about it after Creed made the call, but you were exhausted and we didn't want to overwhelm you."

Serenity sighed. "Please talk to me about anything that concerns me. Don't make snap decisions without at least telling me what you plan to do. I'm going to have to learn to accept that there are three of us and not just me now, you both have to learn that as well. Three, not two. Got it?"

"Got it. I love you, babe. I only want you to be happy," Shayne told her.

"I love you, too." She kissed him, putting as much warmth and affection into it as possible.

Shayne groaned against her mouth and moved her hand to cover his now engorged cock, straining against the material of his jeans. She chuckled. It looked like she could use her powers for more than calming the sleuth. She might just enjoy being the Ursa after all.

Chapter Twenty-One

As Serenity followed Creed into the house, a familiar scent had her stopping in her tracks.

Family.

Who was there? The scent let her know it was her youngest brother, Aaron. She tried to push past Creed, but Shayne wrapped his arms around her and Creed didn't budge.

"Move out of my way, Creed!" she screeched, jumping up and down, trying to see around him.

Shayne's chuckle as he tried to hold on to her still made her want to hit him. "Easy there, babe. Let Creed be Ursus and lay down the law first."

"He's my brother. You're not laying down the law to him, Creed. Move out of my way!" she demanded.

She could hear Aaron laughing on the other side of the big stubborn bear.

"She hasn't changed a bit. I should have known she'd end up an alpha female somewhere," Aaron said.

Creed shook his head. "You're welcome here as long as you pose my sleuth and my mate no harm or ill. You are family to her therefore you are family to us. Don't force us to sever that tie. Now, as soon as we get settled, how about you giving us a few pointers on how to handle her."

This time when Shayne wrapped his arms around her, pinning hers to her sides, he meant business. It was a good thing, too. She was ready to teach Creed what she'd taught her brothers years ago. The only thing serene about her was her name.

"I'd watch my balls for a few days if I were you," her brother drawled before Creed stepped all the way inside and to one side.

The second Shayne released his hold on her, she barreled into the entrance hall and jumped into her brother's arms. He didn't even take a step back to account for her weight. He'd filled out even more since the last time she'd seen him.

"I've missed you so much!" she cried, hugging him tighter.

"Easy there, kitten. You're choking him," Creed pointed out.

She turned an evil eye on her ex-mate and loosened her hold around Aaron's neck.

"Thanks," he choked out. "I've missed you, too. Mom and Dad really miss you. Maybe you can bring your mates and come see them soon. It would really mean a lot to them," he said.

Despite being angry with Creed, she looked over at him before answering her brother. They would make decisions together. She had to embrace that rule as well. When he nodded she smiled and wiggled to urge her brother to let her down.

"We will. There are some things here that have to be taken care of first. They just moved in when everything happened, so they're behind on getting set up."

Aaron nodded and grinned down at her. "I swear, tiger, you've gotten even shorter than you were before. What did you do to shrink like that?" he asked in a teasing voice.

"You've just gotten taller. Are you sure you don't have some giraffe in you?" she asked in retort.

"I'm sure you two have a lot to catch up on," Creed said. "Why don't you take him down to the family den to talk? We're going to find out what all is going on before we join you."

"I can't stay. I was supposed to head back yesterday, but Otto told me you were planning to return today, so I waited. I need to get on the road." Aaron smiled down at her. "When I didn't hear back from you, I loaded up and came to check out what was wrong. I got your e-mail that you were fine but about to move a few hours before I arrived. I wasn't going to just turn around and head back since I was already nearly here."

"I'm sorry. You know how I get when I'm working. I let time get away from me and hadn't checked my e-mail in a while." She hated that it had happened, but at the same time, she was glad. She missed her family, but most of all, her brother. They had always been the closest of all the siblings.

"I'm not going to say anything to our mom and dad since the Rufus might ask them point blank about you. They wouldn't be able to keep anything from him and from what they've told me while I waited on you, he's trying to mess with you. I don't want you coming without your mates with you. Do you hear me?" he asked with a stern expression so unlike his normally relaxed face.

"Don't worry, Aaron. She won't be going anywhere without us close by. We are already making plans where he is concerned." Creed rested a hand on her shoulder.

"Good." Aaron looked back to Serenity. "Love you, tiger. Mind these two. Don't give them gray hair with your crazy shenanigans. I'll see you soon."

Serenity hated that she'd had no time with her brother, but understood his need to return home. If you were part of a den or pack or whatever, it was nearly impossible to be away for too long without the pull of it weighing heavy on you to return. At least that was how it was with her den. For all she knew, that was just because of their controlling Rufus. She'd have to ask her mates about that.

Even as she watched her brother leave with her mates on either side of her, Serenity had the odd sensation that someone was watching them. Before she could say anything to her mates, it had disappeared. She decided it was just her nerves over everything that had happened.

"Before getting deep into business," Bane began. "We want you to see something first."

She frowned up at Shayne as the cinnamon-haired bear led the way to the stairs that would take them down to what she now knew was the family den. Seth was right behind him and the rest of the bears filed in behind her and her mates. It sounded like a freight train as they descended the stairs. What were they up to, she wondered.

Bane and Seth turned the opposite direction from their current suite to walk down the hall leading to their new rooms. He and Seth stepped to the side in front of where her dream spa would one day be so that Creed could see. Then he turned his massive body around and picked her up, twisting her around so that she could see what the bears had been up to while they'd been bonding.

"Oh. My. God!" she whispered in a hoarse voice. "It's perfect. It's just like I dreamed it would be."

Creed let her slide from his arms when she wiggled in an effort to get free. Stepping into the massive spa-like bathroom was like waking up in the middle of a wet dream. She could almost feel herself soaking in the massive pool that surrounded by earthy rock colors and glass that partitioned off the giant walk in shower complete with multiple shower heads, hand holds and a stone bench seat. The three raised sinks looked perfect in the stone counter. Warming bars held towels all along one wall complete with hooks for robes and a place for their house shoes.

She touched and stared at every square inch before slowly turning around and walking out of the room between her two mates. She went to each bear and hugged him, telling him how much she appreciated her surprise. When she got to Otto, he looked as if she was going to murder him with a dull knife, but she smiled and hugged him anyway. Then she turned to Locke.

"Don't look at me. I wasn't part of this. They did it all on their own," he said.

She just shook her head and hugged him anyway. "Nothing goes on that you don't know about and you had to deal with us these last few days while I was, um, indisposed."

Shayne filled in, "While we were fucking like bunnies."

Serenity turned and shot him an evil eye with a slight push of her power. He just took a step back and grinned.

"Speaking of bunnies," Warren began. "Eason thought you might like to know something."

Creed and Shayne both turned to the two bears hanging at the back of the group in the crowded hall. Serenity could tell that Eason wasn't too excited about whatever it was and that had her mate's eyes narrowing as he spoke.

"What is it? What's wrong?"

"Uh, Nothing, I don't think," Warren said, frowning as well. "At least I hope it's not anything wrong."

"Just spit it out, Eason," Shayne said, taking a step closer to Serenity.

Eason licked his lips then spoke up in a raspy voice, "The Ursa is breeding. She's carrying cubs."

Dead silence greeted the bear's announcement. Eason took another step back, his eyes growing brighter as anxiety leaked from his pores.

"Easy," Warren said, moving closer to his friend. "It's okay. They're just shocked."

"How do you know?" Shayne finally asked staring hard at his brother.

"I'm not sure, but I've always been able to tell things about others like when they were breeding cubs or when something was wrong inside of them. I'm not a healer, but sometimes I know things. I get pieces of emotions and stuff like that," he said, slowly regaining control again.

"I'm pregnant? With cubs? No kits?" she asked looking closer at the bear.

He smiled softly. "Not this time. You're having two male cubs and they're hungry."

Chaos erupted as everyone started talking at once. Creed all but smothered her in a hug that Shayne had to make him back off of. Then Shayne did the exact same thing, burying his nose in her neck and inhaling stronger than a Dyson vacuum cleaner.

"Move, everyone. She needs to eat," Creed finally called out, picking her up gently in his arms and carrying her in long swift strides to the stairs leading to the main floor.

Serenity giggled as the bears cleared a path then followed, a returning locomotive roaring up the steps. It was slowly sinking in.

She was going to have cubs. Not kits, but that was okay. How long would she carry cubs? If it was longer than she would have carried her kits there would be hell to pay. She had a business to run. Then she sighed in contentment. She was going to be a mom and have a family just like she'd wanted. Now she could honestly say that all of her dreams had come true. First she'd received her much longed for spa and now she was going to be starting a family with her mates. Life was good.

* * * *

Long after everyone had split up for the night, Serenity had soaked for over an hour in her new tub with her mates on either side of her. They'd laughed and teased about becoming parents and diaper duty, of which Creed certainly would do his share of changing diapers, Shayne informed them. After they'd dried her off, carried her to their temporary bedroom, and made slow, torturous love to her, Serenity relaxed between the two toasty warm bears and contemplated the next few months of her life.

"What has your tongue, sweetness?" Creed asked.

"Because a cat can't have their own tongue," Shayne pointed out.

Serenity rolled her eyes at their cheesy humor and sighed. "I'm just thinking about how much my life has already changed, and how much more it's going to change in the next few months."

"Are you sad about it?" Shayne asked watching her face closely.

"No. God, no! I'm happy. I never realized that I wasn't before. I was just content with what I had before, but now I'm truly happy and excited about the future. I never really thought about the future that much except for dreaming about that spa. Now I have a real future ahead of me," she told them.

"So do we. We wanted our mate but figured it would be months or even years before we found her. Then when we did, I was a little worried about it being too soon. How were we going to get the sleuth set up with a new mate to tend to? But you don't need tending to," Creed said.

"You just need reining in every so often," Shayne added with a grin.

She snorted but grinned. They were both right. She didn't need someone to watch over her every second or someone to tend to all of her needs. She could take care of herself and if she needed something, she knew at least ten bears she could call for help. They still had the uncertainty of what the future would hold in relation to their sons' status and the hunters finding out that their way of life might soon be over. How would the majority of the other shifter groups take learning about the return of a ruling family and council of sorts?

She snuggled deeper between her mates and vowed not to worry about it just yet. She had at least fifteen or so years before they might have to start worrying about that. Right now her only job was to love her mates, bring their sons safely into the world, and manage her business, admittedly on a scaled-back level. Oh, and there was the little perk of being Ursa with inside knowledge on the possible love life of the members of her sleuth. Serenity wasn't about to let everyone think she'd finally grown into her name. She knew of at least two bears who had a crush on a certain wild dog female. She'd start making plans first thing in the morning to rattle some chains.

THE END

WWW.MARLAMONROE.COM

ABOUT THE AUTHOR

Marla Monroe has been writing professionally for about eleven years. Her first book with Siren was published in January of 2011 and she now has over 60 books available. She loves to write and spends every spare minute either at the keyboard or reading. She writes everything from sizzling-hot contemporary cowboys, emotionally charged BDSM, and dangerously addictive shifters, to science fiction ménages with the occasional badass biker thrown in for good measure.

Marla lives in the southern US and works full-time at a busy hospital. When not writing, she loves to travel, spend time with her cats, and read. She's always eager to try something new and especially enjoys the research for her books. She loves to hear from readers about what they are looking for next in their reading adventures.

You can reach Marla at themarlamonroe@yahoo.com, or visit her website at www.marlamonroe.com
Her blog: www.themarlamonroe.blogspot.com
Twitter: @MarlaMonroe1
Facebook: www.facebook.com/marla.monroe.7

For all titles by Marla Monroe, please visit
www.bookstrand.com/marla-monroe

Siren Publishing, Inc.
www.SirenPublishing.com

Lightning Source UK Ltd.
Milton Keynes UK
UKHW02f1351160318
319572UK00006B/957/P